THE HIVE

SCARLETT BRADE

ZAFFRE

First published in the UK in 2022
This paperback edition published in the UK in 2023 by
ZAFFRE
An imprint of Bonnier Books UK
4th Floor, Victoria House, Bloomsbury Square, London WC1B 4DA
Owned by Bonnier Books
Sveavägen 56, Stockholm, Sweden

A CIP catalogue record for this book is
available from the British Library.

ISBN: 978-1-83877-678-7

Also available as an ebook and an audiobook

1 3 5 7 9 10 8 6 4 2

Typeset by IDSUK (Data Connection) Ltd
Printed and bound in Great Britain by Clays Ltd, Elcograf S.p.A.

Zaffre is an imprint of Bonnier Books UK
www.bonnierbooks.co.uk

For Team Strong

PROLOGUE

"WHAT HAPPENS WHEN YOUR REFLECTION isn't your own anymore? When who you were isn't who you are? When the worst things have happened, who do you become?' I ask this in a measured tone, looking straight at my camera phone. I take a sip of tea. The scent of the amber liquid hits my nose. The taste settles on my tongue, meddling with the cigarette I have just smoked. The tea is strong. Heady. Clean in both texture and colour with a warmth that intimately coddles me.

'You're probably wondering what I'm doing here.' I tilt my head, making sure I hit the right angle as my legs begin to tingle with anticipation. 'Why I'm standing in Lincoln Jackson's hotel suite. Streaming live from The Hive of all things. I'm not here to tell you a story you think you already know. And I'm not here for your sympathy or forgiveness. It's gone too far for that to even be possible now. But despite everything you've seen, despite the headlines and blog posts, I can tell you right now – nothing is as it seems.' I pause. My hands are shaking, but I deliberately take another long sip of tea.

'Three things are true. First, this isn't a story – this is my confession and everything I say here and now is the truth. Second, Linc isn't the man you think he is – but I'll get to

1

that, I'll get to all of it. Finally, and probably most importantly, this' – I set the cup down and hold up my reddened palm to show the camera – 'this isn't my blood!'

A moment passes.

I take a few seconds to adjust the phone on the tripod, my agitation rising.

'Heidi Dolak is dead. I shot her. In fact, she's still bleeding out – *see.*'

I step forward, revealing the pale, limp body lying motionless on the floor. The number of people watching jumps from ten thousand, to twenty thousand, to fifty thousand right before my eyes.

'I know a lot of you followed me to see the drama unfold. Laughed at me because . . .'

I pause, my arm feels so heavy I can barely lift it. It's starting. A yielding reminder I don't have much time left. 'Because the man I thought I loved left me for another woman. Misery loves company and I guess you guys are mine. I've read your DMs. The inaccurate comments based on internet gossip surrounding my relationship with Linc. The comments about my life, who I am. The things I've done. The endless rumours. Speculation can be corrosive when it's your skin being burned. The truth is, no one knows what happened between Linc and me. All you know is we were together and now we're apart. He's good at that – making people believe what he wants them to. Using the truth to tell so many lies. It's one of the things I admire about him. One of the things I'll always admire about him – that charisma. It's like seeing electricity for the first time. You've all witnessed it. I guess in some ways you, The Hive, are responsible for it.'

Laughter escapes my mouth. It sounds unnatural, although I'm not quite sure why. I can see my image on the screen. I can hear myself speaking. I may look and sound the same, but I'm not the woman I used to be. Not anymore.

'We weave our lives through social media. *Why?* Why are we so desperate to see ourselves through someone else's eyes? We upload our thoughts, photographs and videos so our followers can live our moments, be part of our hopes and dreams. We let them feel every experience as if they were standing right here with us. Well, I've chosen to share this moment with you. But instead of showing you the best parts, the parts that look pretty, filtered, I'm going to show you the truth – however ugly and distorted it may be.'

I flip the camera to reveal congealed blood sprayed on the pale wall. Then, slowly, Linc ripples into focus. He's on his knees, head down, hands tied behind his back less than a few inches from where I stand.

I refill my cup, the wafts of steam filling the air, making the room seem dense and hazy.

'Why don't you say hi, Linc?'

No reply. No eye contact. Just silence.

I switch the camera back to myself and continue.

'Typical. I guess I'll do the talking then, shall I? They say there are three sides to every story. Yours, mine and the truth, but since we don't have much time together, we'll just stick to the truth. The facts. No one will ever forget what happened here today.'

The next words form then break apart on my tongue like dust. My adrenaline hums, the sudden thrum of fear fighting through my pores into tiny beads of sweat. My perspiration rests in the air along with the only other odour in the room.

Death has a weird smell. And it's hard to concentrate on anything else when Heidi's body is only a few feet away. I regret not putting her in the bath but it's too late to do anything about it now.

'How do I begin to tell you a story when you already know how it ends?'

One deep breath. Two deep breaths. I think I'm going to be sick … I'm running out of time.

'By now some of you will have contacted the police. Probably Instagram too. Their tech teams will be scrambling to end the feed. I wonder how long it will take them to figure out that they can't. Or how long it will take the police to work out I've had help.'

Almost one hundred thousand people are watching now. I swallow, defiantly pushing the vomit back down, and lift my chin high. I've spent my entire life bending to the will of others. Today I wouldn't.

'Attached to The Hive's Instagram story is a poll. I want you to listen carefully to every word I say. Then I want you to decide whether Lincoln Jackson should live or die.'

The camera phone depicts a horrible reflection as I stare into the lens. It shows me with wide eyes, a blank face. Detached. I don't have long, but there's a lot still left to say.

'I can't tell you how to vote but what I will tell you is who I am now isn't who I was at the start of all of this. I guess in some ways it doesn't matter who I am now. Not to you. You only see what's in front of you. How Charlotte Goodwin went from Lincoln Jackson's girlfriend to Heidi Dolak's murderer. But at least you'll understand why.'

I take another sip of tea, before setting aside the cup and slouching back into a chair. I angle the phone down to face me before lighting a cigarette with bloodied fingers.

'How about we start at the beginning?'

kingvince — This has got to be a wind up lol I'm clicking die for bants @thehive #votedie

lee_leeks — @lincolnjackson what in the bunny boiler is going on here??

bernicehawk — This is awful someone do something call the police! #votelive

joancreek46 — Did @charlottegoodwin kill @heididolak ?????

garrymilkybar — @joancreek46 Well who else would she kill other than @lincolnjackson fiancé, she's clearly lost it or are you not watching the same thing the rest of us are?

reecehamiton33 — Who else is voting die just to see if she really does it? #CharlotteUnhinged #thehive #votedie

joancreek46 — @garrymilkybar I just got here, I don't know why ur coming for me like @charlottegoodwin isn't the mad woman about to kill one of the most famous men in Britain on Instagram Live

garrymilkybar — All right luv don't lose ur knickers, I swear all u women are the same, batshit crazy

nevosbrim_3 — Let's look at this logically, this is either a stunt for @lincolnjackson next fight or @charlottegoodwin has really lost her mind, my money's on it being a stunt she's streaming from @thehive not her own account #staywoke

unga45 — For a woman to do this she must be in so much pain, I don't know what happened but I'm praying for you @charlottegoodwin

claytonfook — Wooow u women are psychopaths I don't even know what to say just wooooooooow #votelive

ebonyblue — Everyone vote to save @lincolnjackson, this woman belongs behind bars #charlotteunhinged #savelincolnjackson #thehive #votelive

willsgreen — @ebonyblue I'm voting die, LJs a shit boxer better Instagram than the ring tbh lol #votedie

realcaterg — Lmao how can u be an undefeated boxer but get kidnapped by your ex gf, r u not embarrasseddd @lincolnjackson #thehive #votedie

p_stardust — Oi oi @kandon @frankiereed Lincoln Jackson's being held hostage by some bird looool priceless

CHAPTER ONE

One year earlier

'JESUS, YOU DON'T LOOK SO good. I'm pulling over.'

A sudden, putrid stream of bile erupted from Poppy's mouth into the footwell, as I swerved to the side of the road beneath a row of autumn-coloured trees. The car door swung open, and I watched on as those golden yellow, vibrant orange and fire-red leaves were then permanently soiled by whatever was left in her stomach. I leaned across to my anaemic, wafer-thin friend and stroked the centre of her back. She had her arms wrapped tightly around her midsection. Her face looked grey and tired, and her blonde hair hung limply, clinging to her forehead as she straightened up, ignoring the mess at her feet.

'Sorry, Char. Trix is gonna go apeshit when she sees the state of her car. I'll pay to have it cleaned,' Poppy said in her lilting Irish accent.

'Don't worry about the car, Trix will understand. You feeling any better?' I asked, fumbling in the glovebox for old McDonald's napkins.

'I'm fine. A bit shaken and the car stinks, but I'm fine. Thanks for taking the day off to come with me. I don't know how I would have got through the last few hours without you.'

'We're not through it yet. I've still got to get you home and all these Essex back roads look the same. Besides, I couldn't let you go alone, although you could have picked a clinic a little closer to civilisation.'

'And risk running into someone I know? Or worse, a work colleague? No, Essex was the safer option. I'm just happy I'm not alone.'

'I expected more from Brad if I'm being totally honest with you.'

It was true. I'd barely recognised Poppy when I fetched her from her flat in Bethnal Green that morning. I was racked with guilt since I was the one who'd introduced her to that worm Brad in the first place. An abortion was no walk in the park and Brad hadn't spoken to Poppy since she had texted him the picture of her positive pregnancy test four weeks ago. I felt guilty for him ghosting her.

'I thought he would've been here today. He owed me that much after two years. At least I thought he did. I can't believe he's done this to me. I hate him so much.'

In no way was I blaming Poppy, but Brad was a self-serving dickhead who practically idolised his own reflection. It should have come as no surprise to her that a man like that was incapable of empathy. In fact, I was shocked he didn't dramatise the whole thing and make it a spectacle, in true Brad fashion.

'Some people just don't appreciate what they have in front of them. You're an amazing girl, Pops. What Brad did to you ...' I trailed off, not sure how to proceed, plus the vomit had started to smell acidic and linger heavily in the air around us. 'Well, I wouldn't wish that on any woman. You deserve better, so much better.'

'Thanks. I know I do. I just ... I guess, I just thought we had a connection. I thought I loved him, I thought he loved me too.'

'That's what we all think. I've been where you are too, remember?'

Poppy's blue eyes darted to me as the memories flooded back.

'I remember my mum going nuts because I kept bunking off school with you and Zee.'

It was twelve years ago. I was sixteen. Jason Millington, a so-called drug dealer on our estate, who sold ten-pound bags of cannabis and strange purple pills he insisted were Valium – they were actually multivitamins – lived two doors down from me. My mother, the local council estate drunk, had pissed off for two weeks with Garry, another unpalatable, wannabe replacement for my dad. She left me to fend for myself alone at home. Jason showed up one evening in summer. It was after eight, he had a six-pack of cider with him and claimed his parents had locked him out. I don't really remember what happened after I polished off the first three cans. But I know we had sex. Three weeks later, I missed my period, took a test Poppy and I stole from Boots and discovered I was pregnant. Jason reacted like any eighteen-year-old boy would when I told him he'd knocked up the girl next door. He told me to get rid of it.

I didn't blame him. We were both young and stupid, but what I didn't know, I wouldn't realise until I was in the clinic and it was too late.

I wanted my baby.

I wanted to be a mother. My pregnancy wasn't planned, but the love I felt growing inside me was.

I stayed with Trix at her parents' house after we came back from the abortion clinic, because I was too scared to go home by myself. Poppy came over with watermelon Bacardi Breezers and cannabis she had stolen from her brother's room. We smoked, laughed and watched Harry Potter films while eating pizza. Then we listened to Destiny's Child, belting out the lyrics to 'Survivor' at the top of our lungs. I had soon forgotten about my emotional morning, even the crippling pain had subsided, slipping away as the drugs and alcohol blocked my pain receptors. It was euphoric.

Until I got the urge to get up and go for a piss. A thick stream of red warmed the inside of my leg as I stared down. I had only a millisecond to process my thoughts before Trix came charging in, took one look at me and shrieked, going pale. I knew then the horror of what I had done. It was written all over her face. I had ended a life before it had even begun. I vowed then I would never make that mistake again. If I ever got the chance to be a mother, I would do it right. I would be a good mum.

'Trix's face was a picture. I don't think I'll ever forget it.' I said, patting Poppy's knee.

'I think that was the moment I decided to become a nurse.'

'It was a doctor back then. Remember "paging Dr Leigh"?'

'Yeah, but thanks to you, Trix and Zee I didn't quite get the grades now, did I? Must have been all those uni days I missed, and all those nights I can't remember.'

'Maybe it's best you never do. We were pretty wild back then. But we had lots of fun. That's what really matters.'

'Oh, we had fun all right, but it came at the expense of becoming "Dr Leigh",' she said, air-quoting.

'It's never too late. You're only twenty-eight, Pops. You can always make your dream a reality, go back to uni.'

'Sadly, I think that ship has sailed. Besides, I like being a nurse. The emergency ward is life and death most days. I live for those moments. I love what I do.'

Poppy always took an immense sense of pride in her job. It was one of the things I envied about her. She knew what she wanted and went after it with ferocity. So, if she said she was happy being a trauma nurse at the Royal Free Hospital then I knew she meant it. Besides, if it wasn't for Poppy being such a kick-ass nurse I wouldn't have got my job at the aesthetic clinic. It was just an administration role, but it gave me a brief sense of purpose, and it made Poppy proud of me. That constant surety would often bring me back twenty years to the little girl perched on the red bike just off the corner of my street. She's changed far less than she probably knows. Her golden curls still catch the dregs of what's left of the afternoon sunshine. Just like it did the first time I saw her. From my vantage point on the window ledge across the street, I was mesmerised. I imagined her smile being so bright it could ignite a blaze. But she wasn't smiling. She was crying. Hot, angry tears streaming down her devastatingly beautiful face. Curiosity struck. As I got closer, to what I thought was an angel, I noticed the bruises. Realising my mistake, I asked her what happened and as she spoke, small and low at first, she explained what her father had done to her. Even back then, at eight years old, I wanted to protect her. I wanted to take away her pain and replace it with something, anything that wouldn't hurt her anymore. The more time we spent together over the summer the more the thought of Poppy's father hurting her grated at me. Eventually, one year later, on a bone-chilling winter's night, I grew tired of looking at new water-coloured pigments of greens, blues and purples swirling on Poppy's pale skin. I couldn't take it anymore. I made Poppy's pain go away. Thanks to what I did on that bridge years ago her father never hurt her again.

'Hey, I know today's been hard but just know I'll always be here for you when you need me, even if that means being trapped in a car with your sick. I love you. I also think my eyes are starting to sting. I'll look at Google Maps, get us home. There must be a petrol station in Buckhurst Hill somewhere.'

'Thanks, Char. At least I'll always have you.'

The phone rang. It was Trix, so I answered it as quickly as I could.

'Hey. We're all finished. Just dropping Poppy back to her flat then I'll bring the car back home.' She didn't sound irritated, but without seeing her face I couldn't be sure. She didn't usually mind me borrowing her car, but ever since her parents decided to take her to court for full custody of her son and daughter, she had been acting out of the ordinary. She was upset, felt betrayed by the people she called Mum and Dad, which was understandable since parents weren't supposed to cause their children pain, yet somehow all our parents had managed the opposite.

Trix wasn't a bad mother. She was just too young to have become one, so inevitably she never properly learned how to be one. But her children were her heart and not seeing them was breaking it. I felt so sorry for her.

'You're not gonna believe it, Char,' Trix said, but sounded neither bothered by the car or the time I was coming home.

'What?'

'Poppy's gonna be devastated. Honestly, I'm debating whether we even tell her. She's been through enough today.'

I angled my body away from Poppy, who was close enough to hear Trix's voice booming through the receiver no matter how hard I tried.

'Oh God! What's that arsehole done now?' It slipped out of my mouth before I even knew I'd said it out loud. Even without Brad's presence, he had still found a way to make Poppy's abortion all about him.

'Brad's in Dubai with Sasha.'

'You're joking!' I said, hushed, wishing there was more space inside the A3. I was fairly sure Poppy could hear every syllable of what Trix was saying.

Sasha was our school friend who worked for a huge tech company with offices in Dubai, New York and London. They were major players whose clients ranged from Google to Instagram. We occasionally still hung out with Sasha, because a) while I was good at getting us backstage and in VIP, Sasha was a fucking Jedi. And b) Sasha was arguably one of the most beautiful women in Britain with an eye-watering two hundred thousand followers on three different social media platforms. She was who I wanted to be.

'God's honest truth. Come on, Char, I wouldn't lie to you. Not about something like this. Brad and Sasha are fucking each other, I'm sure of it!'

'How'd you find out? Instagram?'

'No ... Snapchat. They both posted their breakfast in the same restaurant minutes apart. Honestly, I think Brad wanted Poppy to find out. Nobody's that sloppy unless it's done on purpose.'

'Who's done what on purpose?' Poppy asked, as I held up a finger gesturing for her to hold on a minute. 'What did Brad do?' This time I knew she'd definitely heard what Trix said. I saw the glint of tears in the corners of her blue eyes.

'Trix, let me call you back. Poppy needs me.'

I hung up, watching as Poppy's face reduced to a puddle of tears as she tried to speak through fistfuls of air.

'I always hated her. Why on earth would she go away with him? She has no boundaries. What kind of woman picks at her friends' leftovers? Is she a fucking vulture?'

'Calm down, just breathe, we're going to get to the bottom of this, OK? I promise. Let me just take you home.'

'No, call Zee. We should all go back to yours. I need all of you.'

'I don't know, you should probably be resting.'

'I'm not asking, Char.'

'OK. But before we do, I'd better clean up Trix's car. Otherwise, she'll have our heads.'

CHAPTER TWO

POPPY AND I GOT BACK a little after three, narrowly avoiding the rush-hour traffic. I had been living with Trix for almost four years in a converted three-bedroom Victorian semi her parents had bought her for her twenty-first birthday, by which point she was already a mother to a beautiful little girl, Kera. Trix was a tough cookie. I guess she had her mother to thank for that resilient trait. I remembered an adolescent Trix in the blazing August heat. It was a few weeks after my fourteenth birthday, Poppy, Zaheen and I were in the park on the corner of the estate smoking a poorly rolled joint when Beatrix Nolan came barrelling towards us and into our lives. Her eyes were wild.

I asked her who she was waiting for, and when she promptly told me to piss off, I made sure we stuck around to see who she had come to meet. I was enthralled by her. We all were, although Poppy and Zaheen would say otherwise. We had never met anyone like Trix before. Not close up. She wasn't from the estate, and she didn't live near the marshes either. She was something different. Thin and pale with chocolate hair that stretched the length of her back. She had deep dimples in her cheeks and yawning hazel eyes that sucked you into her orbit with a single glance.

Michael never did show up to collect Trix that day, but that wasn't the surprising thing. What was surprising was how a prominent QC's daughter ended up on a dilapidated estate five miles from her affluent home, and how three young girls ensured she would keep coming back.

Her parents hated Michael, who defied sensational odds and became the father of Trix's two children. He was an unsuitable choice to procreate with in their obnoxious opinion. They never thought he was good enough for their only child. Then again, nobody was. Michael being a drug user was the cherry on an already stale cake; he was a smear they couldn't wipe away very easily. But nonetheless they tried everything from rehab to bribery to make Michael go away. They only let me live with Trix because, in their eyes, I was the lesser of two evils, and because Trix threatened to live on the streets unless they let me move in and pay rent. Secretly I think they were just relieved Michael wasn't living there anymore, especially after he tried to burn the house down in a drug-fuelled rage with Trix and her children still inside.

In fact, it wasn't much of a secret. Lawrence Nolan, Trix's father, worked for one of the biggest law firms in London. Her mother, Jennifer, a truly awful human being, ran a number of charities and non-profit organisations, which would be impressive if she weren't such a raving bitch. She was the real mastermind behind having Kera, now twelve, and Kyle, five, taken away from their mother. I guess in her warped mind she had failed her daughter but could still save her grandchildren. Which again sounded good, until she shipped Trix's daughter, aged six at the time, off to boarding school in the countryside. It crushed Trix, but how did she react? She got pregnant with her second child.

A little boy. The sweetest little boy with dark brown hair and hazel eyes. Kyle was clever too. He was forming proper sentences before his second birthday and could count to ten confidently in a rhythmic tone the way young children do. He would sit on my lap and tell me, correctly, all the colours in the rainbow and giggled hysterically when I rewarded him with a ruby-red lollipop for his efforts. Trix would boast about how smart he was and spent hours reading him tall tales about lost treasures and spiders called Anansi. She took him everywhere we went – Zaheen used to tease he was her little handbag – and for a while that's how things were. Me, Trix and Kyle, tucked away in our old Victorian. We may have been an unconventional family but that's what we were: a family. One sweet little boy and his two doting mothers. Even with all her flaws, Trix loved Kyle to the surface of the moon and back. It became clearer to me every day I got to watch her be a mother.

Except Trix's own mother couldn't have that. History was repeating itself, but this time Jennifer was making a legal challenge for full custody, and Michael had given her every right to.

If only I had done more to protect Trix that night, Kyle would still be with us.

Zaheen was already in the kitchen with two bottles of spice-infused gin and botanical orange Venetian tonic water when we arrived. She arranged them on a mirrored tray, along with pristine crystal glasses, ice and dehydrated fruit. Sandalwood candles and hand-tied white peonies in full bloom perfumed the magnolia open-plan kitchen, while what was left of the daylight reflected in flecks off copper pans hanging over the huge marble countertop.

Trix had insisted on cooking, which was the real tragedy of the evening. Given the simplest recipe to follow, Trix could burn water. Regrettably, we dined on overcooked honey and soy salmon, and undercooked coconut rice that could have easily passed for gravel. For some reason it reminded me of the marshes, the long stretch of field about ten minutes' walk from the estate. We used to go there in the summer polishing off one-pound chicken and chips, while some of the older boys from the estate kicked a ball further down the hillside. I'd be seriously worried if I ate chicken and chips for a pound now that I'm in my late twenties and understand the impact genetically modified food has on our body, but back then we didn't give a shit. We ate our poison and smoked weed, Trix telling us garishly how she managed to escape yet another ballet class, catching a train and a bus just to slum it with us. She wasn't being a snob. On the contrary, Trix envied the freedom poverty gave the rest of us. She told us as much one afternoon, half-drunk off Smirnoff vodka.

'My parents have controlled every aspect of my life. They don't get to choose who I'm friends with even though my mother sure tries,' Trix said, looking down and picking at her ketchup-smothered chips.

'Just because we don't have as much money as you doesn't mean we aren't good people,' Poppy chimed in, putting a cigarette to her lips. A click then sizzle followed by a billow of smoke led Zaheen to weave her hand back and forth.

'Maybe we should invite them to dinner?' Zaheen snarled.

'Who? My parents? Are you insane?'

'Of course not, but maybe if they just met us in person, they would see that we are actually a good influence on you.'

'And what exactly are we supposed to serve my mother? A kebab?'

'I have to admit, that sounds like an awful idea, Zee. Let's leave Trix's mum in her ivory castle. I'm sure Trix will find new and other interesting ways to disappoint her parents, not using us.'

'I sure will. Because you three are just for me. My best friends in the whole wide world.'

I smiled as I helped clean up after dinner, letting the memory wash through me. Throughout the years, no matter what life had dealt us, what Trix said that day still held true. The four of us were the best of friends, and we always would be.

It's funny how the biggest moments of our lives usually transpire in the most ordinary ways. There was no crack of electricity in the air, no flashing lights or danger signs up ahead. The moment was no different to any other I'd experienced.

'Poppy's asleep. You sure it's OK she stays in your room tonight?' Zaheen asked, her willowy body half tucked behind the corridor wall.

'Sure, Poppy's been through enough. I'll camp out on the sofa. You staying too?'

She rounded the wall, her hair a billowing sheet of raven black as she moved towards me and smiled.

'I'm too pissed to drive. So that's the more likely option. Is Trix in the shower?'

'Yeah, ever since we got separate bathrooms it's like I don't even see her anymore. Her mother's way of apologising for filing for full custody of the children.'

'I don't get it. Why would they do that then buy her a new bathroom suite?' Zaheen plonked herself onto a stool and started to mix a drink.

'It's complicated.' I waved my hand, throwing a dishcloth over my shoulder and reaching for the mop. 'Her parents think she's more superficial than she actually is. You know, deep down.'

'Are we sure about that?' Zaheen raised a perfectly plucked brow.

'Of course! Trix loves those children. And we didn't exactly help not to give them grounds. Sometimes I think they hate us more than Michael.'

'Nah, they definitely hate him more. Well, Jennifer does. They'll never forgive him for what he did to her. Girls will be girls. I don't know why they're punishing her for that. Trix decided a long time ago to live her life with us in it. We only get one life to live so live it.'

Typical Zaheen. That was her motto. One life to live, so live it as hard and as fast as you can.

Poppy and I met Zaheen in Year Nine after she moved to East London with her father, mother and brother. She was an awkward thirteen-year-old who spent the first six months at secondary school mute. The kids at school used to bully her, calling her 'Zamima', until one day she lost it and cracked an Oasis bottle over a boy's head when he tried to put his hand up her skirt. I should have realised what was happening then. Or at least someone should have.

It was Zaheen's parents who introduced her to Rushil Badoo. When Zaheen's mother, Amrita Shah, emigrated from Mumbai when she was fifteen, she married a man that was almost twice her age. He was Zaheen's father, and also one of Badoo's best friends. Amrita had no visa, or passport, so Badoo created an identity for her. As he got older and technology got better so did his documentation and he became somewhat notorious for his forgery work. Soon Badoo was known throughout the Muslim community for being the man with the magic hands. But an underage Zaheen had known his hands for different reasons.

We eventually met in the head teacher's office after the incident with Martel and the bottle, but Zaheen was no longer quiet; in fact, she told the head to go fuck herself right in front of my face. It was inevitable we would become friends after that. I was the only person Zaheen told about Badoo molesting her. I wanted her to report it at first, but she couldn't go through with it. That's not what good Asian girls from good Asian families did, Zaheen affirmed.

But I wanted justice. So the next time Badoo came over and forced himself inside Zaheen, I instructed her not to struggle or cry. I told her to keep her knickers in a sandwich bag, preserving the DNA.

Then I got inventive.

I convinced Zaheen to blackmail Badoo with the soiled underwear in return for fake IDs, fake doctor's notes to get out of school and just about anything else we wanted. Within six months, he essentially worked for us. It was pretty impressive what two schoolgirls managed to achieve when they threatened a grown man with the prospect of years in prison.

Badoo never touched Zaheen again, and although she had to see him nearly every other day, she convinced herself she felt nothing, because the only person being held down and screwed by then, was him.

Zaheen was fearless. This was a woman who could stay cool and calm in the face of wildfires. She took risks like they were everyday decisions. She would have made one hell of a stock-broker, but Zaheen's passions were a little more criminal.

Cloning bank cards, forging documentation. She had links in Paris and Amsterdam, and was the only one of us that didn't have a single social media account. Zaheen's logic was: that's how you get caught.

'I don't think they disagree with your notion, Zee, I just think they want Trix to live her life according to their rules. They're not evil, they just don't understand her.'

'Oh yes, they are evil.' Trix entered the kitchen, wet and in a cream towel, leaving water marks on the floor I'd just finished mopping. 'They won't even let me see the kids until I take a drug test. Zee, make me one of those, please. I'm in no mood to be sober.'

'Sure, I'll make it a double.'

'Didn't I just see you smoke weed like an hour ago?' I asked, going over my work with the mop for the second time.

'Zee's gonna fudge the results. Don't worry. Plus, I'm stressed. Weed's not even a real drug. It's medicinal.'

'I don't know. Maybe just for now we should play by their rules? It's not like Jennifer's backing down . . .'

'I don't want to talk about it.'

'But—'

'Char, I love you, but I'll gag you with the dishcloth if we keep talking about my mother and the fact she's stealing my children to have a second win at life. They are *my* kids.'

'Atta girl,' Zaheen said, sliding the G&T to her and winking at me. Trix doesn't handle confrontation well, unless she's the one dishing it out. The best thing I could do was let her lick her wounds and come up with a more helpful solution tomorrow.

'*Oh my God!*' I gasped.

'What?' Trix asked me, adjusting her towel.

'A really famous boxer. He just liked two of my photos on Instagram. I liked three of his first, of course, but I can't believe he liked some back!'

'Great. So my life's falling apart, and you're playing Insta tag with a professional boxer. Cheers!' Trix removed the sprig of rosemary and held up her glass.

'Oh, let the girl have some fun. It's Saturday night, Poppy's asleep, she might as well. And look, he has a blue tick,' Zaheen said, taking the phone from me and skimming through his page.

'Gosh, Char, the man's loaded. He drives a Bentley for fuck's sake.'

Trix ripped the phone from Zaheen's clutches.

'Screw the car, have you seen his house?!'

I rolled my eyes and held out my hand.

'We already live in a nice house, or have you two gone blind?' I echoed dryly.

'Yes, but not this nice. He's like *rich* rich. Look at the bathroom. Can't you just see yourself in that bath? And the kitchen. I mean I would never use it, but he must have a personal chef,' Trix cooed.

'OK, that's enough. Give me my phone back. He just liked a few photos, no big deal. Celebs with blue ticks have liked my photos before.'

'That's because you have the biggest following out of all of us. Zee doesn't even have an account.'

'Don't want one, Trixy bear,' Zaheen mused.

'Not the point, *Breaking Bad*. You know I don't have time to post pictures all day, every day, plus I don't want to give my mum's PI any more ammo, and Poppy's a nurse so her priorities are the hospital, but you, Miss Goodwin, already have six thousand followers! Imagine how many you'll have if you took photos in his house every day?'

'I do have a job you know and I do more than take pretty pictures. I also clean, which is something you never do.' I scowled.

'Working admin in a Botox clinic is not a job. It's a hobby you get paid for, and those full lips of yours are the hydrochloric perks,' Trix said, matching my snide comment with her equally snide one.

'That stung.' I pursed my lips together mockingly.

Trix was right though. Most days I sat for hours cropping selfies in the office and snacking on black tea and digestive biscuits.

'Just follow him. See if he follows you back.'

'No. Come on, Trix. That makes me look desperate. He has over a million followers and he's following like ninety people. He's not gonna follow me back.'

'Who cares? Do it anyway!'

Trix rounded the marble island using Zaheen as a body shield as I went after her.

'Done! See, no harm.' Trix grinned.

'You're so silly. Why did you do that? He's gonna think I'm some freak.'

'All right, you two, settle down before Poppy wakes up,' Zaheen said, her words a little slurred from the gin.

'Too late. I can hear you lot screeching from upstairs. What's going on? Did Brad and Sasha get hit by a bus in Dubai?' Poppy floated into the kitchen with a scarlet blanket wrapped around her shoulders and her golden hair in a messy topknot.

'Wishful thinking, but it's nothing. You feeling OK?' I asked Poppy as my phone pinged loudly, and Trix turned and said in a cool voice:

'Holy shit. Lincoln Jackson just followed you back.'

CHAPTER THREE

THE SKY WAS A MUDDLE of blues and purple, and far into the distance the pale moon descended behind a gaping cloud. It had just gone eight and most of the light had faded from the day. The air was warm for a September evening so there was no need for a jacket, which was fortunate since I didn't want to hide my outfit under another layer of material. Especially when I purposely picked a burnt orange dress with minimal fabric.

Poppy was still a puddle of tears when I'd left. Trix, Zaheen and I had spent well over forty-eight hours obsessively watching Brad and Sasha's posts offering plausible explanations for our so-called friend's betrayal. There wasn't any logical reason for Sasha's actions, but I wasn't entirely comfortable with solely placing the blame on the woman, when the man was clearly the one in the wrong. Sasha may have been naive and a little easy, but Brad was the one willing to hurt Poppy. Regardless, we vented over bottles of wild-berry pink gin and smoked pack after pack of cigarettes until the house became thick with smoke, and littered with takeaway containers.

While this was going on, Lincoln and I spoke constantly before he asked me on a date. He was sweet. I listened for hours as he talked about the humble beginning of his boxing career, which was in a garage converted into a gym in Leyton. He liked pop music. Which was terrible, but he knew it and was a little embarrassed by it. I found that distractingly cute. He had just finished training for a huge fight that was called off due to the promoter pulling out at the last minute and had loads of unexpected free time. He said he didn't care about the fight because he got to break his rigid diet and eat Pop-Tarts and Haribo Starmix, but I got the impression that he was a little downcast about it really.

'It must be frustrating when something you've trained so hard for gets called off at the last minute,' I said, pushing the phone closer to my ear and sitting cross-legged atop the kitchen island while the girls slept soundly.

'It is. Boxing's my whole life, all I've ever known. There's nothing like it. I feel terrible for not giving the people what they want, but it really was out of my control. People don't realise all the politics that go on behind the scenes.'

'Sounds complicated.'

'I think people forget we're just humans like everyone else, especially on social media. The trolls, God, I hate the trolls.'

'Can't be all bad … you met me on social media.' I kicked myself later for how desperate I sounded in that moment.

'I did. And I'm happy I did. I don't think I've ever met anyone like you, Charlotte. You're special.'

He asked me about my work, then we talked about what films we liked and where we planned on travelling next year. It was nice just speaking to him, so when he asked me out, I said yes with no hesitation.

Our date was simple. We would sip on fluorescent lychee cocktails and eat hand-rolled sushi, Hyde Park being the perfect backdrop to a night only we would remember – or not, depending on how much we had had to drink. I wasn't usually excited when it came to first dates, but I really liked Linc. He seemed different and it wasn't the money or his fame. He made me want more out of life, and it had only been a few days.

You'll always be able to tell how much a man likes you squarely based on the amount of money he's comfortable spending on you. Or at least that's what my mother used to say before she died. She was a loopy romantic who married for love. Then, when I was eight, my father packed his things and left us for a younger, more vigorous clone of my mother. Seriously, the woman, Ava, was a photocopy of my mum. A tall, wispy brunette with full lips, and an even fuller rack. Dad left with Ava and never looked back. That taught me a valuable lesson. Nothing lasts forever.

Thanks to my eccentric mother I had to experience life's ebbs and flows far sooner than I should've had to. But for the first time I felt like I wanted more. I wanted something wonderful.

Stumbling over my words, I gave the hostess Linc's last name, then declined her invitation to show me to our table. Instead, I followed her through to the private parlour room, sashaying my hips all the way to the high-gloss bar. I caught a glimpse of my reflection in the wall-mounted mirror and smiled, impressed with what I saw. Big doe-brown eyes stared back at me while my dark waves fell to one side of my face highlighting my smoky bronze makeup. I ordered a drink from a twenty-something bartender, with a man bun and trendy tribal hand tattoo, and tried not to look as excited as I felt. I wasn't quite sure why Linc picked the uber-wealthy Mandarin private parlour as the venue for our first meeting, but I was grateful that I had been there on a few occasions with Sasha. I was even more grateful that I was familiar with their strict privacy protocol.

While a name got you inside, no one used them once you were in.

The last time I was there, a few months prior to meeting Linc, Sasha put on a show, dropping dates of when she had been to the parlour, which was so exclusive they didn't have security cameras or any way of keeping track of their discerning clientele. Sasha loved saying that. And Trix wanted to rip her throat out every time she did, but that was the only rule the Mandarin parlour had. *See and blind, hear and deaf.* It was even scrawled on their linen napkins and inscribed at the bottom of their leather menus.

Linc was late, which wasn't a good sign. His last message was an hour ago and he said he was on his way. If I got stood up, it would be my own fault since I'd bought into the ridiculous notion that he was interested in someone like me. Linc was a celebrity and I worked in administration for a beauty clinic in Central London. We were from two very different worlds. So, if he stood me up, then maybe it was because that had become crystal clear.

'Sorry I'm late, parking was a nightmare.' I heard the depth of his low voice before I saw him. Linc stood at almost six foot two inches. His hair was freshly cut low, and he oozed a scent I couldn't put my finger on. His skin looked like whipped butter, pale and soft with the slightest hint of olive. But it was his eyes. Gentle, like ocean waves struck by moonlight on a calm night. He was beautiful.

'It's OK, I just got here,' I answered, steadying my breathing as I looked at anything and everything that wasn't him. 'I would have ordered you one, but I don't know what you like to drink.'

'Scotch.'

He strategically placed a hand on my back, purposely missing the orange material and touching my bare skin. The current from the connection almost made me buckle.

'Sorry I couldn't pick you up by the way. Believe me, I don't usually let my dates take an Uber. Well, not on the first date anyway.'

I smiled then nodded, unable to form the words that seemed to make sense when spoken in my head.

'Y—you can make it up to me on our next date . . . I mean, if there is a next date.'

'I'm sure there will be. That's an amazing dress by the way. I, umm . . . I've got to admit I didn't walk over straightaway. I watched you, Charlotte.'

'Why?' I asked, vaguely registering Man-bun's return as he balanced a tray with Linc's Scotch.

'I wanted to take a minute to admire you before I became the luckiest man in the room.'

'If you're trying to make me blush then you've definitely succeeded.'

'Just being honest. Charlotte, you're amazing.'

I swallowed. 'How about we get some food before my head gets any bigger and I up and float away?'

'Well, I wouldn't want that. I've only just got hold of you. Not ready to let go just yet.'

I turned to Linc and tilted my lashes up at him, our scents mingling as we edged forward, and Man-bun backed away.

'You better hold on then, Mr Jackson.'

We were shown to our table by the hostess who called Linc by his first name, leading me to suspect he had been here more than a handful of times. I ignored a twinge of unease. My stomach was already doing somersaults, and it was hard enough keeping myself together when Linc hadn't taken his eyes off me since he'd arrived.

'How's Poppy doing?' he asked gently, after we were seated in a plush mahogany booth with silvery suede that felt like cashmere against my bare skin. Linc seemed to like Poppy. Well, what he'd heard of her. Which wasn't much, just that she was going through a bad break-up, and needed me and the rest of the girls to be there for her.

'She's OK. Still a little upset, but she's got us girls. We'll be there for her.'

'Good. Real friendships are rare in life. Hold on to yours.'

'I'd do anything for the girls. They know that,' I said, and I meant it.

'A bottle of Dom Perignon, for the mademoiselle?' Man-bun had reappeared holding a bottle I'd neither ordered nor could afford.

'Oh no, that's not ours. I didn't order it.'

'Charlotte, it's fine. It's complimentary.' Linc leaned in, putting his lips close to my ear. 'They give me a bottle every time I come here.' His words were low and raspy.

I swallowed, only now understanding the magnitude of being with someone like Lincoln Jackson.

'Oh OK.' Colour found my cheeks, staining them.

'Can I have a glass, please?' I truly hated champagne, but Linc had no way of knowing that. I could have declined but that felt unnecessary. Instead, I smiled angelically then outstretched my arm, accepting the ochre bubbles. 'Thank you so much.'

'Don't worry, you'll get used to it,' Linc said, declining his glass as Man-bun put the bottle on ice and shuffled away.

'I'm not sure I will. Bubbles aren't really my thing.'

'So, what is your thing?'

'Would you believe me if I said to you that I don't know yet, that maybe I haven't found myself?' I had never said that out loud before, but I had thought it for the past four or so years. Poppy had nursing, Trix was a mother, even Zaheen had an arsenal of contacts at her disposal.

I was lost.

'Maybe now you've found someone to help you find yourself.' Linc's mouth curved into a nervous but somehow dazzling smile that revealed a perfect line of white teeth.

'I hope so. Otherwise you owe me an Uber ride.'

We could have spoken all night, which we practically did. It was after one in the morning when we finally emerged from the parlour. Everything was going great, but then it happened.

Quickly and out of nowhere.

We were photographed.

THE HIVE – Breaking news: Lincoln Jackson spotted kissing mysterious new woman

myworld450 — @lincolnjackson really has a different girl for every day of the week must be nice

qballbigg — Wow she's a looker good on him

d_go_gotta — So you cancel your fight to take chicks on dinner dates you don't deserve your talent mate

bouras.ht — @thehive this one won't last long just like all the others looool

tb3_busy — She's hot what's her @ ????

thehive — @bouras.ht our sources say @lincolnjackson is completely smitten with the mystery woman in his life @tb3_busy we are working on it, sit tight, more soon!!

sweet_chan88 — more celebrity dating news . . . yawn

mk_goharrrd — no one cares this man makes more news outside the ring than inside the ring @lincolnjackson is the worst fighter ever

honeycomb123 — follow me for funny videos and exclusive content

cmg_x — @lincolnjackson I'm your biggest fan

heathergrenich — wasn't @lincolnjackson with a different girl last week?

CHAPTER FOUR

I'm inside. Are you still here?

I READ THE TEXT AND IMMEDIATELY looked up, scanning the crowd for Linc's tall frame. It had been two days since our date and the photos of our first kiss had gone viral. The Hive, the biggest gossip profile across every social media channel, had already tracked down my profile on Instagram and had been direct messaging me for a quote confirming my relationship with Linc. When I didn't respond they took it upon themselves to publish several photos of me with the caption: 'Lincoln Jackson's Mystery Woman Revealed'.

The party was alive with drunk silhouettes screaming along to songs they didn't know the words to as the base thumped the dance floor. Bodies and perspiration mingled, while model-type women flanked the balconies on transparent tables that looked like they were floating from where I stood below under the canopies.

When the pictures broke on the internet, I didn't quite know how to feel. What was supposed to be a rapturous high after our first date was replaced by trending on Twitter and a flurry of Instagram comments. My face was plastered everywhere. Then the fun really began.

The trolls judged me on everything from what I looked like, to what I did for a living, to what I ate for lunch on my work break.

It was brutal.

I wanted to be upset, but all I could think about was Linc. The sudden influx of people who wanted to know about me was overwhelming. I wanted to scream. My following had jumped overnight from a meagre six thousand to a staggering eighty thousand.

It was insane.

I didn't know what to do and Linc was so busy dealing with endorsements I didn't think it was right to ask him to hold my hand. Especially when he said all of it was entirely normal and would blow over in a few days. I didn't want to show him I couldn't handle it. Instead, I got my nails and feet done in bubblegum pink shellac and slipped on a pastel green dress, gathering the girls for a much-needed night out. I didn't know Linc was going to be there, not at first, not until he saw my Instagram story and told me he was on his way and would see me inside.

I was nervous, but at the same time I couldn't wait to see him again.

Where are you?

I messaged back, hopping on the balls of my feet. But when I next turned around, I saw him. He wore a black Fendi shirt, with two large Fs embroidered in brown suede. His jeans were slightly washed out and ripped in typical Balmain fashion. Finishing off his look were Fendi trainers and a pair of absurd Tom Ford Connor sunglasses that hid his gentle eyes.

'I didn't think you were coming,' I said almost instantly as I walked into his embrace.

'I thought I would surprise you. I know the last few days have been a little out of the ordinary for you. My life can be a circus sometimes so I'm sorry.'

'I'm OK, but thanks for saying that. I really appreciate you caring about me.' I was far from OK, but I couldn't let him know that. I had to keep my cool.

'Of course I care. You look amazing by the way.' He let out a low whistle, twirling his index finger to suggest I do the same with my body. I obliged, and felt his eyes slowly slide over me.

'Should we get a drink?' he asked, as he guided me through the crowd up towards the large granite bar with low-level floodlights that blinked from blue to violet and back again.

'What are you having? I promise no bubbles tonight.' Linc's smile was so easy-going and bright it quelled my anxiety.

'Well, slap my ass and call me Sally, you are an Adonis! Oh, don't look at me like that! You look good too, Char,' Trix shouted over the music as she chugged back the remainder of her vodka and slimline tonic.

'Thanks, but are you OK? You don't look so good.'

'I'm fine, don't fuss. We're supposed to be having fun.' She made a face then held out her hand to Linc. 'I'm Beatrix Nolan, although I prefer Trix.'

I grabbed her wrist as she approached clumsily and smiled nervously at Linc. I was afraid of this happening. Trix was drunk.

'I've heard good things. Nice to meet you. I'm Lincoln. Can I get you anything?'

'What a gentleman. Char, you really hit the jackpot with this one. Gin. I like gin.'

37

'And tonic?' he asked, waiting for her to answer.

'Don't be silly! This is a party, straight up will do.'

'Don't you think that maybe you should slow down?' Anxiously, I took a step forward, closing the gap in case Trix lost her footing and suddenly fell.

'Oh, why the fuck would I do that? Not like I have anyone to impress at this godawful party, plus my children have been taken away from me – so chin-chin!'

I gave Trix a pained look. Jennifer had won the first round. The judge had awarded her and Lawrence temporary custody without visitation that very morning. It had pushed Trix right over the edge. She was scarcely holding on by a thread and, although I thought a night out was a good idea, in hindsight, I was quickly regretting the reality.

'I'm sorry, Trix, that sounds awful. Is there anything I can do? Do you have a solicitor?' Linc asked, startling me a little by compassionately putting his arm around her.

'Unless you want to drive me to Portsmouth and help me burn down my parents' house with them still in it, then no. There's nothing you can do, apart from getting me that gin.'

'Wait, your parents took your children away? Why on earth would they do that?'

'It's a long, very messy story, Linc. One we shouldn't be discussing here.' I waved my hand, but Trix burst into tears right in front of Linc, who looked like a deer in the headlights with a weeping woman on his arm.

Goddammit, Trix! I felt the sharpness of eyes on us and started to panic. I didn't want to make this another headline and embarrass Linc any more than I already had.

'Trix, we should go to the bathroom and get you cleaned up. Linc, we'll meet you at the table in a few minutes.' I mouthed a quick sorry to him and whisked Trix away as quickly as I possibly could. But then we were stopped by Poppy, her blue eyes ablaze with rage.

'Pops, what's happened?' I asked, taking a quick glance at Trix, who was drunkenly snivelling into the cuff of her turquoise blouse.

'That bitch is here.'

'Who?'

'Sasha!'

'What, where?' I looked past Poppy's blonde updo and spotted a freshly tanned Sasha in the corner and Zaheen on the approach.

'Oh God. This isn't gonna end well.'

'Pops, you should give her a piece of your mind,' Trix slurred, her mascara running down her cheeks.

'What the fuck, Char? She's a mess. I knew tonight wasn't a good idea. She should be at home trying to think of a way to get Kera and Kyle back, not in some club. Jesus Christ!'

'Yes, I can see now that tonight was a truly horrible idea so I'm going to get Zaheen so we can get the hell out of here before we make fools of ourselves, or, worse, Linc.'

'Wait, he's here?' Poppy asked, as I transferred the weight of Trix's intoxicated body from me to her.

'Yeah, he is, and the last thing he needs is a bloody catfight. I'll meet you and Trix at the front. And thanks, at least you're behaving like the bigger person and avoiding trouble.'

'Believe me it's not without great strength.'

Poppy left with Trix and I watched them disappear into the crowd before focusing my attention on finding where Zaheen had gone. I spotted Linc in my peripheral vision, he was talking to some woman, but I had to get Zaheen out of the building before she did something she regretted. Zaheen hated injustice. And what Brad and Sasha had done to Poppy didn't sit right with her. But it wasn't the time or the place. I had to do everything I could to stop her. As I turned my head to the side, I realised it was too late.

'Excuse me. Hi. Can I have everyone's attention, please? I just want to give a round of applause to Sasha McLean, back-stabbing bitch to us all. Poppy has too much class to deal with you herself, but lucky for you I don't have a classy bone in my body.'

'Zee?' I called out and made my way swiftly through the bemused crowd. Sasha looked both bewildered and upset as she sat there clutching her martini glass as Zaheen's voice belted out over the music.

Everyone stared and then the music stopped.

'They'd broken up. It was just a holiday. Not that this has anything to do with you,' Sasha said in defence of Zaheen's public defamation.

'You slept with your friend's leftovers. Have you no shame? You know I never liked you. Could smell a tramp from a mile off. It was just a matter of time before you showed your true colours.'

'Zaheen, we need to leave.' I grabbed her arm, but it was like I wasn't there. She just shrugged me off and continued to rip Sasha to shreds in front of everyone.

'And, another thing, you're not that cute. Just because you've got a gazillion followers that wipe your ass with compliments doesn't mean it's true. You look like a dog in makeup. But hey, I'm just being honest, something you've never been a day in your life.'

'Zee, please. We really need to go,' I repeated, unable to take my eyes off what was taking place.

Sasha's face changed as her lips twisted together.

'Charlotte, get your criminal friend out of here before I call security and have them throw her out. Matter of fact, we should all check our belongings. She may have stolen something already.'

'Come on, Sasha, you're really not helping,' I said, hoping she would be the one to back off and walk away.

'*Me?* Poppy couldn't do her own dirty work, so she sends her pit bull in to do the job for her. And *I'm* the one in the wrong? It's pathetic.'

'No, what's pathetic is your moral sense of sisterhood. When your so-called looks fade, and trust me they will, there'll be nothing left but that black heart of yours, you stupid bitch. I see you, Sasha. I see you,' Zaheen cried.

'Stop it, please,' I begged Zaheen. 'Linc's here. We need to go.'

'*Jackson?* Lincoln Jackson is here?' Sasha sounded shocked, then rearranged her features, the anger dissipating right in front of me into a beguiling smile.

'Yes, he is. And I would rather he not see my friends fight. So, please, can we go?'

'Yeah, we can go. But not before I do this.' Zaheen upended the silver ice bucket over Sasha's head, water and ice spraying everywhere. 'Now we can leave.'

Zaheen turned, dropped the bucket and walked away while Sasha stared blankly at her. I wanted to stay and help Sasha clean up, but the longer I was in the club the worst my night would get. I trailed behind Zaheen as we met Trix and Poppy at the exit. But there was another person standing with them.

'Linc, I was gonna say goodbye. Was just getting Zee. Sorry, this isn't the best time. This is my friend Zaheen Shah by the way.'

'Charmed,' Zaheen hissed, sparking a cigarette as soon as her foot hit the concrete pavement.

'No, it's OK. From what I've seen you ladies have had a rough night. Let me make it up to you. How about I take you girls to get something to eat. Duck and Waffle perhaps?'

'Sound's good to me. They have a great wine list.'

'Actually I think water's a better choice, Trix,' Poppy answered, as Linc planted a soft kiss on my cheek, making me suddenly grateful he was there for me and my girls.

CHAPTER FIVE

HEN I TOLD LINC ON our first date I'd do anything for my girls, I didn't expect he'd see an example of it play out so soon. Truth was, we'd been through some things together. More than most, more than we should have had to. With perfect recollection I recalled the day Trix broke through a hole in the fence of Rushford secondary school and got into a fight with another student. Some of the other Year Eleven boys had originally made the hole the spring before so they could go out for lunch instead of stay and eat the rancid cafeteria food. But Trix being Trix decided she wanted to spend one lunch break with the three of us at our school. I protested, recoiled by the idea she wanted to spend the day in a school Ofsted recommended be closed.

But Trix insisted.

'You don't get it, Char, I hate my school. I have no friends. It'll only be for an hour and no one will even notice. It'll be like I wasn't even there. No one will know. *Please!*' she begged, sitting in the crooked wooden chair at the far end of my grubby kitchen.

'I have no idea why you're so obsessed with being like the rest of us. You have a good life, parents that do everything for you. I haven't seen my mum in two months. I'd give anything to have your life. Believe me,' I responded, closing the rusting empty fridge and searching the cupboard for a forty-nine pence pack of noodles I would have to split into two if I wanted dinner tomorrow evening.

'Be careful what you wish for,' Trix retorted, seemingly oblivious to the yellowing sheet blinds fixed to the window and the faint smell of damp bonded to the carpet like glue.

'By the way, Dad gave me my pocket money early so we can go shopping after school tomorrow if you like? Get the essentials.'

Ever since Mum left, Trix had been splitting her money with me so I could buy food and keep the electricity on.

'Thanks.' Sheepishly, I turned my back so she wouldn't see my embarrassment.

'In fact, how about you put the noodles away and we get a real Chinese instead, we can plan out my break-in? You know you love planning things.'

She was right, I did.

'You're not going to let this go, are you?'

'Come on, Char, you know me better than that.'

It wasn't just that Trix was helping me survive while my own mother couldn't be bothered, but it was that she never once let me feel bad or self-conscious about it. She was my friend without reservation. So, two days later, Poppy, Zaheen and I broke Trix into Rushford secondary school and were caught by Patricia Liam, a short girl with a pudgy face and horrible cropped chestnut hair. If teacher's pet was a person, it'd be Patricia Liam. She promptly informed the head teacher there was a trespasser on school grounds. Course that was after Trix gave her a backhand to the mouth, and Zaheen took her phone because she threatened to call the police. Poppy and I tried to de-escalate the situation, but it was too late and before we could say 'boo' the four of us were whisked away to the head teacher's office, and Jennifer Nolan was called to collect her daughter.

The recollection made me smile as the butter melted into a pool of liquid gold then sizzled in the pan creating little foamy bubbles. I whipped air into four eggs and added freshly cracked black pepper and rock salt to taste. Linc had an extensive palate and I wanted to surprise him with breakfast and fruit for helping me with the girls the night before.

It wasn't easy, but somehow Linc and I had managed to get Poppy, Trix and Zaheen watered, fed and home safely in their beds without any further incident. Or photos. He had been the perfect gentleman and I was grateful he had been there for me when I needed him. Even if that did mean he experienced a labyrinth of females unravelling all in one night.

My stomach did a tiny involuntary somersault. Was I in love? Did I even know what love was?

Linc had been in my life less than a week and already my world felt like it had been tilted on its axis. After he took me back to his house, which was an impressive contemporary new-build with floor-to-ceiling windows and a colossal rose-gold outdoor water feature, we stayed up all night talking. When we finally did fall asleep, Linc was wrapped around me like a vine. His head buried in my neck, his upper thigh lost between my legs and his arms coiled around my torso. If anyone could have seen us in that moment, they would have said that it was a visual representation of happiness. It was our happiness.

Our bubble. It was so simple, so primitive, but it brought me so much unexpected joy.

'Penny for your thoughts, Beautiful?' All six foot plus of Linc walked in sporting fuchsia pink boxer shorts complete with Hermès insignia and matching sliders. Nothing else.

'What's on your mind?'

'Butter,' I responded, impishly hiding what I was really thinking.

'Butter?' He stared at me, amused, if not slightly confused. I felt a little abashed to be feeling the way I felt so early on, but I couldn't help it. Linc had swept me away.

'Uh-huh, butter, baby. I don't want to burn your omelette. It's the first time I'm cooking for you so I need to concentrate,' I lied. At this point I had all but named the three children we would have and picked out a holiday home in the Bahamas.

'Great, I gotta have some fat in my diet. Although the best part of this breakfast is the view so far. You look amazing.'

'Stop it, I look awful. We were up all night. I have panda eyes.'

'You look beautiful, panda eyes and all. Have you spoken to the girls? Are they OK? They had a tough night. Especially Trix, although the fact she threw up and kept on drinking was pretty impressive. I thought she was going to pass out at one point.'

'That's our Trix. We've thought about entering her in competitions, but she won't go for it.'

He laughed as I filled a chilled glass with orange juice and presented it to him with a wink.

'Trix will be OK. She's a good mother . . . her mother's just a heartless cow who can't stand losing. She has mediation on

Tuesday. Worst-case scenario she gets supervised visitation. Either way, me, Poppy and Zee will be there for her. No matter what happens we always stick together.'

'You really care about them, huh?'

'I do. We've known each other a long time. Since we were kids. Although Trix met us at the end of Year Ten, we all became best friends – that was probably the first disappointment in a long list of disappointments for Jennifer Nolan.'

'I'm guessing that's Trix's mum?'

'You're catching on. Although Trix prefers to call her the devil.'

'To her face?'

The omelette wafted an aroma of cheese and sweet peppers as I set it in front of Linc and sprinkled chopped curly parsley over the top with flare.

'On occasion. Sometimes she calls her worse. They have a very strained relationship. It's complicated, but Trix is not an incompetent mother. I've watched her with those children. She loves them. Of that I'm certain.'

'So, what's the deal with Sasha and Zaheen? This omelette smells amazing by the way. It's perfect.'

I'd messaged Sasha last night at Duck and Waffle, apologising for Zaheen's behaviour, but she didn't answer and had since uploaded a meme about loyalty on her Instagram story.

'It's not really Zee and Sasha with the problem. It's Poppy and Sasha. Sasha slept with Brad ... Poppy's ex. Then they went to Dubai together.' I didn't feel the need to add Poppy was going through an abortion at the time. I trusted Linc completely but Poppy getting rid of her baby wasn't my secret to tell.

'Sasha seems devious. A woman like that. You should be careful.'

'To be honest, I don't know what Sasha was thinking. She's beautiful. She can have anyone. Plus, Brad's a jackass. I can't see why anyone would want him. I don't know why she did what she did.'

'Well, she's definitely beautiful. Maybe she's a hard woman to refuse. Maybe poor Brad was seduced.'

His compliment stung, but I let it go. Sasha wasn't the one making him breakfast, I was. I poured myself some juice, swallowing the lump in my throat before I continued.

'I'm afraid girl groups come with lots and lots of unexpected drama.'

'Well, let's try and stand clear of any drama. Lincoln Jackson does not need any more drama. Trust me.'

'Any news on when your fight will be postponed to?'

'Not yet, but Twitter's been calling me a quitter. They think I don't want the fight to happen. Which isn't true. I want to fight. I want to hear the crowd roar. It's what I live for. It's all I know.'

'Well, I believe in you, champ.' I rounded the island and planted a kiss on his lips. He stroked my hair which had puffed into loose curls. 'I gotta leave soon. I have work tomorrow unfortunately and I need to get ready.'

'No, stay. Please? Come on.'

'I can't. And even if I wanted to, I have nothing to wear.'

'How about I take you shopping, then for food, then I'll take you home? What'd you say?'

'Look, that's really generous of you, Linc, but I can't let you take me shopping.'

'Why not, Charlotte? I want to spoil you. And I will. So go upstairs and get ready.'

'Linc?' I challenged.

'Charlotte!' He stared me down.

'I can't. We've only been seeing each other a few days and – this is crazy.'

'No, your friends are crazy. But even that won't stop me from being with you. Just means I've adopted some crazy friends too. I feel like I know you better than anyone. Please? Don't make me beg, I'm over six foot, it's embarrassing.'

'I wouldn't want to embarrass you. I'll get dressed.'

'Good girl. Now let me finish my omelette before it gets cold. It really is delicious. I might have to fire the chef.'

I guess Trix was right about the private chef after all.

'The secret is paprika but don't tell anyone my secrets.'

'You keep making these and all your secrets will be safe with me. I promise.'

I scurried out through the long corridor, my head in the clouds as my bare feet moved over the oak floors.

This was insane. I was in Lincoln Jackson's house, about to take a shower in his actual shower. My life felt like a film, and Linc was the leading man. I didn't want to think 'why me', but it was a thought that crept into my mind more than I would have liked.

Linc could have had any woman, yet he chose me. He plucked me from Instagram obscurity and changed my life in a matter of days. I glanced at my phone lying idly on the bedside table and was stunned by the amount of new notifications. I had dozens of requests to become an ambassador for brands I had never heard of, and DMs from women I'd never met praising my dress sense. I wanted to ignore my sudden surge to fame, but it was alluring. For the first time I had an inkling of what I wanted to do with my life. And it was possible. I already had the audience. All I needed was a concept, but I couldn't get ahead of myself. I wanted Linc and our relationship to remain private. What we had wasn't for the cameras, it was real. And the public would have to respect that if we had any chance of surviving.

'I figured you probably won't know how to work the shower,' Linc said, startling me. 'It's pretty high tech.' He grinned.

'You're absolutely right. I don't. And I'll need a towel. If you don't mind.'

He stared at me.

The temperature charged with the little distance between us.

'I don't mind at all. But first—'

His arms wrapped around my waist as my small body pressed up against the hardness of his.

'First, I'm going to kiss you.'

'Well, then, what are you waiting for?'

His lips found mine as we locked in an embrace, lost in each other. Linc was fast becoming everything I needed.

CHAPTER SIX

I LOVED ALTO AND NOT JUST because it was nestled on top of Selfridges – although it was convenient and appealing after a full day's work at my clinic, archiving patient files. The decor was rustic Italian chic. Beige basket-weaved high-back chairs, fresh white linen tablecloths and real citrus lemons dangled like light bulbs from the vine-wrapped pergola. Shrubbery and other assorted plants burrowed discreetly in corners creating the illusion of an upscale treehouse. Candles lined the tables, adding to the intimacy with little orbs of glowing amber. It was charming in an unrefined kind of way.

The girls came strutting in one by one, forming a single file of unadulterated ferocious beauty. Poppy led the way in a magnolia bandage dress. It sloped down along her ample breasts, and stopped just above her navel, complementing her pale skin and deep azure eyes. Trix added to the fanfare in a striking red jumpsuit that flared at her tiny waist. It was hard to believe this woman had given birth to two human beings. Her milk chocolate hair was pulled into a sleek topknot and a pair of dark Givenchy shades framed her obviously beautiful features. She could have been a model once upon a time, but Trix never did like cameras. Zaheen kept it on trend in a navy fitted Gucci trouser suit. Never one to underdress, she teamed her look with a Max Mara straw hat I had just seen in that month's *Vogue* issue. Then it was my turn. Dipped in nude. My jumpsuit clenched to every curve of my figure, the delicate rose gold jewellery heightening my cuprous complexion.

'Everybody's watching us.' Trix nudged me, as we took a seat at the table nearest the skyline despite the chill in the autumn air and the sound of evening traffic.

'Do you blame them? We look like models.'

'Models,' Zaheen snorted.

'Strippers more like!'

'Very funny but I think they're looking at Charlotte.'

Poppy was right. Everyone was staring at me, and it wasn't the first time it had happened. Ever since the news of me and Linc dating went public, I kept getting looks and obnoxious stares wherever I went. I'd even caught the nurses at my clinic snivelling at my Instagram page during lunch. It was a nightmare. It wasn't so much that I hated the attention, it was just that I wasn't used to what came with it. Public relationships never went the distance. Social media doesn't belong in relationships and once you invite the trolls in you can never get rid of them.

'Linc said the staring will stop in a few days.'

'Oh, enjoy it a little. You're the envy of every woman. We should order champagne. You know, celebrate a bit.' Trix didn't remove her sunglasses.

'We're not here for me. We are here for you. You have a huge day tomorrow. Mediation isn't going to be easy. How are you feeling?'

'Honestly? I'm shitting it. I found out today my mother, aka the queen of all demons, is having Michael testify against me.

I don't know what I'm gonna do. If we can't work it out then this goes back to court.'

'Wait, back up a second. *Michael's back?*' My heart thumped in my chest. I hadn't seen Michael since that fateful night three years ago, the night I held a knife to his throat after I found Trix covered in petrol, and him standing over her holding a match. Kera and Kyle were soundly asleep upstairs, allowed a rare overnight stay during school holidays. I saved Trix's life that night. I saved all of them. But when Jennifer arrived with the police, she was so infuriated she took both the children, filed for legal guardianship, and hadn't let her daughter so much as glimpse them without her say-so since. Jennifer was on one side and Trix was firmly on the other. Lawrence Nolan sat idly in the middle, watching his family being torn apart while two children were denied their mother. It was heart-breaking.

'Oh, he's back all right. And on the wrong side. My solicitor keeps telling me not to worry but I'm losing my shit. What type of mother does this to her own child?'

'The type of woman who believes she's doing the right thing,' Poppy answered, pretending to cast her eye over the menu.

'So, you're on her side?' Trix looked like she was ready to pounce on Poppy. Zaheen sensed the change in atmosphere and quickly moved the stainless-steel cutlery out of her reach.

'God no! Your mother's a monster, but that doesn't mean she doesn't believe she's doing the right thing. I don't understand how it's got to this. Can't you just talk to her? Sort this mess out.'

'Yeah. Through her solicitor. That's why we're having mediation. She won't speak to me directly, and it's just a matter of time before she has Daddy cut me out of the will altogether. It's not enough she's already killed me, now she's picking at my carcase too.' Trix started to weep into her napkin.

'Oh sweetie, it's OK. You're going to get through this.' Zaheen held her hand, rubbing it slowly.

'It's just not fair. I love my kids. They're the best thing I've ever done. If it wasn't for them then ...' She sniffed. I felt the prickle of my own tears. 'My children saved my life. She can't take them away from me. I won't let her.'

'She won't. We won't let her. No matter what, we will find a way. I promise everything's going to be OK.' Zaheen's words were so kind and gentle, but I was scared they wouldn't ring true. With Michael on Jennifer's side to spin the story of that night any way he wanted, Trix stood no chance. I was scared for her.

'OK, that's enough. This place is elegant but not if we're sitting here crying.' Trix dipped her head, removing her sunglasses for a moment so her eyelashes tilted up at me, reminding me of inky butterflies caught in the rain.

'Should we order that bottle of champagne?'

'OK, Char, but only because you insist, and my liver needs a warm-up before tomorrow.' We all laughed as the waiter stepped into view, readying himself to take our drinks order.

To my dismay, Poppy took the chance to swerve the conversation away from the elephant in the room towards me. 'So, Ms Goodwin, how's work going?' she quizzed.

'Well, those bitchy nurses hate me even more now that I'm dating Linc. So that's new.'

'To be fair they hated you before, Linc's just more fuel for the flames.'

'It's not funny, Zee. But it is true. They were laughing at me today and I caught them on Linc's profile.'

'Do you blame them?' Poppy reached for her water and took a sip, while I looked at her dumbfounded. 'You have no idea what I'm talking about, do you?'

'Not a clue. Should I?'

'I don't even have Twitter, yet I know about Lincoln's tweets,' said Zaheen, adjusting her straw hat to the side.

'Can someone fill me in, please?'

'Char, your boyfriend sent out some rather distasteful tweets a couple of hours ago. It's everywhere. God, have you not looked at your phone?'

Retrieving my phone from my clutch, I opened Twitter and, to my horror, saw the tweets Linc had posted. It was awful.

Lewis 'The Bull' Redmond had got knocked out by an uppercut in the sixth round in a bout two nights before. Lewis was hit so hard he was pronounced brain-dead, sparking a huge online debate about the safety of boxing. Instead of sending well wishes, Linc had mocked the situation, tweeting that if the so-called *Bull* was a better fighter then he wouldn't have been knocked out in the first place. Twitter was in uproar. The trolls were out for blood, and Linc had opened a vein and invited them round to feed.

It was an online bloodbath.

'I don't get why he would tweet something like this.' I shook my head in disbelief.

'I know, it is kind of heartless. The guy's a vegetable, but maybe it's a boxer thing. We all know men like that have egos bigger than their penises,' Poppy said, buttering a crusty roll.

'That's not Linc. He doesn't have an ego. I know what you lot are thinking, but you've met him. He's not like that.'

'Charlotte, are you blind? He's a narcissist! Surely you can see that?' Trix hissed, finally removing her sunglasses altogether because the spotlight had been removed from her and placed solidly on me.

'You were drunk. You're not a reliable witness,' I bit out.

'I may not be, but the girls agree with me. Drunk or sober, Lincoln Jackson only cares about Lincoln Jackson.'

It suddenly dawned on me they had been discussing my new-found relationship behind my back.

'You don't know what you're talking about. I promise you that's not who he is. He really cares about me.'

Zaheen leaned over me. 'I don't know, Char. I'm not sure there's room for the two of you.'

'Thanks, Zee. Nice to know you're on my side.'

'You know me, I have no sides. Be careful. I can't put my finger on it, but just keep your guard up. Men like that will do anything to save themselves and their image.'

'We should be the ones worried about saving ourselves. We've been photographed.'

Poppy's cheeks reddened.

'*What?*' I ripped her phone from her hand. There was a photo uploaded to The Hive fifteen minutes ago. It was of the four of us dining in Alto.

'We should go.'

'Well, no shit,' Trix said, gathering her purse and coat.

'How fucking embarrassing. If this harms mediation tomorrow, I'll have Lincoln's head.'

'Let's just get out of here before there are any more photos,' Poppy intervened, guiding Trix away from me. We paid the bill and left as my phone started to ring in my pocket.

It was Linc.

'Linc! Are you OK?' I hung back, watching on as the girls continued walking.

'They're crucifying me. Char, I don't know what to do. Surely they know it was a joke? Damn trolls, they're never gonna let me live this down. My career is over. What am I gonna do?'

'Just calm down. Everything's going to be OK. I promise. Where are you?'

'I'm at home,' he bit back.

'I'm on my way. Linc, we are going to get through this together.'

'What would I do without you, Charlotte? I really don't deserve you.'

I thought about that. How much of an impact I was having on Linc's life, and how much he was having on mine, but I wanted to be there for him.

'Sit tight. I'm on my way.'

THE HIVE – Charlotte Goodwin grabs dinner with a group of girlfriends amidst the Redmond family's tragedy after Lincoln Jackson's disturbing tweets

bossburts — @lincolnjackson what a fuck up

aylarae13 — so her BF's been publicly disgraced, and she grabs pasta with her girlfriends wow just wow the flipping audacity of this woman

sean.lyim — @charlottegoodwin has some cute friends . . .

rushandchambers132 — @lincolnjackson is a wanker, prayers for @lewisredmond and his family

saira.moon — this is why it's important to pick who you settle down with she obviously doesn't care that his career is going down the drain women like this make me sick

itsmell — @charlottegoodwin is cancelled yawwwwwwn

mscore66 — here for the comments loool @thehive

jiggamantwo — @lincolnjackson I hope someone pisses in your coffee mate #thehive

rellyrenna_2 — no one cares about celeb gossip I just hope @lincolnjackson apologises to his family #bekind

fiona444 — @lincolnjackson is a great fighter he must have been hacked

gelboyfive — @fiona444 if @lincolnjackson got hacked then I'm superman lol

ay90 — I wonder what @lincolnjackson manager must be saying to him like you had one job bro

lucianbay — @charlottegoodwin I don't get how you can date this idiot??? Please explain yourself???

CHAPTER SEVEN

WHEN I ARRIVED AT LINC's house it was dark. All the lights were off, except for the glowing orb shining from the master bedroom suite on the second floor. He buzzed me in, and the Uber drove slowly up the porcelain driveway and stopped a few feet from the Iroko double doors. It occurred to me then that I didn't really know how to proceed or how I was supposed to console Linc. I had never been in that particular situation before, nor did I come equipped with any tools or buffers to help him or myself feel better. We've all made mistakes. Linc never meant any harm, not truly. It was just an ill-timed joke that was getting twisted and blown out of proportion in the media.

It would blow over. It had to. Linc was far too much of an important athlete for it not to.

'Thank God you're here.' His embrace was short. Not the romantic encounter I had envisioned on the drive over here.

'You look dreadful. Is there anything I can do?'

'No, I'm just glad you're here. My phone hasn't stopped all day. I've had more death threats in the last two hours than in my entire boxing career.'

'Why don't you switch your phone off? I'll make you something to eat, we can talk.'

My purse made an echo as I set it down on the marble island. Then I undid my nude jacket, slinging it onto the back of one of the breakfast stools.

'Thanks, but I'm not hungry. God, why did I send those tweets? This could ruin me. It *has* ruined me. What was I thinking?'

'Linc, calm down. Have you tried apologising?'

'Yeah, I put out a public statement straightaway. I said I was sorry for any offence taken. It was just a joke. But the trolls and threats still won't stop.'

I shook my head. 'That's because the public don't want a statement from you. They want one from Lewis's family. You see this isn't about apologising in public, it's about being sorry and truly meaning it. You should apologise in private. Send flowers to his wife and mother. Show them you're sorry and worthy of forgiveness. That'll sway public opinion.'

'Charlotte, that's genius. You're just amazing.'

I stopped my mouth from curling into a smile.

'No, I'm just me, and sometimes being yourself pays off. Now what'd you say to me rustling up a little something to eat? A chicken salad perhaps?'

'You know what, I am starving. Thanks, babe. You really are an angel.'

And that's what I would be, his angel. The person he turned to in times of peril, his confidante and best friend. I could see us five years from now, our future together. I could feel the familiar weight of my diamond engagement ring twist on my left hand as I prepared Linc another meal as I'd done hundreds of times in *our* kitchen. Our wedding would have been a simple affair. The girls in soft blush dresses, our guests chewing on tiny canapés floating atop sliver trays as they swayed in the soft orange glow of a setting sun in lush green gardens, while the scent of rose and applewood from the outdoor firepits tampered the air. By then we would have weathered many storms, shared many memories, but none would be held more precious than the day I would become Mrs Lincoln Jackson, and vow till death do us part.

The house breathed and settled while I put two leaves of mint and red peppercorns into a crystal tumbler. I tipped in a heavy shot of spiced rum and put the bottle back on the kitchen island before collapsing into a stool. Trix had left the kitchen in a state, but I was too tired to do anything about it.

I had been stuck at work all day and hadn't spoken to Linc since I left at the crack of dawn that morning. He was still being torn apart online, in spite of his private letter of apology that was strategically worded to not only ask for the Redmond family's forgiveness, but the public's too.

It didn't help. They hated him, and me by association. I was collateral damage in a battle of words I never started yet was somehow responsible for. I switched my Twitter and Instagram accounts to private after an onslaught of death threats the night before, but it didn't quell the trolls for long. I had over three hundred thousand followers watching my every move, so it was either maintain a wall of silence or face scrutiny for posting whilst a family was tragically suffering.

I needed Linc. I needed him to tell me what to do. How to handle so many people hating me. Even work sent me home an hour early. I'd become a disruption to daily business apparently. It was chaos, and all I kept thinking was I wanted my life back. But I couldn't imagine myself not being with Linc. He was my world, and if the price of being with him was unwanted fame, it was something I just had to face. Even if doing so was becoming a tedious task.

'That fucking prick.' Trix stomped in, greeting me with rage in her hazel eyes, her fists clenched tightly as rivulets of tears ran down her face.

'What'd Jennifer do now?' I asked, knowing mediation went as well as I assumed it would go. I handed Trix my tumbler and immediately began to pour myself another.

'Directly? Nothing. Indirectly: everything. It's not fair. It's not fucking fair.' She gulped back the drink and took the one I had just made.

'Calm down. What happened?'

'What'd you think happened? My mother happened. Michael's cleaned up his act. He's no longer using – been clean for twelve months apparently. He flipped that whole night. Said it was *you* who attacked *him*. Mummy dearest already has temporary full custody – the way this is going it won't be temporary. But I get supervised visitation. In fact, we both do. Not that Michael will use his. She won, Charlotte. It's taken her three fucking years, but my mother finally stole my children, and the worst part is that prick helped her.'

Michael had been very much in love with Trix once. He was always with her, always supporting her, then one particularly obscene morning Trix caught him stealing money from her parents' house in an attempt to pay off his dealer. That was the start of the end for them, but Trix rode it out and had a son before she realised Michael couldn't be saved. In the months and years that followed things went from bad to worse, to at one point plain strange. Turns out you can know a man for a lifetime and still not really have a clue who they are. Or what they're capable of.

'I'm sorry, Trix. I'm here for you.'

'I hate him.' She exhaled, taking the seat next to me, pulling out a cigarette and lighter at the same time. 'I fucking hate him.'

'I hate him too. But at the very least he's clean.'

'It's not fair. How could the two people I once loved so much do this to me? My mother is practically Satan, she really thinks my children are better off miles away at boarding school than with me, and my so-called baby daddy is a reformed junkie who would prefer to make a deal with the devil than let me raise my own children.' Hot tears streamed down Trix's ravishing face.

It wasn't always like that, just like Michael, Trix had loved her mother dearly, but as she grew up and Jennifer tried to force Trix into her mould, she rebelled. They had no relationship at all because both women were too stubborn to let the other be who they wanted. If I ever got the chance to become a mother, I promised myself I wouldn't make that mistake. I watched first-hand how damaging it could be for both mother and daughter.

'You're a great mum. The kids are so lucky to have you, you know that. This isn't fair, but we'll fight this like we've been fighting, and we won't stop till we've won. Come here.'

'No, I'm not. I'm a terrible mum, Char.'

'You're absolutely amazing, Trix – the judge will see how much you love them. It won't be like this forever. Things change.'

She let out a scoff that sounded like a whimper and a cough mixed together.

'It's been like this for years. I've constantly had to battle just to see them. I blame you for this, you should have killed Michael when you had the chance. I would've helped. God knows I regret that now.'

'Trix – you have two kids. You couldn't spend the next twenty-five years in prison.'

'Who says we would've got caught?'

I laughed, but not because I found her funny.

'So, let's say we killed him—'

'With a knife. A very long, very sharp knife – maybe a samurai sword?'

'Then what, Trix?'

'Then nothing. He's dead. Happy days for all of us. We made the world a better place.'

'Yes, but your parents would still have custody. You would still be in the same position you are in now. It's a bad plan, you would never have won.'

'To hell with winning. I've already lost, but at least if he was dead, I'd be able to stomach it.'

I looked at her sympathetically. Trix being in pain was like the out-of-tune notes on a piano. It didn't suit her.

'I'll always be here for you, and we will find a way out of this. You just have to give it time, and I hate to say it, but play by Jennifer's rules for now.'

'I know, Char. Discussing Michael's potential murder seems to bring out the worst in me. I'm sorry.'

'God, you're so dark sometimes.'

'Can't be helped. I hate him so much.' Her face brightened as she stubbed out what was left of her cigarette.

'Really, I hadn't noticed.'

I would do anything for Trix and her children. She was the closest thing I had to a real sister, not in DNA but in tragedy.

'I wish there was a way to make Michael pay for everything he's done to me.'

I saw the small window of anticipation flourish in her eyes as if she was begging me for a solution.

'Do you think he's still on licence for intent to supply class A drugs?'

'Yeah. It doesn't run out till next year. Why? Charlotte, what are you thinking?'

'Do you really believe he's clean? I don't, I think that's just what Jennifer wants us to believe.'

She paused, her brain struggling to connect the direction this was going in.

'I say we ring the police, report an anonymous crime. They'll do a search. We just need to know where he lives.'

'You mean which woman he's scrounging off. I wouldn't have a clue. I was hoping he was dead.'

'Not a problem. I'll get Sasha to pull his IP address from his social media accounts and trace him from there – that's if he still has social media.'

'Michael has an Instagram account. I've already stalked the hell out of it. But wait. *Sasha?* I hate that bitch. The last thing I want is her in my business. Especially after what Zee did to her the other night.'

'Don't worry, I won't tell her why we need it.'

'You better not, otherwise she'll be on my hit list too.'

'Just make another drink. I'm gonna call her now.'

I dialled Sasha and prayed she would answer and be in a forgiving mood.

'What the hell do you want, Charlotte? If you're going to apologise about that misfit Zaheen, save it, I've already had my dress dry-cleaned.'

'Sasha, come on, you did go to Dubai with Brad. To be honest you're lucky Poppy didn't punch you.'

'What'd you want? I'm working.'

There was no point beating round the bush. If Sasha was going to get Michael's address then she wouldn't appreciate the runaround.

'I need a favour.'

'Interesting.'

Phew. There was hope.

'I need a home address. Can you find it using the IP address from a user's Instagram account?'

There was a long pause.

'Maybe, Charlotte. But why would I help you? It's not like we're friends anymore.'

'Sasha, come on. I'm asking you as a friend.'

She paused.

'Do I want to know why? You know since I could lose my job and go to prison for breaching privacy laws. It's crimes like these why companies hire people like me.'

'You and I both know I wouldn't be asking you unless it was important. And we both know you can do it. And that you shouldn't.'

'With a few strokes of my keyboard of course I can do it, but, Charlotte, if I do it then I want an apology from Zaheen, *in person*. Let's say over brunch. Saturday morning at eleven?'

'Done.'

Zaheen was never going to agree to breathe the same air as Sasha let alone break bread with her, but that was a problem I would deal with later.

I had to help Trix.

'Brilliant. I can't wait. What's the name?'

'MichaelBoss66. Michael Wilks. Message me when you have his home address. And thanks for doing this. I really appreciate it.'

'It's OK. And, Charlotte, I really do hope we can put this Brad thing behind us and move on.'

'Consider it forgotten,' I replied, hearing the muffle of a voice in the background as Sasha said she had to go and then hung up.

'So, Sasha's gonna get Michael's address. Of course, she is. Man, I really hate that bitch, but there's no other way to find out where he lives so I'll just have to lump it.' Trix exhaled sharply, knocking back a sugary gulp of rum and mint, the smell of lime and citrus lifting in the air.

It was going to be a long night, but Trix had me to help her through the worst pain any mother could feel. The pain of losing children.

CHAPTER EIGHT

I N AN EPIC TURN OF events Trix had managed to nego-
tiate unsupervised visitation with Kera and Kyle every
other weekend on the condition she passed all home
inspections and drug tests. Jennifer wasn't happy about it, but
it was another small victory. After we reported our suspicions
about Michael to the police, he was recalled to Her Majesty's
Pentonville Prison for possession of class A drugs. It seems
we had been right – Michael wasn't clean; Jennifer had just
made it look as such so she could gain the upper hand. When
the police searched the address Sasha gave me, they found a
few ounces of bagged-up charlie and a few pounds of weed,
as well as scales and oddly enough clear plastic bags with
printed MB emblems. Everything had Michael's fingerprints
on it. He was taken away and Trix and I had levelled the
playing field.

'Charlotte? *Charlotte!* Can't you hear me calling you?'

Linc's shadow lingered over me as I lay in the bath, my
exposed breast peeking out of the milky water. Notes of cedar-
wood and sweet orange rose, as he lowered himself down beside
me next to the freestanding stone resin bath.

'So, I take it you're still mad.'

I remained silent, but sharply moved my leg back so water slouched over the side wetting the back of his head and neck.

'OK ... I deserve that. Please talk to me. I didn't mean to hurt you. You know that. You know it was an accident.'

It was an accident, but that didn't mean I couldn't be upset. It was our second fight in five days. I wanted to go out with the girls. Since Linc's social media outburst I'd been seeing less of them and wanted to have a night out the way we used to. But when I told Linc he practically had a meltdown and accused me of being inconsiderate towards his feelings. If I was being totally honest with myself, I wanted the night off from him and our increasingly public relationship. The Hive was printing ambiguous stories about Linc and me every day, sometimes twice a day, and I was tired. I just wanted one night off from it all. Linc, however, saw it another way, he hammered on about public opinion and then went straight for my throat, insisting that I had used him and our relationship to get famous.

'I know you're sorry but what I can't understand is why you did that to me in the first place. Linc, what was on your phone that you didn't want me to see?'

Our second fight had occurred this morning, rearing its head like a pustule on the brink of eruption. His phone had been vibrating from the early hours. An annoying little buzz niggling away at me as the question appeared in full view.

'Who's messaging you at this time?' I had asked him, tentatively at first.

'No one,' Linc answered, separating his body from mine as he got up to shower.

I'm not proud of what I did next. I didn't want to be that woman. You know, the type of woman who is so insecure that she has to search her partner's phone. I didn't want to be her, but yet somehow that's who I became. Linc's password was the date of his first fight, ridiculously easy since the information was on Google. I knew what I was doing was wrong, but I didn't care. Linc was hiding something. And her name was Heidi.

'What are you doing with my phone?'

The words startled me. My feet felt like they had dissolved into jelly. There was no ground beneath me then.

'Who's Heidi?' I was afraid I would ask that. To me it didn't matter that I was the one invading his privacy, that I was in the wrong for not trusting him. There was a reason for my distrust, an unsettling feeling that something didn't quite fit or belong.

'My nutritionist.' It was short, clipped, but I heard it. An unnatural merging of words and cadence, I was being told a truth and a lie at the same time.

'Why was she calling you so early?'

'I don't know, I never answered it. I was in bed with you,' he deflected.

'I don't believe you,' I said, surly. Every pore was screaming at me that this was something else.

'I don't really care what you believe. I have a press conference in two hours. So get dressed. I don't have time for your hormones today.'

His words stung. He had never been this cruel before.

'I want to know why she was calling you, Linc.' I stood my ground. There was more to this I was sure of it.

'Put my phone down and get ready, Charlotte.'

His words vibrated as the simmering rage in my stomach felt as if it would make me heave.

'Fine, if you won't tell me, then Heidi can.' As my thumb hovered over her name, Linc came barrelling towards me, slamming my back against the wall. With one hand, he clasped me by my throat. I clawed at his wrist, but he looked past me as if I wasn't there.

'You're hurting me, Linc. Stop,' I begged, letting the phone slip from my fingers and hit the ground.

'Don't ever question me again, Charlotte. Do you hear me? I'm not a man you want to fuck with.'

He let me go and I slid down the wall sucking in gulps of air as tears spilled down my face.

'Now get ready.' He picked up his phone and disappeared into the bathroom.

After a few minutes I'd collected myself, stood up and got into the shower with him like nothing had happened. When we returned to the bedroom, he was apologetic.

'Look, Char, you know I would never hurt you. I was just upset. It felt like you didn't trust me, and I . . . I don't know I guess I have issues. I'm sorry, I really am.'

I inhaled a deep breath. I could still feel his fingers around my neck.

'I should have given this to you earlier. I wanted to.' On his knees, Linc handed me a red box with the word 'Cartier' scrawled on it in gold italics.

'Linc, you didn't have to get me anything.'

'Open it.'

The diamond bracelet caught the light from a candle twinkling beneath the shadows.

'It's beautiful.'

'Only the best for you. My world, my everything. Here, let me put it on you.'

I gave him my left hand and looked into his almond eyes. He was sorry. It was an accident. Heidi was just his nutritionist. I had got it wrong.

'Oh my God. I love it.'

'And I love you.' He kissed me deeply then said, 'Mark my words, the next diamond I put on your hand will be a ring. You are the best thing that has ever happened to me.'

'I love you, Lincoln Jackson. I love you now and forever. Always.'

CHAPTER NINE

I HAD BEEN LINCOLN JACKSON'S GIRLFRIEND for three months. It was strange saying it aloud. Even stranger was that I was practically living with him. People followed us everywhere online – our weekend breaks at the Rosewood Hotel, expensive dinners at exclusive restaurants – and internet gossip was rampant that we would be marching down the aisle within a year. Anyone looking at photos of us could tell we were head over heels in love. Stupid in love.

The twelve weeks we had shared together had already been tested, but I proved I could be there for him. That I wouldn't leave his side when our still waters were hit by turbulence. I was his island and wouldn't move until he told me to. In the end, my plan to get the public back on Linc's side worked. At his next fight, I had pride of place sitting in the front row and cheering him on as the rowdy crowd chanted his name, moved by his genuine remorse for the Redmond family. The moment he won all was forgiven. The public loved him, and Linc was on top of the world where he belonged.

Everything was perfect. Picture-perfect.

Poppy had got over Brad too, and had recently started dating Jeremy, a med student who looked like he belonged in a boy band instead of a hospital. He was the offspring of an insanely wealthy Irish family, which Poppy insisted had nothing to do with her dating him. She said he made her laugh. Which was true. They were sweet together, or so I'd heard, but I had honestly never seen Poppy happier.

After weeks of begging, and an eight-course pan-Asian dining experience in the heart of Mayfair, Zaheen and Trix had finally agreed to forgive Sasha. It was still too soon for Poppy, but I wouldn't blame her if she never spoke to Sasha again. Zaheen never officially apologised for tossing a bucket of ice and water over her in the club, but Sasha just seemed grateful we turned up at all. She was sombre and a little out of sorts, prodding me with endless questions about my relationship with Linc. I told her if I had things my way then the public wouldn't know about our relationship. I would have kept it private. We took the opportunity to toast my new promotion as senior marketing administrator. It was a fairly recent promotion. Once the clinic discovered how much traction my Instagram page was getting, they quickly put me in charge of their marketing efforts. I got the added benefit of working from home two days a week which meant I could train with Linc most mornings. The clinic had never been so busy, and I was receiving a generous commission, but that wasn't the only change in my life. And it wasn't the biggest.

I think I knew it before I found out. I don't know how, maybe it was basic human instinct, maybe it was the sense that something had changed, or maybe it was me being in tune with my body. Whatever it was, I knew what was happening to me. I decided to keep it to myself for a few days not wanting to jinx it. Trix was usually the person I turned to when things like this happened, but she was visiting Kera and Kyle and I didn't want to bother her if it was a false alarm.

I felt strange. Not myself. I had been feeling run-down for the past week or so, with no other explanation for it. My breasts were swollen and tender, my skin reacted more quickly in my laser hair removal session. I think I knew it then, but still I didn't want to believe it. I didn't want to find out, because then everything would change. Could Linc and I handle such a big change so early in our relationship? It didn't matter. I missed my period.

I knew what was happening and there was nothing I could do to stop it. I wondered briefly if Linc knew as well. If he could feel the change like I could. We'd been grating at each other. Stupid arguments. Like him spending late nights at the gym. He said he was training, but when he came home three nights ago past midnight reeking of perfume, I knew he was lying to me. Although Linc said he couldn't smell anything, that my insane jealousy was messing with my senses. I was too exhausted to argue, and he was right about his new diet improving his performance. Maybe I was just being silly. I had fought the urge to look up until then and refused to do anything that would break Linc's trust.

We were in love. Sometimes things are difficult. Strained. Our honeymoon period was firmly over but we were still adjusting to the flow of our relationship. Some days it was late-night dinners followed by early-morning sex, and others it was little arguments, because I didn't care which photo looked better for Instagram. Deafening silent treatments followed by feverish make-up sex was our way of dealing with the lesser issues. At every turn, Linc reminded me that he was giving me the world, and that I should be grateful to him for it.

This news would puncture our bubble of love and happiness before we had a chance to float away. The thought scared me stiff, because we didn't know each other; well, we did, but not thoroughly. Not inside out. Not the way you should know a person before life-changing things happen. This would test us to our core.

Could Linc and I survive the storm that was heading towards us? Or would we be swept away?

'What's on your mind?' Linc said, drawing back the sheets as he rolled off. He settled on his side next to me, catching his breath. Shit, I'd zoned out again. 'What's on your mind, babe?'

'Life,' I said flatly, pulling the sheet up over my swollen breasts.

'Ah, I see. What about it? What's getting you down? Tell me, I'm a good listener.'

That he definitely was, but I stared at him blankly before opening my mouth to speak.

'Umm, see, well, I was thinking—'

'Uh-oh, that's never a good sign.'

'Shut up. You think you're so funny, but this is important.' My fist hurt from the mock punch I landed on his chest. He really was sleek and beautifully sculpted like clay.

'OK. I can tell by that face you're serious. You're doing that little wrinkly thing with your nose, the thing you do when you've been concentrating for too long. Whatever's on your mind just say it.'

My stomach fluttered, maybe he did know me.

'I'm all ears, Charlotte. Spill it.'

'Well – and I don't know how to say this, it's not like I planned for it to happen – I'm still not sure how it happened . . .' I trailed off my rambling, because I couldn't lock down the words I really wanted to say. I kept forming them in my mouth, but they became gummy and hard to spit out. 'I was thinking about life, and more specifically how we create it. It's a big thing, isn't it? Creating something special, that's a part of two people.'

'What? We all know how to create life. I just showed you how, but what's that got to do with us?' His brow furrowed then tightened as his gaze held mine.

'I love it when you touch me, Linc, it's not that.'

I planted an open-mouth kiss on his lips, hoping he would relax. He didn't.

'But what if—Linc, what if—'

'*If?*'

'What if we created life?'

He paused for a long time and I instantly regretted telling him at all.

'Charlotte, are you pregnant?'

'I don't know yet, but I think so. I haven't taken a test or anything. I just think – well, I kind of know, I'm pregnant,' I answered honestly, trying not to scare him, although I was the one who should have been terrified. I was the one who couldn't smell the smoke. I had no idea that my house was on fire, or that this was the precise moment Linc lit the match.

'I see,' he said, turning his back to me almost instantly.

'Linc, can we talk about this? I'd really like to, just, you know . . . talk to you about it.'

'There's nothing to discuss. What's done is done. Goodnight, Charlotte.'

I had never felt a man go off me so quickly. If I had a use-by date, it would have read that date at precisely that time. Linc wouldn't even make eye contact with me, but I was absolutely shattered, too tired to try and continue.

I just wanted to sleep. So, I turned over and was plunged into the darkness without either of us saying another word to each other.

The next morning, Linc left before I had woken up, texting me he had to be at the running track for six, which wasn't odd until I thought about why he hadn't asked me to go with him. He always asked me to go with him. It was our weekly routine. Maybe he wanted me to rest. Yes! That was it. I did just tell him that I may be expecting, so he wanted me to rest. Keep me and our potential baby out of harm's way. Perhaps he was being a good dad to our little bundle of joy already. I'd thought it would be best to take the test alone. Linc didn't take the news all that well, but that may have been entirely my fault. It's not like I gave him a definitive answer when he asked me if I was pregnant. I said, *I think*, although deep down I knew.

I quickly got dressed and headed out to the local Waitrose that wasn't far from Linc's house and picked up a digital Clear Blue pregnancy test. I drove back to Linc's, pissed on the stick and waited the all-important three minutes. It took less than sixty seconds to prove what I knew in my heart.

I was pregnant!

I didn't know whether to laugh or cry. I knew what the test was going to say but still, I hadn't prepared myself. I was in a state of shock, or maybe it was excitement. I couldn't tell – my emotions were all over the place. I quickly snapped a shot of the test and sent it to Linc, with tears curling down my face as I sat on the tiled floor of his en-suite bathroom.

My phone rang. But it wasn't Linc.

'Hello?'

'Where the fuck have you been?' The Irish tone of Poppy's voice filled the drum of my ear.

'I know. I'm sorry. I've had a lot going on lately.'

'Like screwing Lincoln half to death. God, do you rabbits ever give it a rest and see the light of day?' Poppy's familiar voice was a welcome comfort.

I just had to tell her. 'Poppy, I'm pregnant,' I blurted out, unable to control the river pouring from my eyes.

'No fucking way. Are you kidding me? You're pregnant – and it's Linc's?'

'Pops—'

'Are you sure?'

'I've just taken a test. It's positive – I'm pregnant.' I sobbed into the phone and heard Poppy take a deep breath.

'It's OK, everything's going to be OK, Char. I'm here for you. You know that. Stop crying.'

'He hasn't called.'

'Who? Linc! You told him already?'

'Kind of. I tried to last night, but he wanted to sleep. So, I sent him a pic of the test a few minutes ago.'

'You should have done it with him on FaceTime or something.'

'What? No. Is that a thing? Do people do that?'

'Not important – what'd he say?'

'What'd you think he said? He's shrugged it off. He's said nothing, but I know he's seen it, that phone lives in his hand.

I should have waited for him to get home. I just wanted him to know straightaway.' I held back more tears.

'So that's why you're crying. There was me thinking it wasn't his baby or something like that.'

'It's definitely Linc's baby. He's the only one I've been with for months. You know that. I love him.'

'I'm just saying you could have bigger problems than having a baby with one of the most sought-after men in Britain. So why are you so upset, Char?'

I laughed through my tears. 'That's the thing: I'm not upset, I'm happy.'

'Oh, sweetie. It's OK; he's just in shock. Remember Brad never texted me back at all. Lincoln's no Brad.'

'That's the door,' I said, hearing the echo of footsteps. 'I gotta go. I think Linc's back.'

I hung up on Poppy, smoothed back my hair and took a deep breath. If a picture is worth a thousand words, then the way Linc looked at me was worth a million.

'Did you get my message?' I began but found it hard to say anything else.

'Well, my number hasn't changed in the last hour. So, yes, I got your message.'

'Don't be like that. This isn't my fault.'

'I thought you were on the pill. That's what you told me. Did you lie to me? Did you plan this?'

'What? No, of course I didn't lie to you. I don't know how this happened. I never meant for it to. This wasn't what I wanted. You have to believe me.'

'Believe you. Charlotte, you've trapped me.'

'Trapped you? Linc, I love you. I would never do something like that. I would never hurt you. Not like this.'

'You know, I thought you were different. I thought you didn't care about money or fame, but you do, don't you? That's what this is, that's what it's always been. I have to admit you work fast.'

'Please, Linc, I never meant this. *Please!* I held out my hand, hoping my touch would make him know the truth. 'I love you.'

'I'm sorry, Charlotte, but I can't look at you right now.'

'What about the baby? Our baby. What do we do?' My lips quivered as I vacantly clutched my stomach.

'I'll make an appointment at the doctor's. Until then, do nothing.'

Linc turned his back on me, walking away, then I was alone with nothing but the sound of the dripping kitchen tap to comfort me.

CHAPTER TEN

THE SCENT OF HAND SANITISER clung to off-white walls as the soft sound of padded shoes on cheap, sheet tile flooring made my skin prickle. Portland Hospital was immaculate. Linc had ensured we used a discreet back entrance and arrived separately, to avoid being seen. He stressed the importance of keeping my pregnancy out of the media, maintaining it was a distraction from his upcoming fight.

'Sorry, I'm late – got stuck in traffic. It's deadlock out there.'

Linc didn't look at me as he trudged in and took a seat opposite me in a teal plastic back chair. It was half past four. He was half an hour late.

'You mean gridlock?' I spat dryly, not looking up from the medical history form I was filling out.

'Same thing.' He shrugged.

'It's fine, they haven't seen me yet. I'm just glad you're here now.'

The dull kiss he'd plonked on my cheek wasn't affectionate in the slightest. It felt like a courtesy, rather than a heartfelt gesture. The air was heavy with scents of sweet huckleberry and floral. A hidden diffuser perhaps? The only flowers I spotted were pristine and artificial. Still, it was all about the little touches. The early pregnancy department at the Portland was costing Linc a cool five hundred pounds for a scan, but I took it as a positive sign he wanted only the best for our child. I'd given motherhood much thought. I would be a good mother. Present for a start. I would never leave my child or do anything to put my baby in harm's way. Considering the drunk of a mother I had, it was surprising there was a maternal bone in my body. But there was. I had a life inside me. Lincoln Jackson's child. Never in my wildest dreams could I imagine I'd be having a child with someone like him. It was like a dream. Instinctively, I placed a hand on my stomach, marvelled by it. That was enough. It had to be enough, because Linc was lying to me. He was wet from a shower he'd just taken despite telling me he was stuck in traffic.

'Are you nervous?'

His face was buried in his phone as I anxiously put down the pen and clipboard. It was our first scan. The first time we would get to see the life we created. Even though it wasn't planned, I was so excited.

'Why would I be nervous? It's just a scan. We probably won't see much, but it would be nice to know how far gone you are if I'm being honest.' His reply sounded nasty. Toxic. He shrugged, then looked down at his knees.

Wavering.

It was like he wanted to run out of there but couldn't locate the exit. I had done my best not to antagonise him, but he was becoming insufferable. I didn't like this version of him.

'You know you could at least look like you give a shit.'

'I'm here, aren't I?'

'Maybe in body, but your mind is somewhere else.'

'Here we go. What's that supposed to mean?'

'It means this is the most you've said to me since I told you I'm pregnant.'

'I'm in shock. Besides, I booked an appointment so we can discuss our options. Isn't that doing the right thing?'

'Options?' It had only dawned on me then that there was more than one. That maybe Linc didn't want to have the baby. But I wanted to. It was sickening to me that he could even think such a thing. Our baby was created in love, not some random night we were both too drunk to remember.

'I'm not having an abortion, Linc.'

'We haven't spoken to the doctor yet. Don't make any decisions. We don't even know if it's healthy.'

I reached for his hand, but he pulled back then stared at his phone.

'I don't know how you can say that. It's like you're hoping that there's something wrong.'

'No, I'm hoping the pregnancy test you took was defective. Charlotte, we've only been seeing each other a few months.'

Seeing each other? Two nights ago I was the most important person in the world to him and now we were merely seeing each other. I twisted the diamond bracelet on my wrist. *Mark my words, the next diamond I put on your hand will be a ring.* The words felt hollow.

I chalked it up to nerves, because of course every first-time father got nervous. He may have been used to being on a big stage with lights and flashing cameras, but this would be the biggest role of Linc's life, and mine.

A nurse crossed our path, the sound of her shoes replacing the words we should have been saying to each other. Linc reached over the space between us and placed his hand on my thigh, gave it a quick squeeze, then turned his attention back to his phone. I wondered for a moment who he was messaging. I tried to dismiss it, because I didn't really want to know.

'Are you messaging Heidi?'

His visible wince was hard to ignore. I didn't mean to say it, but I couldn't help myself.

'I've told you before, she's a nutritionist, Charlotte. She's giving me my diet plan for the next few days that's all.'

It wasn't so much what he said, but the way he said it. Dismissive. The way his voice trailed off when he said, 'That's all.' It made me think there was more to it. It bugged me, but this was supposed to be a happy time and I wouldn't let anyone or anything spoil it. Not Linc.

And certainly not Heidi.

'Maybe she could do a meal plan for me as well. Healthy foods might do me the world of good. I've been so exhausted lately. Heidi sounds nice.'

I tried to laugh but Linc wasn't interested. He was smiling into his phone, unaware of just how bad he was making me feel.

'Yeah, she is nice. Super nice.'

'Miss Goodwin, have you finished filling out the medical history form?' the receptionist asked, breaking our obvious tension with her big eyes, wide smile and soft voice. It was just us in the waiting room.

'Yes, all done.'

I wasn't about to show the discord between us. The last thing I needed was to be embarrassed on top of everything else.

'Brilliant. Miss Goodwin, the doctor will see you now. Third door on your left.'

We went into consultation room five and were immediately greeted by Dr Spairlaz, a petite woman with burgundy hair and circular glasses. She introduced herself, then offered us a seat and began running through the tests and answering some of my questions. Linc was silent for most of it, giving the doctor a thumbs up or a short, clipped answer whenever she asked him a question. Not outright rudeness, but avoidance. I got the overwhelming sensation that he just wanted the moment – our special moment – over and done with. I shook off the deep feeling in my gut and realised I'd been holding my breath for the better part of a minute. Breathing was an important part of pregnancy, so that's what I would do: breathe gently until we were out of there.

'Right. Let's take a look then, shall we?'

I climbed onto the examination table and leaned back, then lifted my top awkwardly to reveal my stomach.

'I'm just going to put the jelly on. It might be a little cold, OK, Charlotte.'

Dr Spairlaz eyeballed Linc, who looked up and gave her his showbiz smile. A pleasant smile. A *practised* smile. Linc was good at pretending.

'OK, I'm just going to take a look around. How have you been feeling otherwise?'

She was distracting me with small talk to fill the space between Linc and I.

'My appetite's decreased lately. I've been feeling really queasy and exhausted.'

'Try to eat small nutritious meals often. It will help with the queasy feeling.' She smiled then pressed the ultrasound to my stomach, adjusting it at an angle. 'Right, just turn slightly, Charlotte.'

Linc raised his head as the lights dimmed and grey blurry images started to appear on the screen in front of us.

'Huh? Oh!' Dr Spairlaz made a small sound then asked me to turn a little more on my side. I heard in her breathing that something was wrong but couldn't bring myself to vocalise a word. Was my fairy tale over before it had even begun? I took Linc's arm and squeezed it. Thankfully, he didn't pull away.

'What's going on, Doctor?' he asked, clearly sensing my panic, and for the first time being in the room with me in mind as well as body. I was wrong – he did care. He wanted to be there for me and our baby. But what if there was no baby?

'Just wait one min—ahh, I just want to see. That's what I want to see.'

'What is it?' Linc spoke for the both of us as my throat closed completely and my mouth went dry. I was expecting the worst.

'Well, well, Charlotte.'

The doctor turned to me with a look in her eye.

'What?' I forced out, confused by the emerging smile brushing against her wrinkled lips. 'Charlotte, I'm delighted to say you're expecting perfectly healthy twins. Congratulations!'

CHAPTER ELEVEN

WET BLADES OF FRESHLY CUT grass shone under a sunset in the stretch of Linc's landscaped garden. It was about eight thirty. Linc's house was silent apart from the sound of ice cubes connecting with crystal in the glass he was holding. I watched him from the window, the man I loved so fiercely. His broad shoulders looked tight as he sat stiffly in the patio chair. Something was bothering him. He hadn't said a word in the car journey home. At first, I thought it was shock. Not even I could prepare myself for the news we were expecting two babies. But as soon as Dr Spairlaz told us, I knew that our babies were the most important thing in the world. Even if I was the only one who could see it. I got up from the stool. It was ridiculous, we were feet away but miles apart, and I couldn't take it a second longer. I loved this man. I loved our babies. That had to be enough.

Tentatively, I interrupted his solitude and placed a hand on his pale arm. 'It's such a nice evening.'

'It's nice enough.' He swallowed the remainder of his icy concoction.

'Can we talk? I mean, we should talk.'

'I don't think I have much of a choice since you're already standing here, Char–lotte.'

He was drunk and angry, his jaw tightening as he stretched out my name.

'I don't want to argue. We should be happy about this. Celebrating. We're going to be parents to two beautiful healthy children. Doesn't that mean anything to you?'

'Should it?'

His body was as taut as his words, the ripples of muscles moving beneath his cream T-shirt as he straightened in his seat.

'Do you want me to apologise? Fine, I'm sorry this isn't the right time. I'm sorry we're having two babies instead of one, and I'm sorry that I'm happy I'm pregnant. OK, I'm truly happy. But I'm not sorry about loving you. This is only happening because of how much we love each other. Linc, look at me.' I took his free hand and held it against the soft podge of my stomach. 'Our babies were made in love. Can't you see that? Can't you feel all our love?'

'You don't understand, Charlotte.' Linc snatched his hand from me. 'None of this is as it looks. I've made promises. I can't just break them. Not for you, not for anyone. I made a promise.'

'To who? And what sort of promise could mean you wouldn't want to be here for your children, our children?' I paused. 'Is it *Heidi?*' I continued as Linc scrunched up his features in disdain.

'You don't know what you're talking about. I told you, she's my nutritionist.'

'Come off it, Linc. You like her, I know you do. I saw you smiling at your phone, instead of being there for me and the babies growing inside me. *Your* babies.'

'You mean the babies you forced me into having? The ones I never asked for.'

'I didn't force you into anything. I thought you loved me?'

'Charlotte, I do. It's complicated. There's stuff you don't know. Stuff I can't tell you. Jesus, God forbid you exercise your choices, then maybe this whole thing can go away.'

I tasted hot bile. 'You mean have an abortion?' A quick flash of memory confronts me. Trix's avocado-coloured bathroom, red between my legs and the pain and hollowness that followed once it was over. 'I'm not killing our babies. I would never hurt them. I won't do it.'

His eyes traced my body.

'Then there's nothing more to say. I guess we'll just have to live with the consequences.'

'And I guess you'll have to live without us.' I turned on my heel, heading for the bedroom so I could pack up my things. It was time to go home.

CHAPTER TWELVE

THE HIVE — Lincoln Jackson has intimate dinner with buxom babe Heidi Dolak while girlfriend Charlotte Goodwin hasn't been photographed in public for months

littlejally — Oh no mate looks like u've been caught @lincoln-jackson

steelreel — @thehive let the man cheat in peace lmao

thehive — @steelreel just doing our job!

misskabe — @charlottegoodwin men like this don't deserve women like you, u'll be stronger after you leave him and know your self-worth stay strong

hanrone — wow another celebrity cheating on his girlfriend . . . yawn

titan213 — @lincolnjackson good choice @heididolak is my dream woman

anngnes — this is what happens when women only date men for their money they become interchangeable #thehive

pop_peach — @anngnes why are you blaming the woman when it's the man that's cheated?

anngnes — @pop_peach oh please @charlottegoodwin knew what she was getting herself into dating a celebrity she's lucky she's lasted this long

pop_peach — wow bitter much????? @anngnes

taran14 — just look at @heididolak how could @lincolnjackson resist

charlottegoodwin — I wasn't going to comment but I feel as if I have to speak up @heididolak is @lincolnjackson nutritionist and nothing more! @thehive Please stop spreading lies

nicoleknoxx — @charlottegoodwin way to stick by ur man when he's taking other women to dinner loool

vinnierichrich — U want privacy so ur celebrity boyfriend can cheat on you? That seems reasonable @charlottegoodwin if you'd kindly change your name to doormat that'd be great #thehive

'I s IT ME OR DOES Lincoln have a death wish or something?' The Irish tone of Poppy's voice rang in my ears as I continued poring through the comments under The Hive's post.

Jasmine floated through the air as the girls tittered around me. I'd just woken up from a syrupy dream that somehow managed to exit my subconscious and stick to me in real life. I was shattered, my feet puffy and raw. I wanted to crawl back into bed but after seeing the photos I would never be able to get back to sleep.

'Say what you want about Michael at least he never had the audacity to embarrass me on the internet. I mean if Charlotte doesn't kill him, I will. How can you do this to your pregnant girlfriend?'

Trix slid a mug of tea in front of me, as Zaheen rounded the island, sitting next to me on an empty stool.

'You know, I don't think Lincoln has a girlfriend.'

I shot her a look.

'Don't get me wrong, you have a boyfriend. But that man does not have a girlfriend. He's as free as a bird.'

'Zee, you're not helping.' Poppy's hand crept up my shoulder.

'What she means is, I think you need to talk to Lincoln about boundaries. It's one thing to cheat but doing it so publicly, it's dangerous. I'm scared he'll force you into doing something drastic.'

The room fell silent. I'd been prone to losing my head once or twice in the past. But this wasn't like before. Linc wasn't Poppy's dad. I was going to be a mother. I had changed.

'You should call him, Char.' Poppy squeezed my shoulder.

'Yeah and tear him a new one. God, I hate that man.' Trix held her midsection.

'Do you all feel like that?' I asked, the smell of burning jasmine from the incense itching the back of my throat.

'Kind of.' Zaheen shrugged.

'He's no good. Just look at what he's doing to you. Pregnant with twins no less. You're literally at your most vulnerable, and I'm looking right at you, I can see how scared you are.'

Zaheen was right, I was terrified.

'You should really call him.' Poppy's blue eyes comforted me as I picked up the phone and departed the kitchen.

A bad feeling crawled into the pit of my stomach and fastened me to the ground. On the fourth ring he answered. My words came out in a rush.

'Do you think this is funny? Why the hell are you going on dinner dates with your nutritionist? I'm five and a half months pregnant for Christ's sake, Linc! Haven't you got any respect for me whatsoever? Worst of all, I had to find out about it on

The fucking Hive?' The wrath in my tone pummelled through the phone as I pushed it closer to my ear. I'd had enough.

'Well, good morning to you too, babe. Look, I didn't know it was going to end up online. I'm sorry.'

'Everything you do ends up there. How was this going to be any different? We can't go on like this. It isn't healthy. It's toxic.'

'If this is about the video of me and Heidi leaving the hotel together last week, then I already told you we had separate rooms. It was innocent.'

It was about the video. It was also about the photos of the pair of them spending an increasing amount of time together. I had spent months trying to justify my leaving Linc's home and returning to Trix's. My pride couldn't take anymore. Leaving was what was best for our unborn babies, and my own peace of mind. It had worked, Linc had calmed down and come round to the idea he was an impending father. He assured me, almost daily, that we were still together and that when the babies arrived, we would be a real family.

'It's about everything. You, making me look like a fool. You've banned me from doing a pregnancy reveal. Even the three women I love and trust most in this world hate you. Linc, you hate that I'm having these babies. It's like I disgust you or something. You're not acting how you should. You're not treating me right.'

The bigger my stomach grew the less interested Linc became. By the time I had begun showing, Linc started spending all his time at the gym. Or with Heidi. When he did meet up with me it was to defend himself from what he called 'delusional assumptions'. Despite the photos, videos and comments, which miraculously popped up every few weeks, showing the father of my children with the woman he preferred, doing something social media deemed as cheating on me. Linc didn't understand that in its own way, spending so much time with Heidi *was* cheating, and although I couldn't prove it, we both knew what was really going on.

'Charlotte, this is insane. You're hormonal. Why don't you come round so we can talk about it? I want to be with you. I want to have a family and make this work. Baby, come home.'

My decision was final. I wouldn't budge unless he gave her up. I didn't care that she was his nutritionist. Heidi was a cancer and the quicker we cut her out, the faster we would heal the rift between us.

'I'll come by so we can talk, but I'm not promising anything. You know my family life wasn't great, Linc, I want better for our children.'

'Come by around seven. We'll work this out once and for all, I swear. I love you.' He hung up and my heart sank.

I loved Linc, but I loved my children more, so I would do whatever I had to do in order to make their journey into the world as smooth as possible.

CHAPTER THIRTEEN

I T WAS A LITTLE AFTER seven when I pulled up in Trix's A3. My car had been on the fritz for months, but I was so preoccupied with hiding my pregnancy – so much so, I had even been working exclusively from home – that I hadn't had a chance to fix it. Linc had promised me a new one. Something bigger that the twins and I would be more comfortable in, but it had yet to materialise, and I was too proud to ask.

The house was darker than usual. The overwhelming scent of floor polish drifted in and out of the air. The fumes were so strong, my stomach churned and bile threatened to violently climb up my throat. The cleaner must have been and gone maybe an hour or so ago. Strong chemicals are not good for pregnant women, or so I had read. I had been particularly keen on reading all things baby-related, especially since I was nearing the end of my second trimester and had found out I was having a son and a daughter. Poppy, Zaheen and Trix were in the midst of planning a very private picturesque baby shower, complete with two three-tier cakes, dainty personalised party favours and walls lined with white artificial hydrangeas. The twins were thriving, and I had genuinely never been so happy about becoming a mother. Even the violent morning sickness and the constant backache were joyful reminders that my children were growing inside me. It was strange how much I had changed in such a short period of time. I had gone from a party girl to a soon-to-be mother of two. All I kept thinking was how lucky I was. How lucky Linc and I both were.

Linc had come over one night when I was plagued with hormones and sickness and said everything he was doing was for us. He had stroked my dark hair and caressed my swollen stomach feeling our little angels turn and twist inside me. He had kissed me deeply and for the first time in months we had made love. Passionate, tender love. He had whispered how much I meant to him and thanked me for the perfect lives I was bringing into the world. He had called us a family, his family, and promised no matter what he would protect us. That memory felt so distant, like a dream that once was.

The house was too quiet. The type of silence that promised unexpected sound at any given moment. Linc's usual pottering was absent, and it was cold. Too cold. Like a window had been left open. Suddenly gripped by fear, I clutched my bump, tightly whispering to my babies that we would call Daddy instead, and head home to Aunty Trix's for a bubble bath and Indian food. I knew something was wrong. I could feel it.

'Linc?' I called out in a shaky voice.

I knew I wouldn't get a reply but shouted anyway. Maybe I just wanted my presence to be known, or maybe, just maybe, I knew what was about to happen. Either way, it still happened.

'Lincoln? Babe, are you here?'

I took several steps forward into the living room past the silver tray of decanters, then changed my mind, turned back

102

and headed for the kitchen. The objects looked alien. Pots and pans foreign to my eyes under the blanket of darkness.

I tried the switch, but the lights wouldn't come on.

I felt like an intruder tiptoeing around in the dark waiting for whatever monster was lurking to jump out and yell 'Boo!' I couldn't figure it out, but all I knew was I wasn't supposed to be there. Not that night. Not by myself.

I quickly turned on my heels and readied myself to leave but dropped my handbag in the process. I knelt to pick it up, my skin hot as I heard the padding of footsteps from behind me.

'Linc, is that you? If this is a joke, then it isn't funny,' I said, standing upright. It felt kind of stupid speaking into the darkness, but I knew I wasn't alone. I knew there was someone out there.

Watching.

I felt the earth shatter, realisation kicking in that my worst thought was true.

I wasn't alone.

'Who are you? W-what are you doing here?' I said, grandstanding the shadowy figure as it sliced away from the darkness. My legs felt like jelly, unable to solidify on command. I was paralysed.

'I don't understand. What are you doing in here?'

The figure just breathed. I took a step back and hit something solid. I turned. There was another figure standing in Linc's kitchen.

The second figure took two steps forward making me take another hesitant step back, then I watched the figures detach themselves from the shadows and become whole.

I couldn't make out faces, just piercing black eyes on the taller one and a slither of dark that may or may not have been part of a ski mask.

'There's lots of money. Please, I can give it all to you. I just need you to take me to the safe. It's upstairs in the closet behind the coat rack.' I pleaded, hoping in vain it would make the slightest difference, but as I felt cold hands wrap around my neck, I knew that it hadn't.

'Please, I'm pregnant.'

Strands of my own hair were stroked delicately as I shook uncontrollably.

I clawed at my neck and carefully pushed the weight of my back against the wall as the figure held me.

The grip loosened around my neck. I screamed, but it came out strangled and distorted. I needed air to scream but not enough was filling my lungs.

'Please, my boyfriend will be back soon. He's a boxer. You have no idea what he'll do to you if you hurt me. Just let me go, you can take whatever you want.'

Using a strength I didn't know I had, I freed myself and bolted, my limbs temporarily unseizing as I whooshed past the bulky figures, bookending the dining table hard as I scrambled for the glass door separating the kitchen from the study. It was the only route I could take but it was locked. I grabbed a nearby candle and smashed through the glass, tripping as footsteps gained pace behind me. My body hurled forward as I struggled against the muscular arms pulling me back, the full force making me fall through the remaining glass at an askew angle.

Spikes of glass fell on top of me as I moaned, light-headed and woozy, half of my body through the door.

Disorientated, I tried to stand. That's when I looked down and saw the huge shard of glass impelled deeply into the side of my stomach.

No!

'Help me. Please someone help me!'

I looked up, pleading with the figures, but I was dizzy and there were now more than two. They just stood there unmoving. Watching me.

My left eye had swollen shut from the impact of my fall and I could only see through a little slit. I was in pain, wanting to hold my head, wipe the blood from my mouth, but I couldn't let go of my stomach.

'Please,' I whimpered harder, clutching at the shard of glass as I tried and failed to remove it, splitting the skin on my hands in the process.

Blood sprayed onto the magnolia tiles. I shrieked in agony, my voice loud and rattled, splinters flying away as I stood and took staggered steps towards the figures. They continued to stare at me.

'For God's sake, please help me.'

For the briefest of moments, I thought of Linc. He was supposed to be here. He had urged me to come home so we could talk. Around seven, he had said.

I love you, he had said.

'Please help me.'

I fell to my knees, the room there one moment and vanishing slowly into darkness the next.

Then there was nothing.

If it was a dream, then I didn't want it to be real, and if it was real, then I wanted it to be a dream.

I opened my eyes. My brain was foggy and blurred. I couldn't make sense of what was happening, even as it happened.

Poppy came into view yelling something to Trix, but I couldn't make out what she said. My ears felt like I'd been swimming underwater, and I could only partially see through one eye. I placed my right hand to my ear and saw blood seep between my fingertips. I opened my mouth to speak but found I couldn't. It was like I had bricks on my chest. Poppy looked scared, her blue eyes moving agitatedly back and forth from Trix to Zaheen and then back to me.

Then I remembered where I was. Why were they at Linc's house?

Poppy said something to me, but it was inaudible. Zaheen was at my side. She had folded towels in her hand which she pressed at my stomach, blood pooling around us as she fought the flow.

Suddenly, the sound came back on. 'Charlotte, look at me. You have to stay awake. I need you to push. Please, Charlotte, push. Trix, where the hell is the ambulance?'

'Ten minutes out.'

'Tell them she doesn't have ten minutes; she needs help now. Zee, apply more pressure. You have to slow the bleeding otherwise she'll bleed out.'

'I'm trying. There's too much blood. Poppy, I'm scared.'

'We don't have time to panic. Her waters have broken and she's crowning now. Trix, get more towels, bed sheets, anything, and find a way to keep her awake. She can't pass out otherwise all three of them will die. Move!' Poppy took charge.

'Oh fuck. Where the hell is Lincoln? She came here to meet him. What the hell happened?' Trix's voice sounded muffled as she disappeared. I felt tender and strange.

'Everything's gonna be OK. We're here; we are not gonna let you die. OK, you've got to be strong. I need you to be strong.'

Zaheen was staring at me, her face contorted with worry as Trix returned.

'Char, please push. Please. If you don't, your babies will die. Do you hear me? You have to push.'

I heard Trix as my body did something I didn't think it was capable of and started to push. The strength inside me grew even as my flesh grew weaker.

'For fuck's sake I can't stop the bleeding. What the hell happened to her?' Zaheen thundered as Poppy handed something to Trix.

It was small. Too small and wrapped in a white towel.

Trix's face looked terrified. She didn't speak but moved out of my line of vision. Whatever Poppy gave her was light, like the weight had been removed and there was only a shell left. I could imagine it floating away on the soft breeze like a feather.

I tried to tell Trix that it was OK. I wanted to see what she had in the towel, but she couldn't hear me. My words were trapped in my head, while everything happened around me.

On hands and knees, Trix worked, her shoulders square and hunched obstructing my view. I didn't know what she was doing. I couldn't see from my vantage point on the floor but whatever she was doing she was scared, more scared than I had ever seen her before. I felt a gush of water between my legs and wondered numbly if I'd pissed myself.

I wanted to look down, but my neck was stiff and wouldn't bend the way I willed it to. Poppy lifted her hands; they were red. The smell of pennies fresh and strong. I felt the metallic tang on my tongue as I breathed in and out.

It was everywhere. The tiles, the cupboard doors. Poppy's blonde hair. My blood was everywhere.

'Trix! What's happening over there?' Zaheen howled, tearing my attention back to the white towel.

'Is she breathing? Please tell me she's breathing.'

Was who breathing? Surely, they could see me breathing. I lifted my arm to wave, so I could show them that I was fine. That I was alive. That I'd survived my fall, but as Trix turned and slumped back beside me, her skin grey, I finally saw what she had buried in the towel.

It was a baby.

My baby.

Except it was too small, its limbs deflated and floppy. Its fingernails barely half a grain of rice. Trix was crying. She held my hand and whispered to me in what I can only describe as a mother's voice.

'I'm sorry. She's gone, Char.'

Every ember inside me wanted to ignite, but I couldn't, I was too weak to fight back. I collected the little fragments of strength I had left and murmured helplessly.

'Please save him. *Please.*'

I felt a tug, followed by pressure from between my legs as Zaheen pushed back her inky hair from her face, covering her cheek with even more red, and resumed trying to staunch the flow from my wound.

I was going to pass out, I thought, as the burning set in and my legs began to shake. I pushed again. Hard. Then there was stillness.

Poppy lay the tiny baby on my chest. He was limp and didn't cry. His tiny hands, like his sister's, were blue.

The room fell silent.

Trix knelt down, putting my daughter on the other side of my chest. My twins lay side by side as Poppy, Trix and Zaheen sat beside me.

I kissed their tiny heads and sang softly.

Sleep tight tonight on Rockabye mountain.
Where dreams come true it's just me and you.
The stars, the sun, even heavens rejoicing.
The angels chose me, then the Lord gave me you.
My reason, my purpose, my beautiful greatness.
Your love is so bright that it lights up the moon.
Sleep tight tonight on Rockabye mountain.
My heartbeat is yours, one day I'll be with you.

Flashing lights was all I remember after that.

CHAPTER FOURTEEN

Beep. Beep. Beep.

I THOUGHT A LOT ABOUT MY mother after I lost the twins. I had certain problems with the way she died. Not the physical aspect of her suicide. I was perfectly content with her reasons for wanting to kill herself. I actually thought I was better off without her. I knew that my life would have been much worse if she'd remained in it. But that's not what infuriated me about my mother's death. It wasn't the cheap hotel room in the belly of Forest Gate she was found in, or the fact she clutched on to a photo of my father like a lovesick teenager who still harboured hope.

It was the vodka. Glen's vodka. A pathetic final drink for a drunk who couldn't even be bothered to leave a note for her only daughter.

Five days had passed when I woke up in the Royal Free Hospital. I'd had an emergency hysterectomy and, although that was the worst of it, it wasn't the end of it. The tubes tethered to me were the only thing keeping me anchored to what no longer felt like the real world.

I felt numb.

Linc had decided he wanted nothing to do with me. The five days I spent hulled up in intensive care fighting for my life changed his mind about a lot of things. Starting with us.

On day two of my stay in ICU, Linc had unceremoniously dropped all my things to Trix's, telling her it was too painful for him to be around me. He said he needed some space and time to heal.

When I first came round days later, he wasn't returning my calls. I called him again praying he would answer. This time, he did.

'You need to stop calling me, Charlotte.'

'How can you even say that to me? I just lost our children. You haven't even been to the hospital.'

'Charlotte, I've been dealing with the police. The kitchen was a crime scene. They don't believe this was an accident. Especially after you told them you saw two people in the house.'

'I did see two people. They had masks on. I tried to get away. That's how I got hurt. It was a terrible accident. You have to believe me, Linc,' I breathed, filtering back my mounting tears. 'Linc, please just come to the hospital. Please, I need you. I love you. My heart is broken.'

'Charlotte, I can't. I'm so sorry for everything. I'm sorry I wasn't at home when it happened, but you need help. Professional help, counselling. I'll pay for it, I don't mind, but I can't be with you. The media will find out. It will tarnish my career. I'm sorry but I just can't.'

'You don't mean that. I've lost everything. I'll never have any more children. They are and will forever be my only babies. I can't get through this without you. Please, don't leave me. Not now. Not like this. I need you.'

Everyone mourns in their own way, so I understood Linc's misgivings about seeing me. I just didn't care. We both lost our son and daughter, we needed to be there for one another. This wasn't the time to fall apart.

'Charlotte, please accept the counselling. Get better and move on. My solicitor will be in touch regarding a non-disclosure agreement. I'm sorry but this can't get out. If you ever loved me or our children, then you'll sign it. Let's not let the media use this to ruin me. Please, Charlotte, sign the papers.'

They speak of the catalyst, the trigger that ignites the fuse. The night I had my accident was the spark.

The line went dead. Linc was gone.

'I had a feeling you'd be here.' Trix's voice was soft, docile like the wind, but I didn't lift my head to meet her eyes, instead I let her voice float away on the breeze as she trod up the steep hill.

'Here, put this on.'

She slung a hoodie over my shoulders, taking the chill off my neck. I hadn't realised I was shivering and couldn't tell her how long I had been on the marshes. I just knew it had been a long time. The sun was setting and the blood that had leaked from my burst stitches on my stomach had dried.

'Could have picked a better outfit for a trip down memory lane, Char.'

Trix plonked herself down next to me. It was cold, most of the light had blenched from the day into dusk. The blue and orange had combined into swirls above London's skyline far in the distance.

It was almost beautiful, in a tragic way.

Or maybe it wasn't the view that was tragic, but the person who was admiring it.

'You feeling OK out here?' Trix asked, but there was no point in answering. I was far from OK. Trix knew that better than anyone. Instead of reprimanding me for discharging myself from hospital – I suspected they had called her hours ago, worried about my fragile state of mind – she sat next to me and produced a hand-rolled blunt that was thick from roach to base. I guess she thought weed would be more beneficial than a therapy session where they asked you how much you wanted to harm yourself on a scale of one to ten.

I was at twelve and climbing.

'I never liked him, you know.'

If Trix decided she hated you, then not even an act of God could redeem you in her eyes. I channelled the anger I felt for the world, Linc and myself but still couldn't find any words to say. The only person I had to blame was myself. I was the one that had fallen through the glass door. I was the one who'd lost them.

'I didn't like him either. That prick has far more muscles than brains, and don't even get me started on the way he speaks.'

We both turned in the direction of Poppy, who, like Trix, was ignoring doctors' orders and handed me a bottle of pineapple-flavoured CÎROC as she sat down on the other side of me.

'Did you get a chaser?' Trix asked, tentatively addressing Poppy.

'Nope, we're all Irish today. No excuses I'm afraid.'

'I wasn't objecting, but it would have been nice,' Trix responded, sparking the blunt, which filled the air with a dense cloud of smoke. We sat there, passing it between us in silence before I spoke.

'I've always liked this place – ever since school. We spent so much of our lesson time out here. Ditching PE. Doing things we weren't supposed to be doing. Who'd have thought this would have happened? Who'd have seen this coming back then?'

'Char, I'm—'

I lifted my head to meet Poppy's blue eyes and knew what she was about to say but couldn't bear to hear her say it.

'I know, Pops. Me too,' I managed, cutting her off but taking her hand, knowing how sorry she was.

'Room for one more?' Zaheen said, slouching down on the other side of Trix.

All four of us sat in a row taking in the view. It had been quite some time since we were all here together, yet somehow it felt like we'd never left. This was one of our favourite spots to bunk school and spend the day lounging in the sun, discussing boys or what we would be when we grew up.

'Dr Leigh. You've got to admit it does have a ring to it.'

'With your GCSEs I think you can be just about anything you want. I'm so proud of you,' I said, poorly braiding her hair into two French plaits.

That day, Poppy had been sad. Her brother, a businessman famed for bringing cocaine to Ireland in crates of potatoes, had been stabbed to death in jail. It had taken the police nearly a decade to catch Shane Leigh and his crew. Operation Gemini was what the police called it, although entrapment was Poppy's description. Her beloved brother was subsequently arrested and later sentenced by the special criminal court to eighteen years behind bars. This had all happened by the time Poppy moved to the estate at the age of seven. Perhaps if Shane didn't go to prison, leaving Poppy and her mother, then the terrible beatings her father gave her wouldn't have happened. Perhaps I wouldn't have had to drop the brick on Poppy's father, paralysing him from the neck down. Perhaps losing the twins was my karma, my sins coming back to haunt me.

We sat on the grass waiting for Trix to make the hour-long journey from the sixth form open day she was attending in Westminster.

'You know I don't get why we bother with Beatrix.'

'Come on, Zee, you know she hates that name. Can you just try?'

'Sorry, I mean Trix. Although my point still remains. She's not exactly one of us.'

Zaheen rested her chin on her knee. Her rich skin golden under the midday sun. She had cut her raven hair into a pixie bob the last term of secondary school but it still hadn't grown back over the summer.

'You mean she's not poor like us?' Poppy winced.

'Hey, I threw some corn, I didn't call any fowls to eat it.' Zaheen held up both hands in protest.

'Look, she's our friend. And so what if she has more money than us, or that she has a "proper family"? She's one of us. Trix has a good heart.'

I finished Poppy's braid as Trix came marching up the hill. Tears trickled down her sallow cheeks and she looked pale and bewildered. Her body was tense.

'What's wrong? What happened?' I asked, dusting the grass off my knees before I approached her. Poppy and Zaheen stayed a foot or so behind.

'It's all gone wrong. This isn't supposed to be happening. This isn't the way my life was supposed to go.'

Poppy looked from Zaheen to me then back again.

'Tell us what's going on, *Trix?*' Poppy stressed her name taking a step forward.

'I—*I'm*—'

'Oh, spit it out already, princess.' Zaheen rolled her eyes.

'I'm pregnant with Michael's baby.'

As I remembered Trix sharing her news at this very spot, I felt a pang in my stomach for my son and daughter. They would never get to grow up like Kera or Kyle. They would never have a first kiss, or a wedding. I would never get to see them smile or take their first steps. All of that had been taken from me and would always be taken from me. I would never experience motherhood. I would never know that joy.

I wanted to go back to a time and place where I was happy, when life was carefree and full of possibilities, but we convened today for an entirely different reason. I was in mourning. My feelings for Linc and our children didn't just go away, they festered, rotting me from the inside out. I was angry, but I could forgive him, we could still be together. I just needed Linc to try. Although the man I loved wasn't sitting beside me, these three women were, and I was more grateful to them than anyone could imagine. After all, they had saved my life.

Even if I couldn't regress back to happiness, they would be my reflection of a time when I had been happy.

'This weed's strong, innit?' Zaheen coughed.

'You know we should get you back to the hospital. Get your scar cleaned up before you catch an infection.' Poppy produced a tender smile, the nurse in her screaming beneath it.

I was fully aware that what I was doing was dangerous to my health, I just didn't care.

'Ten more minutes?' I asked, knowing there was no point in protesting but hoping to delay the inevitable.

'How about fifteen?' Trix said, taking my hand.

I wanted this moment frozen forever.

A field, a lullaby and blurry memories of my children, and the three women who had tried to save them.

CHAPTER FIFTEEN

OPPY'S IVORY HANDS WIPED MY delicate skin in a circular motion. She planted a kiss on my forehead before removing me from the warmth of the bath and handing me over to Trix, who bundled me into a towel. I was ushered on from the bathroom to the stool in front of Trix's dressing table. The bright bulbs illuminated my face and I watched as drops of blood dripped down my shin. Faintly, I heard Poppy whisper to Zaheen, 'I cut her leg while shaving by accident, but I'm really worried, she didn't flinch. She didn't feel a thing.'

'Let's just try and make it through today, Pops.'

Zaheen positioned herself in front of me as she applied my makeup, blending together honey foundation with the vacant tears that streamed down my face.

I didn't name my children.

I had always said once I saw their faces then I would decide on their names. But after what happened I didn't feel like there was much point in them having names. It didn't matter that one was a boy or that the other was a girl. Or that they had dark hair and dimpled chins.

They both became the same thing in the end. Bones and dust.

Death isn't supposed to come in small sizes. Death is for old people who have lived their lives, made mistakes, regretted them. Then made mistakes all over again. Life is an endless ebb and flow of ups and downs, love and losses, but what happened to me meant my happiness was frozen in two almost-formed bodies.

I'd had ideas. Dreams about who my children would've grown up to look like, what they could've gone on to be. Sometimes in the still of the night when traffic has given up and the only noise that penetrates the walls is the sound of wind and insects, I hear them cry. Soft and distant, like I can reach out and touch them if I try hard enough.

I know it's not real. That it can't be real, but for a split second when I wake and my mind hasn't processed what's reality and what isn't, I think they're still with me.

I buried them on a Wednesday afternoon. It was a beautiful day, the sun burned high in the sky by noon, surrounded by nothing but an ocean of blue. It was so unseasonably warm the smell of fresh dirt raised up around me and rested heavily in the air along with the scent of blossom – life and death are never far apart. An unyielding reminder of where we were, and what we were doing there.

Four women dressed in white. It was Poppy's idea. She said it would be a nice tribute, because I wasn't saying goodbye, but saying that I'd see them one sweet day. It was touching. Not that touching tributes and small attentions to detail made things any easier, but the solidarity helped in some small way.

No woman should have to bury her children. Especially alone. Which I wasn't, my girls were by my side, but without Linc I may as well have been.

The funeral was small. Four women, a priest and two tiny white coffins embellished with antique rose gold crosses and lace ivory veils.

The girls had all chipped in to pay for the coffins. In fact, Trix, Zaheen and Poppy had paid for the entire funeral, which made me feel both grateful and a little embarrassed I wasn't in the headspace or financially set to do so. They thoughtfully picked out yellow peonies, amber and patchouli oil candles, and twin grey headstones.

The service was quick. I got the impression that even the priest wanted it to be over. Not out of cruelty – he was an extremely kind man – but for the sadness of the occasion. Everyone recognised the particular tragedy of burying two children who never had the chance to live. Father Nathaniel had dark brown skin and deep creases in his brow and around his lips. He was perhaps fifty, maybe slightly older. He wore a long cream robe, and held a gold crucifix and Bible. He gave an exquisite reading about life and heaven. I was transfixed by the sight of the little white coffins as Father Nathaniel's words washed through me. He compared life to a seed that needed nourishment and water in order for it to grow. He said sometimes an act of nature can take what we've planted away from us. Like a tsunami or an earthquake. He said that a tree can be stripped of leaves to its branches, and although bare, it still lives. It can adapt, produce fruit and grow flowers, even when it looks as though it can't. It becomes not just a tree, but an example of life and what it throws at us.

Obviously Poppy didn't tell Father Nathaniel that I was barren. Or that it wasn't an act of nature that took my children away from me, but the act of two people who scared me into having an accident.

The girls were my rock and I meant that in the literal sense. Poppy, Trix and Zaheen bound together, creating a stable footing for me to walk on. They bathed me, dressed me; they even applied makeup to hide my swollen face and reddened nose. I knew it couldn't have been easy for them, but somehow they managed to give my children the best send-off from the world they never got to see.

'Char, you're squeezing too tight,' Zaheen mouthed over her shoulder to me.

I wasn't aware I was holding on to her. It must have been a reflex since I hadn't taken my eyes off the miniature caskets since they were carried outside the church to the grave site.

'You OK?' Zaheen pressed, noting I hadn't responded.

'I don't know,' I answered honestly, because me saying I was fine wouldn't convince them. We were all broken up pieces of the same fucked-up mirror, our reflection a memory of the two bodies that lay inside those boxes.

I touched the bracelet, the one Linc had given me after our fight. Him not being there was like having my heart crushed, the weight of his absence as heavy as the diamonds on my wrist.

'I know today's hard, but just hang in there. We're almost through the worst of it. You just gotta make it through this last bit, and then I'll get you out of here. I promise.'

Zaheen's words felt like gravel in my ears. I didn't want to leave them. Not here. Not in the dark, damp soil. They were supposed to be with me, not buried with strangers and left in the cold.

'You need to tell this guy to wrap it up. Char's not looking too good. I'm not sure she can take much more of this. I'm amazed she's made it this far,' Trix said to Poppy, who nodded then approached me, her heels getting stuck in a patch of grass as she approached.

'Do you want to say a few words. Maybe sing a lullaby?'

The contrast between Poppy's white dress and blue eyes seemed startling. It brought me back to my surroundings. My children were about to be lowered into the ground, but I could hardly stand, let alone speak.

'I can't.' It was shaky, almost inaudible, but I was sure she heard what I said, because she started to sing 'Carrickfergus'. The ditty was pretty and sad, and I knew instantly why she chose it and was grateful she had. She had an angelic voice although she didn't use it much as she suffered from crippling stage fright. But there wasn't a trace of fear in her that day. She sang from the pit of her diaphragm. She sang for me, and the children I never got to watch take a breath.

I glanced up at the twining trees with running perennial roots and willed myself to be as strong as its branches.

'I ...' My mouth curved to speak but my tongue felt like a weight. The words flapped about then floundered like a fish never to be spoken. Trix's perception kicked in with one look. She paced towards me, her cream clutch perched underarm, eyes wide, lips downturned into a quiver.

'It's OK. You did it. Let's go home, Char.'

THE HIVE — Lincoln Jackson confirms in a tweet that his relationship with Charlotte Goodwin is over

LINCOLN JACKSON @lincolnjackson   22.11
Hey guys. I usually don't speak about my private life, but my house was broken into recently. No one was hurt although @charlottegoodwin tripped during the incident and suffered minor injuries. We are no longer together romantically but I wish her a speedy recovery and all the best in the future

valandrie — No surprise there he's been pictured with @heididolak for weeks

sunshine59 — Poor @charlottegoodwin hope she's recovered from her fall

parkersmith — Good riddance if you ask me

huddleston44 — Another one bites the dust haha #thehive

lucymaddison — No guesses who he left @charlottegoodwin for, I would be so upset if it were me

chestermann — Forget all this nonsense when's he announcing his next fight @thehive

nateyorkshir77 — @lincolnjackson can I get your leftovers mate? Asking for a friend

skinnygirl3 — Be careful @heididolak you lose them how you get them

kareningrid — This is why you shouldn't date celebrities @charlottegoodwin

clayforge — I love @thehive

CHAPTER SIXTEEN

I REMEMBERED EVERY WORD THAT WAS spoken. I remembered crying so hard that I couldn't breathe without hearing a gurgle in the back of my throat. I could have drowned in tears. There were too many tears, and not enough holes to let them out. I remembered Zaheen and Poppy spending the night on Trix's sofas, unable to go home because they were so worried about me.

The funeral was hard but coming home was much harder.

I recalled Trix getting into bed with me, singing lullabies and stroking my hair until no more tears fell from my eyes and exhaustion plunged me into the numbness of sleep.

It was restless, coming in fits and starts. The pain vibrated through me even as my mind tried to switch off. My body wouldn't stop moving, twisting in the bed sheets even as the sutures in my scar stretched open, seeping with blood.

I felt like such a fool. Linc's tweet had gone viral. By the next morning, I had almost five hundred thousand followers. Some offered messages of support, others simply wanted to know why we had broken up.

I had lost two children and my womb, yet Linc described it online as a brief incident where no one was hurt. What was he playing at?

I'd told the police what I had seen that night. I said what had happened when I had spoken to Linc. He didn't believe me, yet there he was, online, admitting that I wasn't lying.

There were intruders in Linc's house that night. They caused the accident.

I had no Linc and no babies. Even the doctors were concerned, urging me to speak to a therapist since I had gone through such an extreme loss.

What the hell did they know about what I had lost?

I had lost my entire family in the space of a few days and then, as if things couldn't get any worse, I was hit with the news that I would never be able to have children again due to the extensive injuries sustained in my accident.

I was twenty-eight and barren.

The only thing that made any sense was that I didn't deserve love, no matter how much I yearned for it. Linc neither missed me nor cared, and I felt it with every breath I took.

So I went through the motions. I brushed my teeth, scraped my hair into a ponytail, and put on clothes. All methodically, all without purpose or depth. Like a memory of things I used to do, my brain and body on autopilot, barely able to hold it together.

I didn't want to cry. It wouldn't bring them back. Crying was just a release if nothing else.

I hid my bloodshot eyes behind sunglasses and left my bedroom for the first time since the girls had brought me home from the grave site.

I needed to get on with life, not because I wanted to, and not because I was fighting to win, but because when bad things happen the world doesn't stop.

There are no choices. You either move with the rest of the world or watch it go by. I was getting a little sick of watching and decided it was time to rejoin.

After all, I had absolutely nothing else to lose.

'Hey, there you are.' Zaheen stood in the doorway carrying a rattling silver tray adorned with toasted sourdough and tea diluted with too much cream. She'd put ruby-red jam in a tiny cylinder pot on the side with a glass of chilled pressed orange juice and slices of cut-up watermelon prettily placed on a saucer next to it.

'I thought maybe you would like something to eat. Wait, where the hell are you going?'

'Are Poppy and Trix back from the station yet?' I asked, picking up the threads of an overheard conversation but ignoring her question. All four of us were due to give statements at the police station about what happened the night of my accident. We had put it off until after the funeral, but DI Kilby, the lead in the investigation, was getting antsy, eager to get it over and done with. He refused to acknowledge that the missing CCTV footage of that night was significant. *System glitches, happens all the time*, he said in a passive voice when he came to the hospital dressed in an awful terracotta suit that had grease stains from what I presumed was that morning's breakfast. He didn't seem to be concerned with finding out who had broken into Linc's house. Since I wasn't the owner of the property, he wasn't at liberty to discuss particular details with me. Even though those particular details led to the death of my children.

It was a shit show. He kept calling it a 'late miscarriage' and shut me down every time I tried to correct him.

I still couldn't remember what had transpired that night. Not exactly. My brain was a muddle of bloodied images and one tender goodbye. Linc's manager contacted Trix to inform her, or rather threaten her, that if any of what really happened that night got leaked to the press, Linc would take legal action against all of us.

The NDA followed. It was unforgivable.

It made the tweet he posted all the more of a betrayal. Linc took away my chance to explain to the public what really happened between us. He had silenced me.

'They're not back yet, but Trix had her interview, I just spoke to her. She's on her way home. You didn't answer my question. Charlotte, where are you going?'

'Out. I'm going out.'

'You sure you're up to that? You know you should be resting.'

The soothing tone in Zaheen's voice made me feel uncomfortable. I knew she was only trying to help but as she set the tray down onto the floating shelf in the mouth of the hallway and slowly approached, I felt even more sorry for myself.

'I'll be fine. The only time I've been out since leaving the hospital has been to attend the funeral. I need some air.'

That was a lie. I wanted to be near my children. I was going to visit them.

'I dunno, Char. Maybe I should go with you.'

'You can't hold my hand every second of every day, Zee.'

'I know I can't, but you need to rest. You heard what the doctor said.'

I didn't. But I was sure Poppy had paid attention.

'If it were me . . .' She trailed off, not finishing her sentence because it wasn't her.

It was me.

'I'm fine, OK? I just need a little air and some time alone without one of you barging in every thirty minutes to check if I'm still breathing.'

'Can you blame us? We're concerned. You're not eating or speaking. You've got to tell me how to help you because right now I don't know how. Please, let me help you.'

I flipped up my T-shirt, revealing the padded bandage that hid the scar from where the glass had penetrated me. There was a perfect circle of blood in the middle that resembled the Japanese flag.

'Don't you see? You can't help me.'

I had only been out of hospital two weeks, my stomach was swollen, my wounds were still fresh, my bruises a watercolour blend of purples and greens. I didn't recognise myself.

'What do you want me to say? It's fine. *I'm* fine. Whatever I say won't help so please just leave me alone. Now, if you'll excuse me.' I barged past her, the tray shaking in my wake as I slammed the door behind me and was hit with a rush of air.

I didn't want to have a conversation, I just wanted to get out of the house.

How do you get over losing the only people you've ever loved completely and unconditionally? How do you begin to start again when so much has changed? You can't get over it. You don't find a way to cope, and it definitely doesn't get easier. If anything, it gets harder. Going about your life, day by day, with no purpose and no hope of things returning to how they were before. You don't get the feeling back.

I hated the memories.

I hated the angry scar that had me doubled over, walking like a cripple, a visual and painful reminder of the night I lost everything. Most of all, I hated the memories of Linc. Those images hurt the most, because when I kissed his lips it was because I wanted to kiss him. I wanted to feel our love radiate through me.

It wasn't an act.

That's what I missed; that's why I couldn't let go.

If I had my eyes open the entire time, I would've seen what was really happening, and just how fucked up it was.

Grief is blind. You can't see past it until you've gone through it, and even then, the pain hurts just the same, but, once the fog clears, you'll see exactly who's to blame.

CHAPTER SEVENTEEN

IT HAD BEEN TWO MONTHS since I had worked and even longer since I'd been there in person, but enough was enough. In a snap decision, I decided to go back, because at the very least I could use the distraction and was getting a little sick of the constant hangover gnawing at my brain in the mornings. So, I called the HR department and confirmed a start date. So much had changed over the past eight weeks, especially me, and it felt like it had been so much longer, like it had been years instead of months. I was slimmer but not in the pumping iron, gym kind of way. My diet had essentially been reduced to gin, vodka and red wine, and it had started to take its toll.

My skin was sallow and dry, rougher than it usually was. My eyes had taken on a tinge and my once-white teeth were stained honey-yellow with nicotine, which had also become a new habit. I would have a cigarette the moment I woke up, needing to feel the fullness of smoke weigh down my chest before I could contemplate the day ahead. By lunchtime, I would have downed half a bottle of something cheap and strong and would be working through a rather large bag of weed. Once all that failed, I would take a sleeping tablet so I was knocked out by the time Trix or Zaheen came in to check on me. Poppy was on night shifts but spent the weekends holed up with me in Trix's house instead of spending time with Jeremy. They were serious now. She was well and truly over Brad.

When had something like this happened?

Although I was moving through life I was still stuck in that moment, paralysed by the night everything changed.

It wasn't easy but I thought if this was the new normal then I might as well get used to it. It was strange being back, acting as if nothing had happened. No one asked me about Linc, leading me to believe everyone had already discussed the hell out of me and my fucked-up situation. Linc had ensured the truth stayed off the internet by posting that tweet, and the girls wouldn't divulge what had really happened to another living soul without my say-so.

The secret of the night I lost my twins remained in my head locked away safe, with Linc having the only key.

None of this stopped Zaheen, Poppy and Trix from giving me sideways looks or tripping over their words just to ensure my fragile shell wouldn't crack from hearing the words 'baby' or 'twins'. They were walking on eggshells, and I just wanted to get back to normal or at the very least some semblance of it. This was another reason I went back to work, to put all their minds at ease. My promotion was just another thing that had been taken from me. HR said it was because I didn't pass my probation period, but what they really meant was I was no longer Lincoln Jackson's girlfriend so I wasn't an asset. Admin it was; the menial daily tasks would be a welcome distraction for my cluttered mind. A small part of me was ready to give the outside world a go, the other part of me just didn't know where I fitted into it.

I wasn't Lincoln Jackson's girlfriend, and I wasn't a mother. I didn't know what I'd become. I felt like someone else.

'How's your first day back going so far?' Arianna, a plump, middle-aged woman with silvery hair and a mole on the left side of her chin came bopping towards me with a wide smile on her face. She was always smiling, and everyone in the clinic affectionately called her 'Mummy' because she baked cakes and was the only person to refill the biscuit tin. She was the head of the HR department and took her role very seriously. It often left her tightly wound but she would always welcome me with an affectionate smile and a steaming cup of tea. She had no children and was always the first one in and the last one to leave.

I always liked her for that. Warm and melty, she reminded me of butterscotch.

'Same old. Nothing's changed around here much,' I answered, not wanting her to know where my thoughts were as I tapped away vacantly on the keyboard.

'Tell me about it. This job gets so repetitive, it's unbelievable. It's like the slush pipe never stops. There's always something to do.'

'Yeah, but I guess I kinda missed the slush. Otherwise, I wouldn't be back. Idle hands,' I said flatly, referring to the giant pile of patient files I had yet to scan on to the internal system.

'Look – I didn't want to make a big deal, considering all you've been through. The last thing you probably want to do is discuss it but, here.' She handed me a white envelope with a lilac card inside.

It wasn't what was written in the card but what wasn't. There was no big spew about dusting yourself off or getting back to life as it was before my accident.

All that was written was – *Sorry*.

'I don't know what to say.'

'I know it hurts. I really am sorry for your loss, Charlotte. No woman should ever have to go through losing a child, let alone twins. You're very brave.'

Legally, I had had to divulge what had happened in order for her to do a risk assessment for me coming back to work. The clinic was bound by employee confidentiality. It was the only clause in the NDA that allowed me to disclose the truth about that night to someone other than Poppy, Trix and Zaheen.

Her eyes raked over me, like she was trying to communicate with thoughts rather than words. The temperature of her smile changed from sunny to chilly, the tears in her eyes reflecting off the light.

Then it hit me.

'How long ago was yours?'

Suddenly I understood her tragedy better than anyone else. It was like we were in some sort of secret club. The barren club.

'He would have been twenty-three in November.'

'I'm so sorry. Does it get any easier? You know, does time really heal all wounds?' I asked, looking at my future and seeing myself through her grief-stricken eyes staring back.

'Well, Charlotte, it doesn't get any harder. But I suppose the pain never goes away. Not truly. Eventually you just become numb to it. You find a way to cope. You already took the first step by coming back to work.'

'I have to pay the bills somehow. Can I ask you something?'

'Sure, anything.' She knotted her fingers together, all those years had passed and she still couldn't reflect on the memory of her child without feeling robbed of being his mother.

'Did you name him?'

'I did. Ben, after my papa.'

'I never named mine. I had ideas – well, one or two – but I wanted to see what they looked like before I gave them names. Now I wish I had instead of just referring to them as "the twins".'

'You will always hold on to the memory of them. I know it's hard especially since you've had such a public break-up, but you are not alone. I'm here if you ever want to talk.'

She was right.

My relationship with Linc had been too public. Our break-up was all over The Hive, on every blog post and in the comments. I was constantly receiving messages, but all I wanted to do was hide from the world. I could have deleted my account but that would just mean the trolls had won, so I did the opposite. I made three fake accounts so I could spy on Linc.

'It's been rough but I'm just trying to make it through.'

'A miscarriage can tear even the strongest couples apart – that's what happened to me and my husband. After Ben, it just wasn't the same. I couldn't forgive myself. We just drifted apart. Soon there was so much space between us it was easier to go our separate ways than stay together and face each other every day.'

Should I have told her the truth? Should I have told her that I hadn't seen Linc in person since I had lost the twins? All I had got was a two-minute phone call as I lay in my hospital bed womb-less and a break-up tweet for the entire world to see.

'He's dealing with it in his own way. On his own,' I hissed.

'Things have a funny way of working out. He'll be back once the dust settles. He just needs time. Men handle grief differently to women. Have you made any appointments to see a specialist?'

'No, I guess I've been a little busy. I haven't had time to book an appointment yet. But I'll get to it at some point.'

That was a lie, I had my second appointment with Dr Kole booked for the day after tomorrow, but I was still a little too embarrassed to admit I was struggling and needed counselling. I only went at the girls' behest, and it didn't go well. That was putting it politely. I spent the first twenty or so minutes high on diazepam wailing Linc's name and making animalistic noises. I ended up leaving my first session more broken than when I went in.

'Charlotte, you should. It'll be good for you. This wasn't your fault; it was an accident.'

'I know, I just haven't had the chance to see anyone professionally yet. But I will,' I said tightly.

'Sorry.'

'No, I'm just a little on edge. First day back. Not sure who knows what.'

'Understandable. And don't worry, apart from me and Gavin in HR nobody knows a thing. Staff confidentiality.'

'Thank you, I appreciate the discretion. I'll catch up with you after lunch. Got to have a quick word with Dr Kapoor about the forms he forgot to sign in his last appointment.'

'Bless him, he's always forgetting. I'll see you later.'

'Yeah, have a good one.'

I had been trying not to go over the events of that night, mentally blocking it out since I had woken up in hospital, but I was aware that something wasn't right. The more I ignored it, the more I knew that something had been wrong. I just couldn't put my finger on it. Linc had asked me to come by that night. Which was odd. Linc usually stuck to a pretty strict schedule: track first thing, usually Lea Valley, followed by break-fast, then an afternoon nap. Linc would then go sparring, which took at least two hours, making him get home just after 7 p.m. But he didn't come home that night and he didn't go sparring either. Trix checked with his coaches when she was trying to get hold of him to tell him what had happened. So, if he hadn't been sparring then where had Linc been the night of my acci-dent? I had been afraid to ask myself this question, scared of what the answer would mean.

'There you are!' Zaheen interrupted me at my desk, my growing thoughts simmering as they reached boiling point.

'Yeah, I'm here. I thought we were meeting after work?'

'Yeah, I know, but I got a late meeting so thought I'd check on you first. Coffee? Everything OK?'

I thought about lying and if anyone else had asked, I prob-ably would have, but Zaheen had this look on her face. One I was all too familiar with.

'No. Actually everything's not OK. In fact, it's very wrong.'

'What's on your mind? Talk to me.'

'Why did you guys come to Linc's house that night?' I hadn't asked that question before, but it had been niggling at me for weeks.

'You're joking, right?' Zaheen raised one perfectly micro-bladed brow and waved her hands back and forth.

'I know I hate talking about it, and I said I never wanted you guys to mention it again but ...'

'It's OK. To be honest, it always struck me as weird you inviting us round that night. We hated Lincoln, but thank fuck you did. Imagine if Poppy and Trix never got your message.'

'Invite you? I didn't invite you. What are you talking about? Zaheen, what message?'

She paused, confusion flooding her features.

'Why are you screaming?' She closed the office door. 'Look, you hit your head pretty hard that night, so you probably don't remember much, but you sent Poppy and Trix a message.' She pulled her phone from her snakeskin handbag, scrolling through her WhatsApp messages until she found the photo. 'This message. See. The girls screenshotted it to me. This is precisely why I don't have any social media by the way.'

She turned the screen to face me. And there it was. A message from me in our Instagram group chat, asking Trix and Poppy to call Zaheen and come over and have a girls' night in Linc's cinema room. The message came in around the time of my accident.

'I didn't write this.'

'You were concussed. Maybe you just don't remember,' Zaheen said, replacing her phone.

I took her by the shoulders and looked straight into her eyes.

'I didn't send that message.'

'So, if you didn't, then who the hell did?'

CHAPTER EIGHTEEN

I RAN FASTER, MY HEART BEATING so hard, I could have sworn it was going to burst straight through my chest, but I kept going. Sweat dripped from every pore in my body, as I felt my muscles tighten. I pumped weights, still unable to relieve myself from the adrenaline coursing through my veins. When that didn't work, I left the gym and headed for The Rose pub at the very top of Poppy's street in Bethnal Green, and messaged the girls along the way to meet me there as planned. While I waited for them, I soaked up the smell of lager and battered haddock.

The lump in my throat hadn't cleared since Zaheen showed me the Instagram message sent from my account, a few hours earlier. I never wrote it, nor could I figure out why anyone would. It was strange because I knew whoever sent it must have known about the break-in. Or maybe they were behind it.

'Over here,' I called out. Trix waved, herself and Poppy quickly approaching the wooden table at the back as I stood up to greet them. Zaheen couldn't be there for at least another hour due to her meetings but promised me she would get there as soon as she could. I'd learned over the years to never ask Zaheen anything when she said she was busy. She did things her own way and I was very much OK with that.

'What's this all about? Your message said we should hurry so we got here as soon as we could,' Poppy said.

Her snowy-blonde hair glistened even under the glare of dim lights as she plonked herself into the seat opposite me, her violet jumper making her look younger than she was.

'It's about the night of my accident.' I sat back down, removing a notepad and pen from my bag. If we were going to go over the events from that night, then I would have to do so detached from my emotions. I had to treat it like it wasn't me it had happened to. I had to see it through fresh eyes.

'You both received the same group message on Instagram, asking you to come to Linc's to meet me for film night. Right?'

'Yeah, and it's a good thing we all came together. You could have died if we hadn't found you in time. All three of you could have died I mean …'

Trix rested her leather jacket on the back of the chair and proceeded to drop a sugar cube into my lukewarm latte. It made a plopping noise before it dissolved.

'You've completely lost me.' Poppy's face didn't change, although her tone did. She was confused and I didn't blame her. What I was about to tell them sounded crazy even as I said it.

'Two men broke into a house, the house of a famous boxer, yet rather than rob the place blind, they scared the life out of me until I fell and then they left me for dead. Then you guys showed up after receiving a message from me on Instagram. It doesn't add up.'

'I'm still not following,' Trix said quizzically.

'Don't you see? I didn't send the message,' I said, staring them down. 'I didn't ask you guys to come round. It wasn't me, which means the men that broke in must have sent it.'

'Don't be silly! It came from your account. It had to be you.'

'Quiet, Trix – so if it wasn't you then it must have been them? Why?' Poppy cut in, her blue eyes darkening as her brain saw the direction this was heading. 'Who were they?'

'I don't know yet, but if I figure out who sent that message then I'll know who's responsible for the death of my children.'

'But DI Kilby said it was probably a couple of kids messing about. It was a horrible accident. That's all.'

'The police got it wrong, Trix. Wouldn't be the first time, and I doubt it'll be the last. Come on, it's not like they've had any leads. Or found any suspects. It's like they've brushed it under the carpet.'

She was rendered silent, but I could tell she wasn't convinced.

'I don't get it. Why would anyone want to hurt you, or your twins?'

'That's a good question, one I can't answer because this whole thing makes no sense to me, but someone deleted the CCTV footage. That's not a coincidence.'

I turned to look at Poppy to confirm what I was saying was true. Her face was sombre at first, but then it looked like she was trying to swallow a huge pill that had become lodged in the back of her throat.

'What is it?' I asked, knowing there was something she wanted to say but was too afraid to say it.

'Nothing,' she replied, an air of fear tightening her tone.

'It is bloody something, Pops – spill it! Honestly, it can't get any worse now, can it?'

'You're not going to like it, Char.'

'Well, I don't like being in the dark either, so do us all a favour and shed a little light. Poppy, whoever did this took away my only chance of having a family. I need to understand why. Please, I need closure.'

'But it'll hurt you – and besides, I don't know, it's just a feeling. A sick, twisted feeling.'

'Nothing can hurt me anymore. I'm unhurtable – just say it. You can't cause me any more pain.'

She stared at me.

'For God's sake, Poppy, say it already. This shitty latte's running straight through me,' Trix tutted.

Soft and gentle, Poppy spoke as if every word was a misshapen step and she had to tread extremely lightly in case she fell.

'I think Lincoln did it.'

'What?!' I spat, unable to control the disgust in my voice.

'You said it yourself, he wasn't acting like a prospective father. He was distant and—'

'So, you think he caused the accident because he was scared of becoming a dad? I've never heard such bullshit in my life, Poppy. That's ridiculous. He wasn't even at home.'

'I told you, it's just a feeling. Lincoln was acting odd from the moment you told him you were pregnant. Then two men break into his home and focus the entirety of their efforts on you. He didn't even bother coming to the hospital let alone the funeral, and let's not forget the NDA. It's suspicious!'

I turned to look at Trix, waiting for her to jump in, to defend Linc, to defend our relationship – hell, even to tell Poppy to shut the fuck up – but she didn't. She just nodded along absently.

'He did this. I know he did it, and if he didn't, then he's mixed up in it somehow. Mark my words, Lincoln Jackson is far from innocent.'

'You don't know what you're talking about, Poppy. This isn't one of those crime books you love reading – the husband did it – it wasn't him. Linc wasn't home that night, and he doesn't know the password to my Instagram account.'

Poppy snorted. 'Coincidently. Yet he told you to meet him at his house at precisely the same time as the break-in.'

'OK, you two. Let's all just calm down for a minute and talk about this,' Trix said, taking on the unusual role of mediator.

'Something about this doesn't feel right. I'm not trying to hurt her on purpose, but you know it too. You said it yourself.'

'You've been speaking about me behind my back?' I said to neither of them in particular but both of them at the same time.

'No, you're not trying to hurt her, Poppy, but she just lost her children. Accusing their father isn't exactly helping right now, is it?'

'*Hello?*' I was pissed off. 'I'm sitting right here, if you're gonna talk about how fragile I am at least have the courtesy to wait until I'm out of earshot, or is that another thing you discuss behind my back?'

Poppy leaned forward.

'Charlotte, sweetie, you don't need me to tell you how strange he was acting and deep down you know that Lincoln wasn't who you thought he was. That's why he won't face you. That's why he won't face any of us because he knows what he's done.'

I hated to admit it, but she was right. Looking back now I could see all the little signs that Linc wasn't ready to be a father.

But still, could Linc really have done it? Did he set me up?

'Someone group-messaged us to save you that night, someone who knew your Instagram password,' Poppy hissed.

'You all know my password. It hasn't changed in years, so should I be accusing you lot as well as him?'

'Come on. Are you for real? Why would we do that?' Trix screeched, gobsmacked.

'Maybe you were jealous.' I sniffed, folding my arms. I didn't want to hurt them, but they were attacking Linc and therefore, by extension, me. Suggesting that somehow I was to blame for what had happened.

'Even if you believe we are capable of doing that to you, and I'm hurt you'd for a second think that was possible, we couldn't have. From the moment we picked up Zee we were all together, we found you together, and whoever sent the Instagram message knew the security code for Lincoln's house. You never gave any of us the code. *Ever!* It couldn't have been me, Trix or Zee.'

Poppy was right, it wasn't them, nor did I ever think it was. Not really. It was just easier to hurt them than to admit they could be right.

'I don't know what I'm saying, I'm sorry,' I admitted. 'I know it wasn't you, or you, Trix. I just can't stomach the thought of Linc having anything to do with our children's death. He's a selfish prick, but this level of evil is surely too much even for him. You see that, right? We were their parents. We loved them.'

Trix and Poppy exchanged a look.

'And how would you know that? You two were only dating three months before you got pregnant. You don't know him, or the things he's capable of, Char. You can't swear for him, you can't swear for anyone.' Poppy sounded like she was about to cry.

'So, what do I do?'

Trix and Poppy both looked at each other, waiting for the other to answer. In the end it was Poppy who spoke.

'You can either forget about Lincoln, about what happened and move on, or you can let this thing eat away at whatever's left of you and make him pay for what he did. No matter what you decide, we are always going to be here for you, like we were there for you that night. We got through that together, we got through the funeral together, and we'll get through this together.'

She was right. Poppy had delivered my children as I lay in a pool of blood on the brink of death. To this day, she, Zaheen and Trix were the only people other than myself to have held my twins. All four of us went through it together, but there was one person who wasn't there.

And that, I couldn't ignore.

'What's it gonna be, Char?' Trix asked, the words swollen, waiting to see which path I would decide to go down, then my phone pinged.

It was a notification from one of my fake accounts.

Linc had posted a photo.

LINCOLN JACKSON — Happy birthday to the love of my life @heididolak. I'm so lucky to have you with me on this crazy journey called life. In the short time we've been together you've shown me what true unconditional love looks like. There's no one I would want to spend my life with other than you, I love you baby

anniekaper2 — wasn't he just in a relationship with @charlotte-goodwin like a week ago???

mazzydean — @anniekaper2 these celebs and their constant need to go Instagram official with their partners yukkkk

lisaoakley — @mazzydean if you don't want to see it then delete your account #bekind

martinjustmartin — wow you 2 look amazing together

smokeme — Happy birthday @heididolak

valandrie — @lincolnjackson bought her a Range Rover I can't even get my boyfriend to buy me flowers lol nice for some

vinnierichrich — now we know why @charlottegoodwin was always defending her relationship, I feel sorry for her she looks so stupid

francescabrernice — @heididolak you look amazing so happy you've found the love of ur life

liamgreen43 — when's your next fight? @lincolnjackson

sharonlovespasta — @vanessaflynn77 don't you love @heididolak dress I want something like that for my bday!

yannablake — nooooo @lincolnjackson I'm your real wife kmt I'm sad now . . .

CHAPTER NINETEEN

INC'S TWEET WAS A SLAP in the face, like everything else he had done since the night I lost our babies. I still didn't have a clue who had sent the Instagram message or why they had wanted to save my life. It didn't add up; everything about that night remained in darkness.

'Ms Goodwin, you can go straight through to Dr Kole's office on your right.'

I looked up at the sound of my name. The receptionist, bright in magenta, looked at me dazed for a moment. I had completely forgotten where I was and what I was there for. Collecting myself, I got up and paced towards the small windowless corner office observing the paper-thin walls as I did. It was the first week of March and outside the weather was considerably warm for an early spring day, meaning I'd opted for a Tiffany blue sundress accented with pearl accessories and white sandals.

London revellers were gearing up for the impending weekend with their usual animated vigour. I used to be one of those people, thrilled for the weekend, ready to see which club or restaurant I would end up in. I would drink wine I couldn't afford, eat food I couldn't pronounce and wake up in hotel suites with men I couldn't remember fucking. Those were some of the best nights of my life. They always ended the same way: with Zaheen, Trix and Poppy, making memories we could hold on to forever. That was until I got pregnant, then the best parts became Linc and our unborn children.

'Have a seat. Is it OK if I call you Charlotte, or would you still prefer I go by Ms Goodwin for today's session?'

'Charlotte will be fine.'

The room was airless. The only outside light smattering through a huge pane of frosted glass. Dr Kole wasn't a slight man. He was bald and podgy with red spots on his face and neck. Specks of silver lined the stubble on his chin, while the pale blue shirt that struggled to encase most of him helped bring out downy green eyes. He smelt like an old man. Earthy and ancient. I was in no mood to deal with him though, and once I regained my surroundings, was pissed off that I was even there to begin with. But painstakingly session two began.

'Would you like a tea? Coffee? I've got some Jammie Dodgers in the desk drawer. I won't tell if you don't.' He rubbed his full stomach and chuckled warmly, adjusting himself in his seat.

'I'm fine, thank you. I had a big breakfast.' Smiling, I realised I had just lied straight to his face within seconds of entering the room. I hadn't actually eaten anything solid for at least seventy-two hours and didn't intend on doing so anytime soon. I quite liked being day-drunk, it gave me something to do other than mourn.

'Ah, so you're eating, that's good. You seem less lethargic. Quite an improvement to our last session.' He was referring to our first meeting last week where I'd started screaming and, once I'd started, I didn't think I'd be able to stop.

After my wailing, I had sat in silence for the rest of the hour, hearing the slow tick-tock of the clock. By that point I didn't want to talk. Hell, I didn't even remember how to talk.

'Yeah, it's great. I'm like a bottomless bin. I just eat and eat and eat,' I said, welcoming the small talk. If I kept it up for long enough then the entire hour would pass before I had to speak about anything real. While I knew I needed to talk about things, this was the new way I dealt with my feelings. By letting others speak about themselves all I had to do was sit there and nod. Agreeable.

I even found myself doing it with the girls. The other night Poppy had passed by Trix's after work. She had been doing that a lot, checking in and popping by, this time she came armed with a ridiculous story from work because she was sure it would cheer me up.

'One of the patients in ICU came back to life today.'

I paused then burst into mock laughter, as if what Poppy had said was the funniest thing in the world.

She had to be joking.

'What'd you mean, came back to life? That can't happen, unless your patient's name is Jesus of Nazareth,' Trix declared, obviously baffled and rightly so. Poppy hadn't even finished her gin and tonic yet.

'That's what I said at first. But he was dead, and now he's alive and absolutely fine. Just frostbite – bad frostbite might I add. But that's all, can you believe it?'

'No. Poppy, to be honest, I'm struggling to follow.' Zaheen dubiously raised a brow, her mind swimming with questions.

She loved a good mystery, but this seemed too much even for her.

'OK, start at the beginning. What happened? How did he die?' I made a good effort at feigning engagement, leaning forward to mix another drink as the three of them picked at matching chicken pomegranate salads. Mine hadn't been touched.

'He didn't die. That's what I'm saying. Or are you not paying attention? We thought he was dead.'

Sometimes it annoyed me that Poppy thought she was the most intelligent person in the room. That was one of those times. Or maybe my drinking was getting out of hand. I couldn't really be sure.

'You know what I mean. What happened?'

Frustrated, I pulled out the adjacent stool and sat down, the legs made a horrible scraping sound against the wood, setting my teeth on edge as Poppy spoke.

'This man – well, he's more of a boy than a man. He's a teen-ager, like seventeen – anyway he was pronounced dead a few days ago. Drug overdose or some other experimental shit like that. You know kids these days, anything from LSD to synthetic marijuana, they wanna try it all. Fuck the consequences. Anyway, he passed out at college and was taken to hospital. He was dead, or at least looked that way by the time the ambulance got there. We put his body in the morgue, recorded time of death, informed his parents and offered counselling – all the normal things we do when a kid dies. Then, seventy-two hours later he woke up.'

'How's that even possible? What'd you mean he woke up? Like in the freezer?' I asked, the alcohol etching my words.

'Yes, in the freezer. One of the nurses heard banging coming from inside. She opened the door and he came at her like some savage dog. His skin was blue and bleeding. He was so mad but he came back to life!'

'So, what is he? Some sort of resurrecting demon? I've got it. He's Merlin's son,' I quipped.

'Very funny, Char. Close but no cigar. Turns out he was never really dead to begin with, just in some deep comatose state. Barely alive, but not dead either. Somewhere hovering in between. It must have been awful come to think about it. It's spooky.'

'Surely you guys checked his vital signs before pronouncing him dead? It's the NHS for Christ's sake, not a mud shack in Mexico. Although you know I only do private healthcare,' Trix challenged, still in disbelief, but not shocked enough to remind us she was wealthy.

'According to the nurses on shift that night, he had none. He had no pulse or signs of life. He was dead. Well, not literally, but well you get it. It was like he was dead. They couldn't tell the difference. Whatever he took it almost killed him though. He's lucky to be alive.'

'How creepy. Honestly, stuff like that makes me feel so uneasy. Gives me the shivers.'

Zaheen tried to pour tonic water into my gin but I declined. The smell of citrus rested in the air as I did my best to block out the nattering. I wished my own children could come back from the dead.

'So, how have you been? How's work?' Dr Kole interrupted my thoughts. What he meant to ask was, how was work since I gave birth to two dead babies on my ex-boyfriend's kitchen floor.

'Work's great! It's a good distraction. It's nice to be a part of the real world again.'

He jotted something down disapprovingly, so I manufactured a more convincing smile, positioning pre-prepared lies on my tongue ready for his next line of enquiry.

'Exercise has really helped, you know, mentally, physically. I feel like I'm in the best shape of my life.'

'That's good. How are you sleeping? Have you had any nightmares or panic attacks?'

'Not one, guess I'm one of the lucky ones. Everything's back to normal. No complaints.'

It didn't seem necessary to tell him I locked myself in the staff bathroom struggling to breathe for two hours that morning. I mean surely that was completely irrelevant and frankly none of his business. Even if he was my doctor.

'You know, Charlotte, all you've said is "everything's fine". Do you think maybe we should go a little deeper under the surface? What'd you say? Just for today?'

No, fuck that. We were not going anywhere, especially under the surface. That's where I kept all the bad things. The things I told myself weren't real.

'I'm good,' I said firmly. My smile was gone.

'You went through an extreme trauma. It's only natural to have strong emotions, whether they are good or bad, sad or happy. Our emotions are the one unpredictability in humans. It's OK to feel something, Charlotte.'

'I'm fine, Dr Kole, honestly.'

'That's the thing – sometimes our minds can play tricks on us. Our brain needs to find a way to cope with trauma, so we block out how we really feel as a coping mechanism. That way we protect ourselves from the truth.'

'Well, I'm certainly coping.' I meant that because I was there, so I was coping on the outside at least.

'So, have you had any contact with Lincoln?'

The question threw me. I wished I was more prepared for it. But I wasn't.

'Can we not speak about him today, please?'

I remembered our first session a little more clearly then. Me curled up in a ball howling Linc's name. At one particularly embarrassing point, I pulled out my phone and showed him pictures of us together so he would believe it was really him. That I was really with Lincoln Jackson and it wasn't all just some fabrication by an insane woman obsessed with The Hive and celebrity culture.

'We should speak about him. He suffered too you know. It might be helpful to talk about someone else's pain if we can't talk about your own.'

I hadn't spoken to Linc since that phone call while I was in hospital. I was the last person who knew what he was going through.

'I can't talk about him, I just can't.' It was the most honest confession I had made in two sessions.

'OK. But we have to talk about it at some stage.'

'No, we don't.' I shook my head. 'Talking about Linc doesn't benefit anyone. Especially me. But fine. The love of my life hurt me. I loved and trusted him, and he hurt me. Can we move on now?'

'Not quite. How did that make you feel?'

Was Dr Kole fucking with me?

'Are you for real?'

'Yes, how did it make you feel, Charlotte?' Dr Kole's chin moved a little as he pronounced every syllable of my name, his eyes fixed to mine.

'I can't have children! I can't do the single most important thing I was hoping to do,' I snapped venomously. 'You think this is easy for me? Watching my ex-boyfriend publicly move on knowing I never will?'

'So, you're angry at Lincoln?'

'Yes, I'm angry. I'm also sad. I'm sad all the time. They are the only babies I will ever have, and they're gone. Everything has been taken from me in an accident, but where's my justice?'

'That's the thing with accidents, there really isn't anyone to blame . . .'

I wished Trix, Zaheen and Poppy had let me bleed out on Linc's kitchen floor that night. I wished they had never come to my rescue.

'This whole thing is a joke. You're not making me feel any better.'

I got to my feet, readying myself to leave.

'Charlotte, please sit down. We have another forty-five minutes.'

'That's forty-five minutes I can spend alone not answering your absurd questions. I miss my children. You can't bring them back so there's no point in talking about this anymore, OK? I'm done.'

'I'm sorry for striking a nerve, but that's the point of therapy. To talk about the things that make us feel uncomfortable.'

'Stop wasting my time. I'm done!'

I picked up my bag and left without another word.

I was fuming. Where the hell did Dr Kole get his PhD? All he seemed interested in was making me hate myself more than I already did.

Linc had offered to pay for these sessions, but it was the girls who suggested I do them so I had continued support, but I had never felt more alone or more worked up in my entire life. I pulled the cigarettes from my handbag and lit one, letting the smoke dance across my chest until it felt tight and hard to breathe. When the fag had run its course, I lit another, balancing my phone on my pinkie finger as I perched my back against a wall. I clicked on Linc's Instagram profile from my fake account and instantly wished I hadn't. There was a smiling selfie of Linc with a stunning blonde under his arm. *Heidi.* They were cuddled together while the turquoise sea crashed on the shores behind them. They were in Bali, the tropical paradise where Linc had promised to take me for my babymoon. I had the stupid thought, maybe a daydream, that Linc would have popped the question on the beach they were standing on. I had imagined posting our newly engaged photo on Instagram with the caption: *I said yes.* I was going to swoon from all the congratulating messages and finally announce the pregnancy I had desperately been hiding. This was supposed to be my trip, yet there he was with her. Taunting me.

Heidi fucking Dolak, Linc's innocent nutritionist, was living my moment with my man by her side.

It wasn't fair. How did I manage to lose everything, while Linc's world stayed so perfectly intact? It was like I was never even pregnant, like our son and daughter had never existed. Linc had erased us from his life. Linc had replaced me.

How the hell could I have been so stupid? Poppy was right, he never acted like he wanted to be a father. I finished my fag then lit another before walking to the bus stop. But then I stopped as I realised something significant. Everything was fine until Heidi came along. Linc and I may have had our problems but that was just love. I resumed walking, now plagued by some very different thoughts. Thoughts of killing Heidi Dolak.

CHAPTER TWENTY

MY SUNDRESS WAS HALF OFF, half on when they found me.

'Easy, Char, take small sips.'

'Shouldn't we call an ambulance?' Zaheen narrowed her gaze at Poppy as she tipped a half-filled glass of water to my lips.

I was shivering beneath a white sheet, my lips chapped and tinged blue as the smell of my own sick hovered around the four of us.

'I got her to bring up most of it. And she's conscious so she should be fine – well, physically anyway.'

'Damn it, how much did she take?' Trix was clutching her phone, readying herself to dial 999.

'Half the bottle by the looks of it. Charlotte, what were you thinking? Why would you try and hurt yourself? We might not have found you in time. You could have died.'

Woozily, I sat up in bed not knowing how to pinpoint the origins of my stupid, failed suicide attempt. The truth was, I had no idea what I was thinking. After my therapy session with Dr Kole that morning, I realised I just wanted it all to stop. All the pain and humiliation online. Everything I felt for

Linc. Everything I wanted to do to Heidi. I just wanted it all to stop.

'For God's sake, Charlotte, explain yourself!' Trix's voice was shrill, but even that failed to mask the fear that shadowed her.

'It was an accident.' I knew they wouldn't buy such a flippant excuse, but it was all I had to offer. I was ashamed.

'Do you think we're stupid? You took half the bottle. I swear to God, Char, I'm not attending your funeral. First, I lose my kids to my parents, then you lose yours ... I'm not losing you too. You better snap out of it, because I am not burying you.'

'OK, Rottweiler, back off. She doesn't need tough love right now.'

'Zee—'

'I said back off, Trix.'

The mattress sagged a little as Zaheen sat on the edge of the bed, shaking her head before she spoke.

'You know we love you, and we are all here for you. But please don't ever do anything like that again. We can't lose you. We can't take that. That hurts us, and I know you don't want to hurt us, Charlotte.'

I nodded as Poppy pulled me closer to her, wrapping her arms tightly around me, but I wished it was Linc who was holding me.

'Come here. You gave us such a scare. Don't ever do that again.'

I watched the online symbol hover below Linc's name and wondered aimlessly who he was messaging. Was it Heidi? Or was it someone else?

One thing was for certain, he wasn't messaging me. He didn't even have my new number, which was a cunning ploy on my part since he couldn't block what he couldn't see. I could see him though.

I applauded WhatsApp for the nifty 'online' feature. It was really helpful when it came to working out whether or not you were being ignored. If you've sent a message and the other person's online, then you can guarantee they've seen the message even if their read receipts are off.

I had found a way to stay connected. I had found a way to lurk in the background, affiliated through a phone app without Linc being any the wiser.

I missed Linc. I missed speaking to him and cooking him his favourite deconstructed carbonara, minus the heavy cream, because that wasn't part of his diet. I missed waking up in the morning in his house, Linc snoring ever so lightly beside me. It was the small things I missed, the tiny interactions. It wasn't the sex. It was the stolen looks and soft kisses that were burned into my skull. It was as if I was desperately peering through a glass door, staring at the life I used to have.

'How long do we have to stay here?'

Poppy had barely left my side after she came home and found me passed out with a bottle of sleeping tablets clutched in my palm. She was worried about me; they all were, which was ridiculous. I hadn't been trying to overdose, or at least that's what I'd convinced myself. I just liked mixing sleeping pills with alcohol and went a little too far on that occasion. Everyone had their vices, their methods of coping. Booze and pills just happened to be mine.

'Until he comes out. We have to be patient. Please, I just want to see him,' I said, staring out of the window at the barbers Linc had gone into twenty-seven minutes earlier. I realised that

I needed closure and without seeing Linc just one more time I could never hope to move on. I needed answers that only he could give and no matter how present the girls were, they could never really understand what I'd lost and counselling was only making me worse. Linc was the only one I could turn to. He had lost the twins too. And months had passed since he told me he couldn't see me. Back then the trauma was too raw for him, I understood that now, and now I'd given him space to start healing, I knew he would need to see me. We had to talk. But even I was shocked that I had managed to convince Poppy to go with me. Trix was always up for getting her hands dirty, but never Poppy. She was the practical one. Level-headed and less irrational than Trix or even Zaheen at times.

'We've been here ages. I'm hungry and you need to rest. Trix heard you pacing around at 4 a.m.'

'Well, if someone hadn't taken away my sleeping pills then I would've been asleep instead of up in the night pacing.'

'Yeah, and risk you trying to kill yourself again? No thanks. We need to keep you healthy, baby girl.'

'Why? Not like I'll ever have kids of my own, so I don't need to be healthy for anyone else. I'm practically extinct – last of my kind.'

'I didn't mean it like that, Char.'

'I know you didn't. It's just always at the forefront of my mind, I guess. Like a damn nightmare I can't wake up from.'

She was silent for a long time after that, neither of us able to fill the space between us with words.

'There he is. What did I tell you? Patience.'

'Yes, well you've seen him, so now we can leave?'

'Not a chance in hell. I gotta talk to him.'

I was out of the car before Poppy had a chance to pull me back, and across the road before she could call my name. I heard her curse from over my shoulder but was too focused for it to register in my brain.

'*Linc!*' I screeched. He spun round and looked as if he had seen a ghost.

'Jesus Christ. Are you following me, Charlotte?'

'No.' Yes. But he couldn't prove that. Could he?

'What are you doing here?'

Linc looked amazing. His skin was clear and buttery soft, flushed slightly from the unusual spring heat. He wore a dark tracksuit and matching trainers with designer insignia.

'You know what I'm doing here. It's not like you've given me a choice.'

'I've said all I have to say to you. I really don't have time for this. I need to get to training so please just leave me alone.'

'"Training", or do you mean Heidi? I see you've promoted her from nutritionist to girlfriend.'

'Heidi's none of your business.'

'Like hell she's not. I don't understand how you can be so heartless. We lost our babies, and you act like we lost a damn puppy.'

He turned his back on me, readying himself to slide into his Bentley, but I was quicker jumping into the driver's seat the moment the doors unlocked.

'Charlotte, get out of my car.'

'No,' I bit out then folded my arms like a spoilt child on the verge of a nuclear tantrum.

'This is unbelievable. I don't want to talk to you. Haven't I made myself clear?'

'But I *need* to speak to you. Don't you get it? This thing, this terrible thing happened. It changed us.'

'I'm with Heidi now. There isn't an "us" anymore, Charlotte, and there should never have been an us to begin with. I'm so sorry.'

'You pumped-up little prick!' Poppy's cheeks were stained bright red. She had stormed towards us, her blue eyes wild with fury. 'This woman treated you like a fucking king and you abandon her when she needs you most. Who even does that? You're nothing more than a selfish little shit.'

'Poppy, don't!' I shouted, then shot up out of the driving seat a fraction of a second too late as she came face to face with Linc.

'Nice to see you again, Poppy,' Linc mocked. 'You know I always thought you were the classiest out of Char's friends. Turns out you're just as trashy as the rest of them.'

'What'd you say?' I wedged myself between the two of them, but Poppy reached over me to grab Linc. I managed to stop her just in time. She needed to remember he was a heavyweight boxer and could knock her out with one punch if he wanted to.

'Poppy, please, just let us talk?'

'He's not worth it, Char. I swear to God I could kill him. You hear that, Lincoln, I'll fucking kill you.' Her Irish accent was thick.

'Please, Poppy, I have to do this by myself. I'll meet you in the car.'

I turned back to Linc, who stood with a smug smile on his face and his hands in his pockets. He waved at Poppy, and she gave him the finger calling him a 'fucking prick' as she slid behind the wheel of her turquoise Corsa.

'Your friend is batshit crazy by the way. Matter of fact, you all are. Birds of a feather.'

'Do you blame her for being upset? Look at what you've left me to deal with by myself,' I said, then lifted my top to reveal the jagged scar. 'They were ours, Linc. You just abandoned me. Left me to pick up all the pieces of this fucked-up situation. Why did you do it?'

He looked blankly at me as if I had not only struck a nerve but severed it altogether.

'I thought it was obvious. I didn't want to be with you anymore. I had no choice, so I did what I had to do, and I don't regret it.' His tone was toneless, lacking any and all emotion.

Goosebumps ballooned despite it being so warm you could fry an egg on the pavement.

'You're a mess, Charlotte.' Relief slapped his face, and I couldn't work out why. What did he do to me that he didn't regret? Why did I mean so little to him? 'Heidi's waiting at the gym. I have to go. She's my priority now.'

'So, that's it? You're not even gonna apologise for making the worst thing that's ever happened to me a million times worse. Do you hate me that much?'

'I'm sure you'll bounce back, and even if you don't, it's really not my concern, Charlotte.'

I swallowed back my tears. Tried not to let that blow hit me as hard as it did. But it was too late. Linc had delivered a knockout without raising his fists. I didn't say anything after that, just watched him jump into his car and drive away.

How could I have been so stupid? This whole time I thought if I could just get him alone, talk to him face to face then things would go back to how they were. I thought Heidi would be out and me back in, but he was done with me, like I was a withered rose and the only place for me was out with the rubbish.

'Are you all right?' Poppy asked, her voice so low it was almost inaudible as I sat down in the car beside her.

'Can you take me home, please? I'm really tired,' I said, unable to manufacture the pretence of being OK. I was far from it.

'Sure, let's get the hell out of here.'

'Thanks, Pops. I don't know what I would do without you.'

Suddenly I understood how I was feeling. Seeing Linc hadn't given me closure. He had given me something new and dark. It felt strange at first, like the texture was rough against my skin, but it was different. It was real.

What I was starting to feel was hate.

CHAPTER TWENTY-ONE

THE NEXT DAY, MY MEETING with Linc was still swirling through my mind. He had been so cold. Distant. Nothing like how I remembered him. He hated me. And I couldn't figure out what I had done to him. Why was Heidi so important to him yet the woman who carried and lost his children meant nothing?

'*Deadpool* one or two?' Trix mumbled from behind the closed bathroom door.

I'd been sitting on the tiled floor for little over an hour staring at the razor blades in the cabinet above. My eyes were raw and puffy from the eight-hour crying session I'd put myself through last night.

Trix opened the door looking lovely, fresh and airy in a ribbed cream maxi-dress. Her face had no makeup, but Trix didn't need it, she was naturally pristine.

'Two, but Ryan Reynolds is funny in both.' My response came out too quickly, like I'd been caught doing something I wasn't supposed to be doing. 'We could always watch both? Not like we have anything better to do today.' That was a lie.

It was Sunday. Trix would be having a visit from her social worker tomorrow so the last thing she should have been doing was babysitting me. If all went well then Trix would be granted overnight visitation. Meaning I would have to camp out over at Zaheen's one weekend a month, but they hadn't told me that yet. They'd just discussed it, at length, in hushed tones when they thought I was sleeping.

'Sure. Although we'll need popcorn if we're gonna get through both films.'

'I'll tell Poppy and Zee to stop at Sainsbury's and pick some up on their way over. Wine too? Or do you fancy something stronger?'

'Vodka. I fancy Vodka,' I said in an enthusiastic tone. Maybe if I acted like I was all right then they would believe I really was.

'I'll text them now.' Once she'd fired off the message, Trix looked up from her phone and eyed me warily. 'You're making that face.'

'What face?' I asked, quickly rearranging my features and grabbing a stiff flannel off the radiator as the water ran, drowning her out.

'Like there's something on your mind. You wanna talk about it? You know we can talk about anything right?'

She wrapped me in another layer of cotton wool then put on her kid gloves to deal with me.

'I'm fine, really I am. It's just been a rough day—week, it's been a rough week, if I'm honest.'

'Poppy told me what happened with Lincoln.'

I wasn't even surprised. I was just surprised she hadn't said anything up until then.

'Oh. She did, did she?'

'We both know Pops wasn't gonna stay quiet. I've actually never seen her so pissed. She would have ripped his head off if you weren't standing there. She really hates him for how he's treated you.'

'I should never have gone there.'

I couldn't look at her, so I scrubbed at my face instead.

'I'm surprised you didn't punch him. I would've punched him, maybe even run him over with my car, and that's me being lenient, which is way more than that shithead deserves.'

'I think Poppy would've done it for all of us if I'd given her the green light.'

'Do you blame her? The man's pure evil, and again, that's me being kind.'

'I don't understand why he hates me. We used to care about each other so much. Was it just a lie? I mean, we were about to have a family together. That has to count for something, doesn't it?'

'Of course it counts. It was real. It was real to you. You should hold on to that, for the sake of your children's memory. They were so loved and wanted. I would've spoilt them rotten. Me being their favourite auntie, of course.'

'You're like my sister, Zee and Poppy too. We're like our own little hive.'

'Like?' she scoffed disapprovingly. 'Hell, after what we've been through, we *are* sisters. We may not share the same DNA, but we share a bond, and it can never be broken. You're us, and we're you, don't ever forget that. What happens to one of us happens to us all.'

We both stood in silence for a few minutes as my face dried. I knew what she wanted to say but was grateful she didn't mention how sorry she was. Not just for the twins but for Linc too.

The doorbell rang and Trix disappeared to get it, offering me a reassuring squeeze on the shoulder before she set off.

'Oh.'

I could hear Trix from down the hall.

'Yes. Can I help you?' Her voice sounded flustered.

'Detective Inspector Kilby. Is Charlotte Goodwin home?'

DI Kilby's voice travelled through the crack in the door.

'*Char!*' Trix called out, slightly alarmed. 'Come here for a moment. That cop from the hospital wants to have a word with you.'

'What? The police are here?'

Quickly, I uncurled my T-shirt and threw it over my head. I took a deep breath and made my way to the front door.

'What's this about? Have you found the people who broke into Linc's house?' I knew I sounded desperate but after my run-in with Linc yesterday I felt like I needed some good news.

'No. We're still investigating the alleged break-in and will keep you updated if we make any arrests. Or if we get any new information. Although, as previously explained, we will not be able to supply you with any specifics as it was not your property that was broken into.'

'Are you shitting me?' Trix flared. 'Then why are you here? Two babies are dead. It's been months and you and the rest of the Met have done fuck all about it. Do you have any idea what Charlotte's been through?'

'Like I said, we are still investigating the accident and alleged break-in and will follow up with Miss Goodwin in due course.'

'If you're not here to tell me who broke in, then why are you here?'

My brow creased and I got the imminent feeling things were about to get worse. Much worse.

'We've received a complaint from Mr Jackson.'

'A complaint, what type of complaint?' My voice was hoarse and uncontrollably cracked at either end of my words.

'Mr Jackson says you've been following him. He also alleges he's been receiving various messages on social media from accounts all named "Charlotte Goodwin".'

'That could be anyone. He has millions of followers. Not to mention Charlotte is a very common name,' I said defensively, then stared at Trix to back me up.

'She's got a point. Lincoln has so many followers it could've been anyone leaving him abusive messages.'

'So, Miss Goodwin, you've had no contact with Mr Jackson?'

'Don't answer that, Charlotte. This is harassment. If anyone should be making a complaint it should be her.' Trix pointed at me, her arms waving back and forth as she got more and more upset. 'How dare you come barging in here throwing around accusations to a woman who's just lost her children. Have you no shame?'

I was grateful for Trix's ability to flip every situation on its head. It was part of her charm, but every so often became part of her wrath. She was more like her mother than she thought she was.

'Linc and I spoke. Nothing more,' I said abruptly.

'Mr Jackson has contacted the Met in order for us to put a stop to any further contact with him on your part. This is an official warning. Any further contact and he will be within his rights to take out a restraining order.'

'Why?' I said, more shocked than upset. 'He was the father of my children. I have every right to speak to him. How would you feel if you were in my shoes? If you'd lost everything and the man ... or woman you loved wouldn't even speak to you?'

'This is complete and utter bullshit. He needs to talk to her, not send you pigs round here to do his dirty work. My opinion of Lincoln Jackson has always been pretty low, but this ... this takes the biscuit.'

'Trix, please. Anger won't get us anywhere.'

'It's advisable for you to listen to your friend, Miss Nolan.'

'It's advisable for you to piss off, DI Plum.'

'Trix, please! That's really not helping.' My voice was low.

'Please what? They practically want to arrest you for talking to that hateful dickhead.'

'We never said anything about arresting you, Miss Goodwin. This is a verbal warning. If you go anywhere near Mr Jackson, online or otherwise, then you'll be arrested.'

At precisely that moment, Poppy and Zaheen came bursting in, hands full of fluorescent orange carrier bags.

'What the hell's going on? Why's he here?' Poppy asked, her distrust of police ever present because of what happened to her brother, Shane.

'They're here to stop Char from seeing Lincoln. He's made an official complaint. Can you fucking believe it?'

'That sick son of a bitch. He really has no heart, no fucking heart.'

'Poppy, please don't start,' I said in a less audible tone. I was embarrassed and tired of the bickering. I just wanted it all to stop.

'Poppy Leigh.'

We all turned to face DI Kilby.

'You are also not allowed to have any contact with Mr Jackson.'

'You're breaking my little heart. I wouldn't spit on that man if he was on fire, trust me!'

'Like I said.' DI Kilby's arms were up as he backed away from the door, the four of us semicircling him like alley cats. 'This is an official warning.'

'Too right it is,' Zaheen scoffed. 'When are you lot gonna do your job and find out what happened the night of Charlotte's accident? You pigs make me sick.' She grimaced, dropping the last two shopping bags on the floor.

'We are still investigating.'

'You keep saying that, Detective Inspector Plum.' Trix took a step forward.

'It's DI Kilby, miss.'

'It's get the hell away from my house. That's what it is.'

'Have a good day, ladies.'

Trix slammed the door behind him once we'd turned away.

'What a prick!' said Zaheen as she pulled me in for a long hug.

I couldn't believe Linc had taken such lengths to keep me away from him. Did he really not care about the twins at all?

HEIDI DOLAK — So I have huge news! I've partnered up with @sleekinterior to give @lincolnjackson home a makeover. I'm so excited to put my stamp on our home, stay tuned for the fabulous results #ourhome #future #inlove #justthetwoofus

bonnie46 — oh my gosh @lincolnjackson is the gift that keeps on giving

xenaprincess22 — wait I'm confused! Wasn't he just posting pics of @charlottegoodwin like a week ago?

bonnie46 — @xenaprincess22 they broke up months ago . . . where have you been?

xenaprincess22 — @bonnie46 sorry must have missed the latest episode of celebs trade in their girlfriends for supermodels looool

coolandcold — keep us posted can't wait to see what you do with the place

littleheidi33 — go girl, I'm ur biggest fan so happy for you

thehive — wishing you and @lincolnjackson all the best with the redecorating

bluejay — @lincolnjackson u are one lucky son of a bitch @heididolak is a keeper lool

heididolak — @bluejay I tell him this everyday lol

lincolnjackson — @bluejay I'm the luckiest man in the world @heididolak you are my queen

houghton88 — looks like there may be wedding bells in the air for @lincolnjackson and @heididolak they would make the cutest babies ever

CHAPTER TWENTY-TWO

I SAT UPRIGHT ON THE EDGE of my bed. It was Monday morning and I'd already called in sick, complaining I had a stomach bug. Heidi's Instagram photo was like a slit in my heart that slowly leaked, all that was missing was red blooms of fresh blood. How could Linc have asked her to move in with him so soon? It was one thing to not call or speak to me, but replacing me so quickly and then calling the police to give me an official warning cut deep.

Repelled by the sudden smell of cured bacon Trix was using to smoke me out of my room, I blinked back the tears I'd been holding in since DI Kilby showed up last night and warned me never to go near Lincoln Jackson again.

I felt violated.

It was as though Linc was doing everything in his power to ensure he never had to face me again. As I stood, blood roaring in my ears, I watched Heidi post a photo to her Instagram story with the irritating caption:

HEIDI DOLAK – Ready to hit the shops you have no idea how much a heavyweight eats lol #emptyfridge

It was never my intention to purposely go looking for her, but she popped up on my fake account and I had this overwhelming urge to see what she was like for myself. I'd built a picture up in my mind based on what she posted online, but I knew better than anyone that was only ever half the story. I wanted to know what she had that I didn't. Why was Linc so enthralled by her that he gave up the chance of being with me? It wasn't like anyone could give me the answers, but hopefully seeing Heidi would show me the pieces of the puzzle I was missing.

And DI Kilby hadn't warned me not to see her.

Since my accident I'd always felt like I had only fragments but never the whole picture of that night. There was so much hidden. I could feel the strings tugging at my limbs even as I sat there unable to take my eyes off the woman who was breaking my heart. Thoughts of hurting her swirled in my mind. I could wipe that pretty smile off her face. I could ...

'Can I come in?' Trix didn't wait for me to answer as the white frame of the door bounced back off the doorstop making the walls vibrate. It was just enough of a distraction for me to hide the phone and wipe away my tears. My mind had been taking a dangerous turn and I felt foggy. 'Sorry. I swear I need to get that thing fixed, but that would mean an awkward audience with the baby snatcher, or as I like to call her, Mum. Hey, you OK?'

'Fine. I thought you two were getting on better lately.'

'Oh, please, that lasted all of a week. We can always count on my mother to be a total bitch if nothing else. Her greatest joy in life is making me miserable. That's why today has to go well.'

Trix set the tray down and approached me, concern etching her features.

'I said I'm fine, Trix. Stop looking at me like that. You should be getting ready for your visit with the social worker. If this goes right, it's the start of getting Kera and Kyle back.'

'Yeah, over my mother's dead body, but you're right, I should be optimistic. I'm ready – nervous, but ready.'

'Good. I'll get out of your way then,' I said, glancing at my phone quickly as if I was checking the time, then pulling a T-shirt over my head, forgoing the shower. I would have to be quick if I was going to catch her.

Heidi was already in her car showing off all the fine details Linc had customed just for her birthday. It made me sick.

'Where do you think you're going, missy? They're not going to be here till three.'

'Out. I need some fresh air.'

'Splendid. I'll join you, then, shall I?' Trix eyed me, suspiciously.

'Thanks, but I would rather go alone, then maybe head over to Zee's for a bit.'

She made a sudden noise, then took a few cautious steps towards me. I eased past her thinking that would be the end of our conversation, although I could still feel the weight of her eyes.

'What?'

'I don't know if you think I'm stuck on stupid, Char, but I know you're up to something. You look guilty as shit.'

I stared at her, damning her power of deduction. I thought about lying, trying to convince her otherwise but it was point-less. Trix knew exactly what I was up to and she wasn't going to let me out of her sight, social worker visit or no social worker visit.

'I just want to see her. I'm not going to say anything. I just have to see her in person. You get that, right?' I confessed, then watched Trix take a step back, putting up her hands to protest.

'Charlotte Goodwin you are like a dog with a damn bone. This isn't a good idea. The best thing you can do is leave them both alone. Let karma deal with them.'

Karma? I'd be waiting a lifetime for Heidi the homewrecker's karma to catch up with her.

'Look, I'm doing this. If anyone should know how I feel it's you. You're a mother too.'

Folding my arms, I watched as Trix let out a low huff. She knew I was right.

'Get your coat. We'll take Poppy's car, you nutter. You're lucky hospital car parks charge an extortionate amount for parking because my car's getting serviced, and just so you know, this is a terrible idea.'

There are two reasons why updating social media in real time is a stupid thing to do. Reason one: someone who wants to know where you are may be watching. And reason two: that person might want to hurt you.

Waitrose wasn't far from Linc's house, and it took about twenty minutes to reach the almost empty car park. We stopped a few spots away from Heidi's white Range Rover. According to her Instagram story she was in the fruit and veg aisle showing her dense followers how to tell when an avocado is ripe.

I got a pang in my stomach as my thoughts tangled. Maybe being there stalking Heidi wasn't such a good idea, but she had told the world where to find her and I hadn't gone looking for the information – that was fate, surely? It wasn't her fault she fell in love with a man who was already taken, maybe she wasn't to blame, but she knew about me, she chose to cross that line, so then again maybe she was.

The car door swung open, startling me.

'It's pissing down out here; I wish you lot would do your stalking from inside.'

The leather squelched as Zaheen slid into the back seat.

'Did any of you bring a towel by any chance? Tissue ... anything?'

'Trix? You told her where we were?'

'Well, I wasn't going to lie to her, now, was I?' replied Trix angrily, the disdain clear in her voice.

'So, that's a no to the tissue then. Cheers. I don't know why you're so upset. I actually agree with you. I think you should confront Heidi.'

Zaheen fixed Trix with a look of sheer defiance.

'Keeping things bottled up isn't good – believe me, I've been there.' Zaheen was right.

'Look, I just want to see her, that's all. I don't even want her to see us.'

The sky got dimmer, the clouds preparing to burst into an even heavier rainfall. Fat droplets had already begun to release in a rhythmic beat on the roof of the car.

'Then why don't you just watch her from a screen like a normal social media freak? Trolls don't leave the house; they do this shit from their bedrooms. I don't see why you need to be different.'

'Come on, Trix, we've stalked Michael more times than I can count. Let her have this one.'

'That's different, Zee,' Trix protested.

'How exactly is that different?' Zaheen shot back.

'It just is. We have kids together for a start.'

The moment she said it I saw her face fall apart.

'Shit, Char, I didn't mean it, I just meant—'

'It's all right. I know what you meant.' I cut her off.

'At the end of the day, if this is going to help you heal then I'm all for it,' said Zaheen as she tried to dissolve the simmering tension.

'It will. I just don't want her to know it's me.'

'Oh! In that case, I have just the thing.'

Zaheen removed a paper bag from her LV tote.

'What the hell are these?' Trix asked, unimpressed.

'They're Anubis masks.'

'*What* masks?' Trix's brow tightened.

'Anubis masks, like the ones from Egypt.'

We both stared at her slightly perplexed.

'Half man, half jackal – protector of the underworld. Wow, obviously you guys didn't pay attention in history whatsoever.'

'What are we supposed to do with these?' Trix's upper lip curved down.

'Wear them – *dur*.'

'Don't "dur" me. If Poppy was here you two would be outvoted.'

Trix was right, Poppy would be more practical. Level-headed.

'Well, she's not and I am. Masks on, ladies. CCTV and all that.'

And with that said Zaheen was out of the car first.

'Crazy bitch,' muttered Trix, who, despite all her protesting, hopped out second shoving her mask on.

'*Pssst* – over here.'

The three of us bent down behind a red Astra. Even though it was daytime it was dark, and the sound of water droplets on my mask made me feel like I wasn't myself anymore. Like I was someone else. Someone hidden.

'Look, there she is,' whispered Zaheen.

I lifted my gaze to meet Heidi's slender frame. She was taller than she looked online, with her long strawberry blonde hair swept into a high ponytail. She was wearing grey yoga pants and a cropped Adidas jumper in white. She was carrying two shopping bags that looked bigger than she was, and her face looked unblemished like a petal. She was elegant. Beautiful. And everything I wasn't. As she hurried across the car park to avoid getting too wet, she managed to juggle the shopping into one hand and fumbled in her pocket for her car keys. She tapped a button and the car lit up on her command.

'Well, Linc certainly has a type,' whispered Trix, who was less than a foot behind me, adjusting her mask underneath the flood of rain.

'Tall and sexy is not a type. It's a *preference*.'

'Whatever, Zee. Can we leave now? I have that important visit in case you two have forgotten,' Trix asked eagerly.

'Guys, I want to get a bit closer,' I said, edging out from our hiding place and on to a blue BMW.

'Char—*Char*. That's too close, someone's going to spot you. Charlotte?'

It was too late, I couldn't hear Trix anymore. Heidi was a mere few feet in front of me, her car door open as she took out her phone, shielding herself from the rain with her free hand.

I don't know why I did it. It was like I couldn't control myself or rather I was being controlled. I didn't understand it, but I was on my feet standing behind her before my brain recognised what my body was doing. I snatched the phone from her hand and threw it with all my force on the ground, smashing the screen into pieces. Heidi screamed, and for a moment I forgot I was wearing the mask. I thought she could see me. See what Linc had done to me.

'Please, take whatever you want. Please don't hurt me.' She screamed again, but my skin bloomed into goosebumps.

Trix and Zaheen joined me, gathering around Heidi in a triangle so she was caged in. The three of us just stood there watching her quiver in fear. I wanted to hit her, drag all that pretty blonde hair from her scalp, because she took Linc from me. I balled my fist, but Trix must have sensed it was getting ugly because she put her hand on my shoulder and shook her head. Underneath the mask I could feel the burning tears beginning to fall. That's what got me moving.

I took one last look at Heidi and made a promise to myself that it wasn't over between us.

CHAPTER TWENTY-THREE

THE SMELL OF RAIN LINGERED as the three of us huddled together on a laminate corner table on the outside terrace of the Mona Lisa cafe. It was a little after ten a.m., the day after we had confronted Heidi. I sat inanimate, my mind swirling with thoughts of the woman who had taken everything, and what I would have done to her if Trix and Zaheen hadn't been there to stop me. Like oil, these thoughts seemed to slip away just as quickly as I could grasp them. They scared me at first, but the more I thought the more it made sense. If Heidi was gone, Linc would come back to me. I'd had dreams about her for weeks now. Sickening thoughts of the different ways I could peel back her skin while she was still alive. The sounds she would make, the utensils I would use. Happy thoughts.

Pecan French toast dotted with robust blueberries and a generous dollop of crème fraiche was presented to me by a slim redhead with a tight smile and a rushed-off-her-feet demeanour even though it wasn't busy. The food I wouldn't touch. In my opinion, it was inedible, but nowadays most foods were if they didn't come in liquid form with a percentage attached to the label. Maple syrup oozed, creating a golden pool of liquid, as Zaheen spoke to me distantly at first.

'Smells good. Maybe one bite. Hello – Char?'

'I'm not hungry.'

I understood how it must have looked to them. The jealous ex that couldn't let go versus the new woman who was seemingly perfect in every way. I was unbalanced in mourning when everyone else, including Linc, had moved on.

'Please, just a little.'

'I said I'm not hungry, Zee. I'll eat when I'm ready,' I managed to say with a tiny puff of irritation and shoved the plate away from me.

'Fuck! It's all over her page.'

Poppy came sweeping towards us, a slight gust of wind caressing her blonde hair as she slumped in the chair across from Trix, who hadn't made eye contact with me all morning.

'What is? Whose page?'

Trix lifted her head from her spiced Americano. She had been giving me the silent treatment since last night. Not only was she late to her home visit with the social worker, but she was so distracted by what had happened with Heidi that she accidently spilt scolding Earl Grey tea in the social worker's lap causing a second-degree burn. It was a disaster, and the social worker was yet to make a decision about overnight visitation given the circumstances. Trix rightly blamed me.

'Heidi. She just posted on Instagram and it's – well, it's about what you guys did to her.'

Poppy handed me the phone.

HEIDI DOLAK — Yesterday I was attacked. I was pinned to the ground by three people. I managed to defend myself and send all three of them running with their tails between their legs. Thank God @lincolnjackson taught me how to punch with impact. In light of my tragedy Lincoln and I have decided to run an all-women's self-defence boot camp. DM me for details and stay safe, you never know what sickos may be out there #boxersgirlfriend #notscared #selfdefence #youshouldhaveseenthemrun

Ran? Nobody ran. We walked away!

'I thought you guys said you didn't touch her. Charlotte, you said you just smashed her phone.'

We passed Poppy's phone between us, reading the highly inaccurate statement, and each made a noise of either horror, surprise or disbelieving laughter.

'We didn't touch her. That bitch is lying,' muttered Trix angrily, curling her fists tightly then banging them against the table.

'After reading this, I wish we had. This is exactly why I don't have social media. Her followers can't really believe this drivel,' Zaheen added, also unimpressed with Heidi's wildly misleading statement. It was so far from the truth even I was shocked at how low she'd sunk to garner sympathy from the public.

'She's practically a stick figure, just look at the size of her. How was she supposed to fight off the three of you?' Poppy pushed, then stared at me waiting for me to open my mouth.

'She's lying to make herself look good. She's an actual sociopath.' The disdain in Trix's voice was hard to miss.

'Actually, she's pretty smart,' I said, half expecting the gaping looks they were giving me.

'What? Char, did you bump your head, sweetie? Or have you just completely lost it?'

'Heidi took an opportunity we presented her with, Trix. She made it work in her favour. Not only will her so-called attack be on The Hive in less than an hour, but she will start this bootcamp thing, her followers will pay and she'll reap the benefits. Like I said, she's pretty smart.'

I didn't take my eyes off the untouched French toast as a wayward pecan swam in the golden river.

'How can you sound so calm about this? Are you not mad that she's lying?' Poppy sounded wounded.

'Not really.' Nonchalance seemed the appropriate attitude to take.

The more Heidi and Linc ruined my life and humiliated me online the less I seemed to fight back. My grief was embalmed in me. It took everything I had just to get through each day without going mad. I just wanted a day off.

'Why? Why the hell aren't you mad?' Poppy snapped her fingers in front of my face. 'Hello? Charlotte!'

'Nobody knows it was us. Besides, I think she was the one who sent the Instagram message to you and Trix the night of my accident.'

'You think she sent the message? Why would she do that? Not to mention how would she know your password? It doesn't make sense for it to be Heidi. Why would she save your life?'

Poppy had a point, and perhaps she was right. I was just trying to piece together the fucked-up situation I was in, trying to place blame any- and everywhere I could. None of it made any sense, but I knew Heidi was involved. I just hadn't figured out how yet.

'I'm not convinced,' Zaheen said in her sure voice, which was rare as she was almost never sure of anything.

'If she was dating Lincoln while Charlotte was pregnant then it could have been her. She had the most to gain, if you call getting Lincoln Jackson gaining that is. Either way we can all see how manipulative and calculating she is. I definitely wouldn't rule her out.'

'But why would she send us the message? She didn't even know we were friends,' Poppy added, yet another level of disbelief.

'Of course she did. It's all over your pages – we're inseparable, a quick social media search would prove that. I always told you guys social media was dangerous.'

'You're right, Zee, there are still some holes though, but I agree, I wouldn't rule her out. Not that any of this matters. All we do is talk about this all day, every day. I'm sorry, but I'm sick of it.' Trix waved her hands.

'Who put a bee in your bonnet?' Poppy asked.

'My children are probably going to be taken away from me for good after yesterday's performance, and all you guys are worried about is who sent that stupid Instagram message. Can't we just thank God someone did and move on?'

Poppy focused solely on Trix. 'I'm sorry, sugar. We didn't ask. How are you holding up?'

'Does it matter? If it's not about Charlotte and her problems then it gets swept under the rug, just like your abortion did the moment Charlotte met Lincoln.'

'That's not true. You know we love you. You know we care,' Zaheen said in a sing-song way that I knew would only make

Trix more irate. She didn't want consoling or sympathy. She just wanted someone to scream at and we were the only viable candidates.

'Yeah, just not as much as you care about Charlotte, right? You lot can fuck yourselves. I'm going to fix my makeup before it falls into my eggs Benedict. In the meantime, I suggest you all think about how to be better friends because right now, you suck.'

She got up and beelined for the ladies' room while Poppy took a bite of my toast.

'It's really good, Char. You should have some.'

'No thanks. Trix is mad at me, and she should be. I put her relationship with her children at risk.'

'No, you were just looking for answers. No one can blame you for that. You're the victim in all this.' Zaheen kept her voice a whisper.

'She had motive, and the most to gain.'

'Who?' I asked Poppy. She had an unreadable look on her face.

'How do we prove that Heidi was the one who broke in? Maybe once this ugly mess is put to bed Charlotte can finally have some closure and we can all move on. Because Trix is right – this craziness has got to stop before it gets out of hand and someone gets hurt.'

Poppy lifted her Sicilian lemonade to her lips.

'We can't prove it. That's the problem,' Zaheen spat, a little defeated.

'Yes, we can.' I reached for Poppy's phone. 'Heidi posts every day, right?'

'Yeah, that's right. She's a slave to Instagram like bloody Sasha,' Poppy scoffed, leaning over to take another bite of my French toast.

Zaheen raised an eyebrow slowly.

'Don't look at me like that, Char Insta stalks Heidi all day every day. I just look at Sasha's on weekends.' Poppy produced a tight smile.

'Anyway, all we have to do is scroll back to the night I was attacked and see if she posted anything.'

'That's not a bad idea, but it's not definitive. She could have been anywhere doing anything.'

At that moment Trix returned looking grey and we fell into silence in unison. Then, in what I can only describe as slow motion, six uniformed officers entered, followed by DI Kilby in an awful shit brown suit. He marched towards us, with an air of superiority in his step.

'Ladies, I'm glad you're all together. Saves me making more than one trip.'

'What the hell do you want, DI Plum?' Trix said, never one to back down in the face of trouble, which in this case we were clearly in a lot of.

'Miss Nolan, it's DI Kilby, and I'm here to bring you all in for questioning.'

I gasped then remembered the warning he gave me last time.

'For what? Charlotte and I haven't seen Lincoln.' Poppy's voice was a mixture of fear and outright shock.

'This isn't about Mr Jackson. This is about the stalking and intimidation of Miss Heidi Dolak.'

'Who? I don't believe we know anyone by that name.' That was Zaheen's way of warning us to keep our mouths shut. We were to say nothing.

'Sure, you don't.' DI Kilby was patronising us, in a whiny tone that quite frankly didn't suit his Pugsley face. 'How about we all take a trip down to the station and figure out who knows who? Up you get, ladies.'

We stood and a female officer held Trix by her upper arm.

'Get your hands off me. I'm perfectly capable of walking. You wait till my father hears about this, DI Plum. Then you'll be sorry.'

The female police officer escorted Trix past the stunned diners. A few had already begun recording on their phones, meaning our only course of action was to go quietly.

That's the thing with grief and pain. There are no days off.

CHAPTER TWENTY-FOUR

THE AIR FELT STIFF, THE room holding the pungent smell of foetid bodies. It would be dark soon, I thought, as my head pressed stickily against my forearm. I felt weak, helpless. A tiny critter trapped between the paws of a cat probably had more fight in them than I did at that moment. Things had got worse. Much worse.

DI Kilby separated all four of us as soon as we got to the station. He said it was best we didn't corroborate our stories, which was ridiculous since everything Heidi had told him was a lie. Police stations always had the ability to move at a glacially slow pace, maybe it was done deliberately. Desolation used for a purpose.

Isolation was a form of interrogation. Torture even. I had read that in a book somewhere. Humans were not made to be on their own, we were built for companionship. We needed it. We are co-dependent organisms whether we liked it or not. We needed one another.

I started to get antsy. My hands hadn't stopped moving since I sat down. It was bad enough Heidi lied to her followers but lying to the police was a different matter entirely.

That bitch! It wasn't enough that she had taken my place, she was trying to ruin my life too, I thought, then condemned my irrational decision to go after her in the first place. Linc had already beaten me in the great game of life, it was just a matter of time until Heidi did the same. I should've never gone anywhere near that woman. But she drove me to it, taunting me with the life that once was mine.

DI Kilby burst through the door, pulling out a chair opposite me and slouched into it with a familiar thud.

'Miss Goodwin, sorry to keep you waiting.'

On closer inspection, Kilby was a slightly wrung-out man, with bloodshot eyes and jittery hands, which I suspected was the result of too much caffeine and not enough sleep. My suspicions were confirmed by the purplish bags that bulged under his eyes.

'Am I under arrest?'

'No. We're here to discuss Miss Dolak.'

'What about her?' I replied as disinterestedly as I could manage.

'We've received a complaint from Miss Dolak, Mr Jackson's new girlfriend, who claims you and a couple of friends attacked her yesterday morning in a Waitrose car park. The incident wasn't captured on CCTV, but Miss Leigh's car was spotted at a nearby petrol station in the area, therefore I am required to follow up on Miss Dolak's complaint.'

'We didn't lay a finger on Heidi despite whatever lies she's concocted.'

'OK, let's take it back a little bit—'

'You can take it back as far as you like, Detective Inspector, the answer remains the same. We never touched her.'

Although right then I wished I had. Thoughts of killing Heidi were becoming more frequent. Visions of my hands wrapped around her slender throat, squeezing it until she went floppy and still. My only solace in an otherwise bleak situation.

'So, why did you and your friends go to Waitrose?'

'We didn't. I have no idea what you're on about. We went home and watched *Sex and the City*.'

'Miss Goodwin, your friends have already admitted to being in the car park. Do you wish to continue lying, or do you want to start telling the truth?'

Goddammit, girls! I cursed internally. Hadn't they ever heard of plausible deniability?

'All right, so we were there. But we still didn't touch her, therefore we've not done anything wrong apart from going to a supermarket, which last time I checked wasn't a crime.'

'Actually, it is a crime if your intention was to cause bodily harm or emotional distress to Miss Dolak.'

Emotional distress? Was he shitting me? If anyone was going through emotional turmoil it was me and not that silicon, airhead, sodding Barbie.

'Well, it's a good thing none of those things occurred, isn't it, Officer?'

'It's Detective Inspector. And that's not what your friends have said ...'

Shit!

'What have they said? Honestly this is such a waste of resources. Don't you have better thing to do than arrest innocent people?'

'Like I told you earlier, you are not under arrest. I'm just trying to establish the facts.' He cleared his throat then bent forward.

But I didn't allow him to see how much he had got to me. I wouldn't allow him to see me falter, especially when there was every chance we would get away with it.

'So, what are they saying?' I asked tentatively.

Something had started to bug me. I got the feeling he wasn't here on official police business. Which was strange since I was in an interrogation room. But the interview wasn't being recorded. And DI Kilby hadn't offered the same platitudes I was accustomed to at police stations. Just like the other kids who grew up on the Oliver estate, I'd had my adolescent brushes with the law. I had been arrested, I had been detained in several police stations, and I had definitely been interviewed. But unless I had bumped my head this wasn't how interrogations usually went.

Not even close. Our whole interview felt informal.

'I'm saying that your friends . . .'

He made a show of flipping through his notepad. The same notepad he was yet to write anything in.

'Poppy Leigh, Beatrix Nolan and Zaheen Shah, they've been making accusations.'

'Accusations about who?' I swallowed, pushed the lump down in my throat then leaned forward, squaring my shoulders to brace myself for impact.

'Lincoln Jackson.'

Fuck!

'What about him?'

'They're saying he was the one who arranged the break-in that caused your accident, Miss Goodwin.'

I clenched my fists until my knuckles were white and raw.

'They said that you know Mr Jackson was involved. They said you have evidence and you want to make a formal complaint.'

I stayed silent.

'Do you want to make a complaint, Miss Goodwin?' His eyes narrowed but his tone was flat. He was either very bored or patronising me. I began to suspect the latter.

'What's this really about, Inspector Kilby?'

'Whatever do you mean? I'm an officer of the law. If a crime's been committed, then it should be reported. Although reporting crimes can come with its own set of tribulations—'

'*Like?*' I interrupted him, sensing the real reason I was here was about to be revealed like a terrible magic trick.

'Solicitors, judges, the press, and believe me you think a court case is bad, try being trialled by the public. It gets ugly – *fast*.'

Did DI Kilby just threaten me?

'Lincoln Jackson is a huge name. He's a national icon even. His ex-girlfriend throwing around heinous and, in my professional opinion, completely baseless accusations may lead to you being more on trial than him. Then there's your friends. Miss Nolan has an upcoming custody case against her parents scheduled for the end of next month. Be a shame if she lost it because you decided to breech your NDA.'

My mouth felt dry. DI Kilby knew about the NDA and Trix's custody case. Which meant this wasn't what I thought it was. It was much worse. If I talked then Trix would lose everything.

'Miss Leigh – she's a promising nurse, but I'm afraid the NHS frown on staff having a criminal background. She'll lose her job.'

'Poppy wasn't even there – there were three of us, not four.'

'Yeah, but which three? Maybe you weren't there at all, Miss Goodwin. Maybe you really were at home watching *Sex and the City* as you claim. Maybe, just maybe, it was all of them and not you. It's a plausible explanation. The car is registered to Poppy Leigh so it's easy for any judge to buy what I'm selling.'

That time I didn't have to question myself. DI Kilby had definitely threatened me. I didn't know how Linc had managed to get a cop to intimidate me, but he had, and it was working.

I was scared.

'That's not what happened. It was all me. The girls had nothing to do with it.'

'Ah, but with Zaheen Shah's extensive criminal activity that would be hard to prove. Wouldn't you say so, Miss Goodwin?'

I remained silent. He had me.

'Where are my manners. Can I get you something? Tea, coffee?'

'*Go fuck yourself!*' I screamed, jumping to my feet and looking him dead in the eye, realising that the girls may have been right. Linc had something to do with my accident or at least he wanted to cover it up. I needed to know what DI Kilby knew so I decided to fight fire with fire.

'You can't intimidate me. Linc knows what he did and, judging by what you're saying, you know what he did too, so why don't you do your bloody job and arrest that son of a bitch for the murder of our son and daughter.'

Unmoved, DI Kilby stared at me smug and tight-lipped.

'Bravo, Miss Goodwin, but theatrics won't get you anywhere with me. You had an accident. No crime was committed, certainly not murder. You tripped and fell.'

'How many times do I have to say it? There were two other people there that night. They're the reason I fell. They're why my children are dead.'

He put a hand up and silenced me before I could continue.

'It's not what you know, it's what you can prove. That's how the law works, and you can't prove a damn thing since I personally handled all enquiries surrounding your unfortunate accident.'

It was true. Linc was covering up what really happened that night. The earth moved beneath my feet as the realisation set in: the man I loved had betrayed me.

'I almost lost my life. He asked me to come to his house that night. Linc has blood on his hands. You have to see that. Why else would he go through all of this? Why else would he want to silence me?'

'Maybe this is your fault and no one else's. You tripped and fell. That's the end of it. Move on, Miss Goodwin.'

I could have gone for him. Taken the stupid tie dangling around his neck and used it to choke the life out of him while I used my thighs to pin back his flaying arms. It's what he deserved. For a brief moment I rationalised using the twenty-five-to-life prison sentence to finally get the gym body I'd always wanted, but instead I stood still and watched on as he spoke.

'Move on, Miss Goodwin,' he repeated. 'Final warning.'

'I can't,' I said in a rush, my eyes blurred by hot, angry tears.

'You have to. Mr Jackson has millions of followers online. Once he informs his army that his psycho ex killed his children with the help of her jealous friends, they'll come for you. All of you. First the public, then the Met. We'll take everything from you. Just walk away.'

Christ! He was right. It didn't matter what Linc had done to me, people were going to take his side over mine no matter what.

'So, what now?' I said as he paused, letting the bottom line sink in.

'Just go home, Miss Goodwin. Live the rest of your life and forget about Mr Jackson and Miss Dolak. Let them be happy.'

I readied myself to leave.

'And the girls?' I asked, trying not to sound flustered.

'You keep your mouth shut, and this complaint disappears – win-win. Just forget what happened.'

'DI Kilby?'

He lifted his chin defiantly and gazed at me. He didn't look so spiteful then.

'Yes, Miss Goodwin?'

'I'll never forget what happened to me.'

THE HIVE — Charlotte Goodwin releases shocking tweet claiming she has nothing after break-up with Lincoln Jackson

CHARLOTTE GOODWIN @charlottegoodwin   19.13
One day the world will know what you've done to me. I loved you and lost you, now I have nothing

jakerome — someone sounds suicidal @thehive
shannikemp — poor girl she's been thrust into the limelight and now she's unravelling #bekind
trevmack — forget @lincolnjackson he's a shit boxer @charlottegoodwin can do better
solomonride55 — don't be mad @charlottegoodwin I'd leave my wife for @heididolak too
sevenlenny — @solomonride55 cold blooded but so would I lol
ralphsimpson — I'll marry u if ur up for it @charlottegoodwin
indigoskyee — this is just sad we all know she's referring to @lincolnjackson #thehive
yorkflanagan — why did they split up? @thehive
winnieume — damn girl what'd that man do to you? @charlottegoodwin
hilton2010 — @lincolnjackson looks like your ex-bird wants to spill her guts on the internet
thehive — and we'll be here when she does @hilton2010

CHAPTER TWENTY-FIVE

I T WAS QUARTER TO EIGHT and as twilight approached, the final dregs of light fighting a losing battle with the forthcoming darkness. There were still sections of pink and orange far into the distance. It was beautiful yet eerie. It taunted me. The atmosphere romantic yet unkind given its beauty and my circumstances. It surrounded me but couldn't penetrate through my darkness.

No one was out on the marshes when I got there after leaving the police station. I got out faster than the others, although I knew they would be coming for me. I spent my time wondering what Linc would do after seeing my tweet. I wanted to tell the world what had happened, what I'd lost, but Linc had finally succeeded in silencing me.

'I knew you'd be here.'

'When did they let you go?' I replied, keeping my gaze fixed away from Poppy and on the horizon.

'About an hour ago.' She shook her head and narrowed her frown as she edged closer to me. 'Glad to see you're doing OK. I thought you might have come here. I know these fields mean a lot to you, so when you didn't answer your phone, I knew this was where you'd be.'

'I guess I'm becoming predictable.'

'I thought they might have kept you longer than the rest of us.'

'For what? I didn't attack Heidi. That woman's a pathological liar, but you already know that.'

'Easy, Char. You guys did spook her though. Maybe she was just scared.'

'So, she reports us to the police. How did she even figure out it was us? We wore masks; she didn't see our faces.'

'Lincoln must have told her it was you. She looks dumb enough to believe whatever that jackass tells her.'

Poppy let out a tiny huff then folded her arms disapprovingly in her lap as she sat down next to me.

'What'd you want, Poppy? I really can't be arsed to do anything other than sit here and take in this view. I don't want to talk about Linc, or anything Linc-related for that matter.'

I was tired, defeated and quite honestly over all the drama. A terrible thing had happened, but I needed to put it to rest and move on before more people I loved got hurt in the process. DI Kilby was right. I needed to move on.

'I want you to tell the truth. If people knew he lied about what really happened that night, then maybe Lincoln would be the one getting hauled in for questioning not us.'

'We don't know that he's done anything wrong. Like it or not we have no proof.'

DI Kilby's words rang in my ears, if I wanted to protect my friends then I had to get them off Linc's trail. It was far too dangerous, and I couldn't lose them too.

'We have no evidence he's guilty of anything, Pops. Just leave it alone,' I said, reiterating the point that we just couldn't take him on and win.

'I don't get it. Why are you protecting him?'

'I'm not protecting anyone,' I hissed sharply.

An unwarranted tear rolled down my cheek, curled around my nostril and eventually settled on my chin.

'Poppy, I lost more than I ever thought I could. Those babies were my whole world, and all I have left is this' – I lifted my top revealing the angry raised scar on my stomach – 'a permanent reminder that I was a mother and I'll never be one again. And that's thanks to myself. Not Linc. So quit passing the blame because I'm responsible for that night. Even if I never meant to be.'

From the moment I said it I regretted it. I knew the words would shatter her, but I had to hurt her to save her. It was messed up, but I had to be the bad guy. Not Linc. I had to be the one to blame.

'We saved your life that night, the three of us. We saved you. You gotta understand how scared we were. Jesus, Charlotte, you were gonna die. You are not the one to blame. We didn't save them. We couldn't save them. We had the chance to save your babies and we failed you. I failed you.'

'You should have let me die with them. You think this is living? I'm barely surviving. Each day is like a fucking dagger in my chest because they aren't here. They're never gonna be here. I'm never gonna get to hold them, or kiss their little hands, or smell their heads. They're just gone and I'm still here. Existing every single moment of every single day without them.'

I lowered myself from the bench and sank to my knees like I was tied to an anchor that had just been slung to the bottom of the ocean. If I had the slightest doubt that Linc had something to do with my accident, it was snuffed out the moment DI Kilby interviewed me.

The threat of hurting the girls was an admission of Linc's guilt. Why else would he go to so much trouble to keep me quiet? That confirmed everything, and although I was yet to know why Linc was entangled in the death of our children, I knew he wasn't innocent. But there was just nothing I could do about it without ruining the lives of the women who had saved mine.

'Ay, come 'ere.'

Poppy got to her knees, cradling me as I wept into her chest.

'It's all gonna be all right. You're the strongest out of all of us. You've always protected me. And I'm here for you now and forever no matter what. We're sisters. Through thick and thin.'

I understood her implication, and I was grateful she was still there for me. I was glad they all were. The four of us bound together by our mutual tragedies. From Michael trying to burn down Trix's house with her and the children still inside, to me dropping the brick that crippled Poppy's dad when he wouldn't stop beating her, our lives were full of pain.

'Well, that was the most uncomfortable few hours of my life. All that and they didn't even arrest us. Wait until my dad hears about this.'

Trix appeared out of nowhere, her brow creased as she took in the sight of me.

'Oh, Charlotte, this can't go on. You're in bits.' Trix's voice broke slightly, but she held her composure.

'You don't understand – we can't. There's nothing we can do. He's Lincoln fucking Jackson for Christ's sake!'

'Well, we have to do something. God, is there no justice in this fucked-up world? Char, I know you loved him, but Lincoln's torn you apart. You're a shell of yourself.'

Trix's eyes grew dimmer, and her words pinched.

'It's torn us all apart,' I replied.

'Oh goody, the gang's already here.'

'What took you so long?' Poppy asked, turning to face Zaheen, who looked a little tired and more pissed off than the rest of us.

Zaheen tossed a clear plastic bag of cannabis on the grass in front of us and took a seat on the bench. 'Made a pit stop first. Thought we might need a pick-me-up considering the police wanted to charge me with everything from money laundering to grievous bodily harm. Don't worry they let me go with an NFA for now.'

'That's grand, you just got out of the police station and the first thing you do is break the law.' Poppy shook her head disapprovingly. Poppy always seemed disappointed: at life, at me, at herself. I wasn't the only one who had been dealt an impossible hand.

'Don't be such a prude, we needed it. It's been a fucked-up day, so spare me the lip because I'm really not in the mood,' Zaheen spat.

'Grand, if I don't lose my job for getting mixed up in this mess, I'll lose it when they drug test me. Grand, just fucking grand.'

'Oh, stop whining, it's only a bit of weed. It's not like it's crack, although after yesterday's antics with Heidi I did consider it,' Zaheen said, and they all laughed and it was real. Natural. I missed laughter.

'Do you think things will ever go back to the way they were? Like, do you think I'll ever be happy again? Without them? My babies I mean.'

'This isn't the end for you.'

Trix's hand squeezed mine but provided little to no comfort whatsoever. I wasn't the same, and I never would be again.

What happens to a person when the unthinkable occurs? What's left after everything's been stripped away? Can anyone really survive when nothing holds its weight or significance anymore?

'I think you should go and see Dr Kole again. Maybe now he can help. We can't lose you, Char. And this, this isn't healthy,' Poppy pleaded.

Zaheen quietly rolled a joint, making eye contact only with the white sheet of Rizla paper.

'We can't hurt Linc. Not now, not ever. You have to promise me. You have to swear – you all have to swear not to take Linc on. You'll lose. Can't you see I've already lost everything?'

My warning was the only thing I could do to protect them. For the first time, I could see how much my accident had affected them. I guess in some weird selfish way, I thought that I was the only one who got hurt that night. I thought I was the only one who lost somebody they loved. Yet as I sat there surrounded by the only three people who had ever been family to me, I realised that they'd lost somebody too. They'd lost *me*.

'OK, Char. We won't do anything to Lincoln.' Poppy's face softened, but her tone was icy.

'And what about you?' I asked, turning my head.

'*Me?*' Trix snorted. 'I'm not making you any promises, but if you really want us to stay out of it then I swear on Kera's and Kyle's lives I won't do anything without your say-so. But if that prick does even the slightest thing to you, I'll kill him with my bare hands. And that's a promise.'

Maybe it was what Trix said, or how she said it. I couldn't quite put my finger on it, but for some reason, for the first time in our friendship I believed Trix was capable of anything.

I leaned forward.

'Please tell me we are all in this together?'

'Yeah, Char, we got it. No more Lincoln. We just let it go. Just like that. Like nothing happened,' Zaheen said then continued rolling.

'I know you're upset. I can hear it in your voice,' I coaxed, as I watched her forcefully spark the joint and suck in a big draw, which made streams of smoke exit her nostrils. She reminded me of a dragon.

'No shit, Sherlock, I'm fucking thrilled all right. We are doing exactly what Lincoln wants us to do.' Zaheen's sarcasm was unmissable, but I couldn't divulge the real reason I wanted them to stay out of it. I couldn't let them know Linc had succeeded in destroying me, although it was painfully obvious he had.

I looked out beyond the horizon. The pinkish clouds simmered with blue, and in the distance the stars twinkled. Tiny specks glittering among the mixture of colours. It was so beautiful that I thought if this was the last thing I ever saw, then I would die with the image of unimaginable beauty right before me and that would have to be enough, because I had nothing left.

CHAPTER TWENTY-SIX

A S THE WEEKS WENT BY, everything started to get harder. I could no longer go through the motions of appearing fine. Putting on clothes, going to work, even maintaining my mainly liquid diet became a tedious task riddled with irritation. Nothing tasted like it used to; and even if it did, I simply didn't have the capability to enjoy it. Life was simply a means to an end and the happy thoughts of hurting Heidi were only increasing in their intensity. So, I decided to try and catch myself. Save what little of me I still had before there was nothing left to save. I'd hoped Dr Kole's was the place to do it, even if our previous sessions hadn't been exactly successful. If a professional couldn't fix me, then nobody could.

'Miss Goodwin, can you hear me?'

I lifted my head to meet the receptionist's dull eyes. She was younger than the woman that greeted me on my past visits.

'Yes. Sorry, I was miles away.'

She offered me a tight smile that didn't quite reach her almond eyes.

'Would you like to go through? It's the third door on your left.'

'I know. I've been here before, thanks,' I replied, grateful there was no small talk.

'Good morning, Charlotte. Please come in, take the load off. It's been a while since our last chat. How have you been?'

The leather squelched as Dr Kole slipped familiarly into his seat. Silver specks of stubble sprouted from his face reminding me of cat whiskers.

'I'm coping.' I mentally instructed my face muscles into a smile, but it didn't reach the surface. Would I ever truly smile again? Or was smiling a functional default designed for everyone to believe I was all right, when in truth I was anything but?

'I want to apologise for my outburst last time. I've been through a lot, but that wasn't me. I'm sorry.'

'That's quite all right, Charlotte,' he said evenly. 'Our last session was quite intense. You've had some time to reflect. Maybe we've made progress after all. It's good to see you coping.'

In truth, I had struggled more than coped, but maybe that was the idea. I had kept going. It wasn't supposed to be easy, maybe that was coping.

'I hope so.'

'Well, Charlotte, you've had to readjust. That takes time and perseverance to some extent. Are you sleeping?'

'A little better, Dr Kole.' That was a lie. A flat-out lie. I wasn't sleeping at all, just dozing when my body reached the level of complete exhaustion. My insomnia had become so intense that I had taken up internet surveys in order to gain a little extra cash and keep my mind preoccupied at night. That's when I wasn't drunk or flying high on a double dose of Valium. I wanted his help, so why couldn't I tell the truth?

'What about eating? You've certainly lost some weight since I last saw you. Actually, quite a bit of weight.'

The ink from Dr Kole's pen spilled out as he spoke. It left a blue blob the size of an M&M on his index finger and thumb distracting me from his question.

'I've been trying to eat more. It's hard sometimes to have an appetite.'

He made a note.

Hopefully, I'd said something that didn't make me sound like I was unravelling. Although I realised that's what was happening. Every day I unravelled slowly, piece by piece, atom by atom, sense and sensibility eluding me.

'Charlotte, is there something bothering you? You seem off. A little more optimistic than usual. But off. Is there something in particular you would like to discuss?'

I haven't been myself in quite a while, Dr Kole, is what I wanted to say but didn't. Or rather, couldn't.

'I'm fine. I'm learning to let go,' was what I went with, coupled with an induced smile. I thought if I voiced those words they might come true, but I couldn't even convince me, let alone a trained professional.

'To be honest, you don't look fine. In fact, you look rather sad. Maybe a bit agitated. I call it as I see it, Charlotte. And while I think you want me to believe you're moving on, in reality I don't think you are. It's a facade.'

'I'm . . .' I began but didn't continue. I slouched my shoulders instead, picking invisible threads from my mustard-coloured jumper. I was defeated, tired and ashamed. It was all becoming too much, the sound of my heart drumming a steady beat in my ears.

'Say something, please? This is a safe place. Everything you say here will be kept within these four walls, I promise you.'

'I can't.'

I paused again. No follow-up to my omission that I just couldn't continue. I took a tissue from the box behind me and tore it apart in my lap.

'Heidi. Linc's new girlfriend. She made a complaint to the police. She said we attacked her.'

'We?'

'Me and my friends. She said we hurt her.'

'Did you?'

'No. She's lying.'

'I see.'

'You don't believe me. Do you?'

'Whether I believe you or not is irrelevant. How it makes you feel, however, isn't.'

'I didn't hurt her. I wanted to. I wanted to do bad things to her. But I didn't. I know the difference between right and wrong. Hurting Heidi is wrong. It's a bad thing to do.'

'Were you arrested?'

No, I was threatened.

'We were questioned and let go. But because of what she did, the lies she told, I'll never be able to see Linc again. She made sure of that.'

'And that bothers you?'

Dr Kole chewed on the inside of his cheek, scribbled down another note and underlined it.

'Even though we're no longer together, he'll always be the father of my son and daughter. I'll always love him. I just need to talk to him. Everything will go back to how it used to be.

I want to know if his head is as messed up as mine. I want a conversation. That's all.'

'But he doesn't want to talk to you?'

'No, he doesn't.'

I figured it was best to leave out that Linc also made a complaint to the police. It wouldn't help me to admit it, and I wasn't sure Dr Kole needed all the facts. Besides, maybe it was too soon. I ambushed Linc that day with Poppy, but I felt like I had no choice. We weren't united in our grief like we should've been, we were separated by it. Like a wall had been built between us.

'Linc must have been terrified when he saw the aftermath in his kitchen. There was so much blood. That's what I remember – the blood. The smell of wet pennies rising up to swallow me. I'll always remember. And I can only imagine how it must feel for him to still live in that house, every day to walk past the white tiles and remember what we've lost. I don't think I understood it before, I didn't realise how it must have affected him. But now I do, I understand his pain.'

'I see.'

Dr Kole jotted down another note.

'How does Lincoln's reaction make you feel?' he encouraged.

'I don't know. I'm ashamed. Upset, sad, a little angry – but mainly I just feel rejected.'

'Why do you feel rejected?'

'We lost our babies and we've never had a real conversation about it. I mean, does he hate me that much? Does he blame me? Did he hate our children because they were mine and not Heidi's? Or was he just scared?' I waited a beat, catching my breath to regain something that resembled composure but couldn't quite nail it. 'Heidi is Linc's girlfriend now. They live together, just like we used to. That was the house we were going to raise our twins in. I was going to come home, then we would've been a real family. We were gonna have a nursery – we'd already decided on the colours. Grey and beige. I didn't want pink and blue. I wanted it to be neutral, but that doesn't matter now. It's their house, and I'm left on the outside. Alone. So yeah, I feel rejected.'

'Does it feel odd that Heidi's living the life you were supposed to be living?'

A lump came to my throat. 'She's not pregnant! So, it's not my life she's living. It just looks that way. To the public. To *The Hive*.' I struggled to contain the anger from erupting out of my throat like hot lava. 'Heidi isn't in the same boat we were in. It's different. Entirely different, Dr Kole. You have to see that she's not living my life.'

I wasn't aware when I stood, but I now registered I was standing. My shoulders were squared and hunched as my face twisted with disgust.

'Charlotte, just calm down. Have a seat. You and Lincoln got together pretty quickly. So did they from what you've said. I was just making the comparison.'

'Linc and I were in love; it wasn't just a publicity stunt. We were going to have a family that was real. Their relationship is just for Instagram, or at least that's the way they make it look.' I pulled my phone from my pocket. '*See!*'

I scrolled down to the loved-up posts of Linc and Heidi littered all over his profile. Shots of them kissing and eating pasta in Venice. We were supposed to go to Venice. He had promised me that once upon a time too. *Bastard!*

'Charlotte, please calm down. Just sit back down.'

'No, I'd rather stand,' I said, my tone tight and voice hoarse. I wanted to scream.

'Fine, have it your way. We will stand if that makes you feel more comfortable.'

He adjusted himself as he got to his feet.

'The question I was working up to was, now that the family you so desperately wanted can't happen, what do you do next?'

'I can't be a mother, and that was the one thing I always thought I would be. Now, I'm just Charlotte, with no idea where my life is going. I don't like this version of myself very much, but it's all that's left.'

'I can understand why you're at a loss,' he said, but didn't divulge further.

'Dr Kole, I can't seem to attach myself to the life I used to have. The things I used to do or enjoy. Everything is different now.'

'Why do you feel detached?'

'Everything's changed, I guess. I don't really recognise myself anymore. My body feels foreign to me – like I'm some sort of alien or something.'

I paced agitatedly back and forth, my mouth dry.

'How long have you had this detachment from yourself?'

That was an impossible question to answer because, to be honest, I'd always had a kind of detachment from myself. I'd never had that family support growing up so the least I thought I could do in life was create my own family. The real question was, when had I ever felt attached to my life?

'I don't know,' was the simplest answer I could give.

'I see.'

He reached for his notepad but, this time, I failed to hide my irritation. With the torn-apart tissue scattered like confetti at my feet, I snatched the notepad from his plump fingers.

'What are you writing, huh?' I flipped through the pages then saw what it said. 'I don't understand. What the hell is this?'

'Charlotte, calm down,' he said, neither defensively nor offensively, but as a matter of fact.

'What the hell is this?'

'Honestly?'

'That's kind of the point of these sessions, isn't it? So, tell me, Dr Kole, why have you written that you recommend I be held for psychiatric evaluation?'

'Because I believe it's true. In my professional opinion, I think you're unravelling, Charlotte. I think you've buried your grief so deep that it's just a matter of time before you can't contain it anymore. While you still recognise the difference between right and wrong, the more detached you become, the more that line will blur, and eventually you'll snap. You'll either hurt yourself or others. I want to help you before that happens. Please, let me.'

A tendril of a smile began to form.

'You can't help me. I have to go.' With those final words, I left, because he was right. Even if I didn't know it yet.

CHAPTER TWENTY-SEVEN

I HAD WITNESSED IT BEFORE. THE lights, the cameras, the loud hum chanting in unison. I had been in awe of the fireworks, felt a tug of satisfaction as I became someone important. I had been close enough to smell the perspiration, to see the blood seep from open wounds made from punches that connected to the right piece of tissue at the right time.

I saw from a comfortable distance the pressure being applied, the determination, because boxing was no game. It was war; Linc had once stressed that to me. Each a single soldier, ready to go to war and fight to be the best. And I used to be his queen, his prize.

I used to sit in the front row, cheering, willing him to win with every bone in my body. He was mine and I was his, and after it was all over, after the crowds had gone back to their mundane lives and desperate routines, we would escape the battlefield, just the two of us.

Boxing – it's deeper than flesh, it was deeper than us, at least that was the way I understood it. There was a mental factor to fighting, it was strategic and planned. Linc had once told me that going into a fight unprepared was like driving a car with no brakes.

I hadn't known it then, but soon I would gear up for the fight of my life and there would be no brakes on me either. There would be nothing to stop me.

'Do we have to tune into this nonsense? Like, honestly, hitting myself in the head with a rusty hammer seems more appealing than this crap.' Trix wasn't a fan of boxing nor was she a fan of any sport in general, despite the number of athletes she'd dated on rotation.

I guess that always amazed me about Trix: she could have had anyone, yet she ended up having two children with a junkie from the estate that she only fell in love with to piss off her parents.

'I want to watch it. It's Linc's big moment. I can't miss it. We'll always have a connection, you know that.'

My legs dangled over the arm of the grey sofa as I sat up to reach for the remote before she could get to it.

'I assure you, there are serial killers with better connections to their victims than you and Lincoln.'

I didn't rise to Trix's sarcasm. I knew what she was getting at but didn't have it in me to fight her. At least she was speaking to me since she'd got an all-important court date for unsupervised visitation. I was happy for her.

'This is important to me. Please can we just watch it?'

'For fuck's sake, Char. I thought you were moving on. Letting go.'

'This is part of moving on, doing so with no animosity or guilt. I need to do it with a pure heart, and my heart still belongs to Linc. So just let me watch him fight, just this once.'

Trix shook her head. It reminded me of one of those mantel bobble heads, or maybe that was her new graduated bob which made her look older despite her twenty-nine years.

'I'm all for you moving on, but we don't need to cheer. Can't you just move on without needing to watch? It's embarrassing.'

'No, I can't. Everybody moves on in different ways. This is just my way of doing it. He's let go, I know that, but that doesn't mean I have to do it the way he did.'

There was a tiny piece of friction that burned in my chest when I admitted that. Linc was gone.

'I really don't get you. I swear I feel like you're losing it sometimes.'

Her brow furrowed, her lips a hard line as she tried to resist saying more.

'You tell us to stay away. We all know what Lincoln did to you, yet we can't do anything about it because you've decided this is a better way of letting go. Marvellous, Char.'

'Trix, I know it doesn't make sense to you—'

'You bet your arse it doesn't make sense. It's like a weird case of Stockholm syndrome or something. You're protecting the one person who's hurt you most,' she snapped.

I could see how it must have looked to her. How foolish I must have seemed, but unbeknown to her, and even myself, I was getting smarter.

'Oh God, am I interrupting?' Zaheen entered, holding a litre bottle of Smirnoff and elderflower-infused tonic water.

'Nope, not at all, maybe you can talk some sense into Charlotte, because I must either be speaking Latin or nonsense. One of the two. Or perhaps it's both – either way I'll be in the kitchen making us some drinks.'

She snatched the bottles from Zaheen and disappeared down the passageway.

'What have you done now? Are we getting brought in for questioning again? Because if we are, I'm going home now to change. I had to throw away my Gucci trousers after last time. Police stations are so unhygienic.'

Zaheen's eyes focused intently on me.

'Nothing. I haven't done anything. I just want to watch the fight – that's all. Trix thinks I'm nuts.'

'Please tell me you're not talking about Lincoln's fight?'

'Zee, you know that's the fight I'm on about.'

Trix re-entered on cue.

'Fucking hell. Did I miss something? You were practically drilling us after the thing with Heidi, saying we should stay away from Lincoln, now you're just casually watching him on telly. Have I smoked crack by mistake or is this a bad dream?'

'It's not like that,' I protested. I couldn't explain it to them because I couldn't explain it to myself. I was angry at Linc, but I still loved him, and although I suspected him, I trusted that he would never do anything to hurt me. It was confusing. On one side the worst thing that had ever happened to me, and on the other the best thing that had ever happened to me, but in the middle there were secrets and lies. Questions that only Linc could answer.

'So, if it's not like that, then why are we watching him?'

I should have anticipated Zaheen's question, but I didn't. I knew they wouldn't understand the truth or understand why I was struggling not being a part of Linc's world anymore. My world had been taken from me.

'It's all over social media. It'll be damn near impossible to avoid it so I figured we may as well give in and watch it like everyone else. Why should I be different?'

'That's a dog-shit excuse and you know it.'

'Damn, Trix, that's a little harsh.'

Zaheen placed her hands in the air and shook her head. She knew better than anyone what a firecracker Trix could be when she was upset.

'Oh, I'm calm, fucking chilled over here. But really, Char? FOMO? I just can't.'

Trix retreated back to the kitchen. I could hear the cupboard doors being slammed a few seconds after she entered.

'She'll calm down.'

'I know, Zee. And it's not like I can't see why she's upset. But Heidi's the one who made the complaint, not Linc,' I said, then folded into myself a little. It was best to leave DI Kilby's threats out of it.

'Heidi was just copying Lincoln. He made a complaint about you and Poppy first. Doesn't that make you angry? Or at the very least pissed off?'

I *was* angry. I could feel it deep inside me like toxic waste bubbling up, trying and failing to escape. But I couldn't let it – I had to supress it because Linc would hurt them, and fear tops anger every time.

'I'm past all of that.'

'It happened less than three weeks ago, Char.'

'Exactly, we should leave it there and move on. It's what's best for all of us.'

Zaheen picked at an imaginary piece of string from her grey knitted jumper.

'And what about Poppy? She could have lost her job over this. She was already on thin ice; this could have meant the end of her nursing career, and it's all Lincoln's fault.'

'She saved my life. I won't let her lose her job. She risked everything for me. I'll always be grateful to all three of you for that.'

'You risked everything for me. I'll never forget what you did, Char. I wouldn't even be standing here if it wasn't for you. You're my best friend, I just can't stand to see you in this much pain. It hurts me too,' Zaheen confessed, but I was lost in a memory as I saw Linc step into the ring.

I'd realised over time that Linc and I conceived the twins the night he successfully defended his world title against Dennis 'The Bruit' Robinson. We made sweet love that night after he knocked Robinson out with a mean right hook in the second round that left the crowd breathless. It was the best night of my life, not just because he won but because I felt like we won together. And then the twins were conceived in that happy, healthy bubble of love. I had never felt so important. That's why I had such an affinity for boxing, that's why I couldn't let go.

Linc thanked me after the fight for everything I did for him. I told him how proud I was. I thought then that that moment would never end, that I would be his love for all time.

I was wrong.

'I don't want the night I lost the twins to define me, or the rest of my life. It's just so hard to let go. It wasn't like they were sick or deformed. They were healthy, which only makes it worse. If I hadn't gone to Linc's that night, then all of this could have been different. I would never have had the accident.'

My stomach began clenching. Other than a few watery cups of tea I hadn't consumed anything in days. I touched the bracelet under the cuff of my shirt, my reminder that Linc would always be with me.

'We can't live in the past, Char. We have to live in the here and now, with the people who love us. The people who love you.'

'And I love you guys too. But I seem to ruin everything I touch, Zee, even when I don't mean to.'

'It's starting. Let's hope this dickhead gets blinded by one of those floodlights and knocks himself out, then I'll be happy we watched. Ecstatic even.'

Trix reappeared holding a tray with three glasses, some chopped up lime wedges and blush tonic water. She proceeded to make the drinks as me and Zaheen got comfortable, our conversation over for the time being.

Everyone thought I watched so I could see Linc win, but that wasn't the reason.

Not the real one. I watched because I wanted Linc to lose.

THE HIVE — Lincoln Jackson successfully defends his world title against Paul 'the Loon' in an astonishing third round knockout

falcon36 — did you see that right hook? I swear @lincolnjackson would be a decent fighter if he didn't have such a big mouth!

theoriginalblade — @falcon36 lmao he got lucky mate, @paultheloon had him first 2 rounds and he's a journeyman let's not forget

kev_boxgym — @falcon36 @theoriginalblade he still won lads and by the looks of it he's winning out of the ring too, did you see his new bird? Fitttt! @lincolnjackson

theoriginalblade — don't care if he won @kev_boxgym he's still a shit human being @lincolnjackson won't win another world title not with his attitude

falcon36 — @theoriginalblade @kev_boxgym shitty person or not @heididolak can suck my nob any day, total upgrade from the @kimkardashian clone he had before smh

kev_boxgym — @falcon36 @theoriginalblade haha @charlottegoodwin was scary @lincolnjackson dunno what u was thinking u date trash u'll fight trash lol

theoriginalblade — least we can all agree on that @kev_boxgym @falcon36 lmao @heididolak is a 10 out of 10

adrianelliot55 — @theoriginalblade @kev_boxgym @falcon36 oh come off it the last one was hot, I quite liked her bum @lincolnjackson

theoriginalblade — @adrianelliot55 no one asked u mate!

CHAPTER TWENTY-EIGHT

L INC ALWAYS VISITED HIS FAVOURITE cafe the day after he won a fight. It was a stupid compulsion he'd superstitiously kept without fail. He confirmed it on his Instagram page with a post on his story of him heading there in his car. I'd watched the screen and knew he wasn't far from me, and that if I wanted to see him I could.

It was like a bolt of lightning had ignited in my veins. I had to see him, even if it was from a distance. I wanted to steal a glimpse of the man I still loved desperately. I knew it was wrong, forbidden in the literal sense – it could cost me everything – but I couldn't ignore the ebbs and flow of my wanting for him, of my need for answers, to understand the man who took everything from me. It's strange, how much you can want something once it's gone. Even when it's broken you. You still yearn for what you had. It's a psychological response.

I missed us. The us Linc and I used to be. When Linc and I still had a future, but now he hated me. He wouldn't even speak to me. I was the mother of his children, then because of an accident I became the bane of his existence. Ambushing him at the barbers with Poppy caught him and myself off guard. I may have wanted to see him, but I wasn't ready to. But now was different. We were on neutral territory. Linc would still be riding high from his win the night before, meaning he'd be more inclined to talk to me.

A contemporary vision of teal cushion-back chairs and drooping artificial vines made up the interior of Grind. It hummed in the middle of its afternoon rush of local business millennials. The twenty-something women half picked at their smashed avocado toast they begrudgingly ordered for the picture they posted to their socials when in truth they were craving the buttermilk chicken burger.

I fingered my hair, scraping it tightly into an untidy topknot then dabbed at my lips with Vaseline. Pinching my cheeks to add a little colour, I sat upright and looked out for Linc.

I looked terrible. Unkempt, but that was best since I wanted to remain incognito to everyone apart from him. I didn't want anyone to recognise me, or I would be at risk of DI Kilby coming back and ruining everything. Though I was prepared to argue our meeting was coincidental, a part of me knew the excuse was thin. My heart was in my stomach and my body felt like it could leap at any given moment as I sat there in a basic white T-shirt and skinny ripped jeans waiting for Linc to appear. Golden slivers of light slid over the white tables like luminous cloth. Had I not minded being noticed, I would have found it comforting. A tranquil place I could sit and get my fucking head together. But since I was trying to remain invisible to everyone but Linc, it was just irritating being out in the open.

Forensically, I examined the menu, staring up at the door in ten second intervals until I saw him from the corner of my eye. He came through the glass double doors with his head down, staring intently at his phone. A wisp of a smile hit his lips, but it vanished the moment he spotted me.

'What are you doing here, Charlotte?' Linc paced towards me. He was in grey joggers and a matching Trapstar sweatshirt, which strained against his taut muscles.

'I—' was all I said. I had planned on seeing Linc, but I hadn't planned on him seeing me so soon and I hadn't practised what to say. Despite longing for this moment for so long, I was still woefully underprepared.

'You're not supposed to have any contact with me. Do you think this is a game? This is harassment. I'll have you arrested in one phone call if you don't get out of here.'

'No, I—' I needed to regain some control. I was wavering and it showed. 'Linc, I just wanted to congratulate you. For winning last night. It was one hell of a fight. One of the best knockouts I've ever seen.'

'You watched?'

Whether he was angry or not I could always rely on Linc's ego to need stroking. I could trust him to hang around long enough for me to do at least that.

'Yeah, of course. That's why I had to see you. Just quickly. Maybe you can take a seat and do what we should have done months ago.'

'And what's that?'

'Talk. Linc, I just want to talk.'

I gently pushed the chair out with my foot, gesturing for him to sit. I didn't think he would, but when he slumped himself into the seat, I knew this was probably the only chance I would ever get to talk to him face to face.

'What do you want? And just so we're clear if the Powerpuff Girls come busting in here I'm leaving and calling Kilby.'

'I told the girls I was going to the gym. It's just you and me. Lovely way to greet the mother of your children by the way.'

I couldn't help it. It slipped out like a knee-jerk reaction.

'Our children are dead, Charlotte! You mean absolutely nothing to me so spare me the guilt trip. I'm doing this as a courtesy. Or charity, however you want to see it. By the way, you look like shit.'

My stomach knotted, but at least he was talking, even if it was to insult me.

'I'm not sleeping.'

'I can see that.'

'I've been through hell. You'd look rough too, if you cared. They were our children, Linc. Someone broke in and because of that I had an accident. None of this is my fault.'

'Let me stop you there. I have no interest in talking about the past and that's what you are: the past. I've moved on.'

That hurt, and I could instantly feel the tears pricking my eyes. My lips felt dry, so I licked them, but the panic and fear had already set in. Was this what Dr Kole had warned me was coming?

'Is that what I am to you? The past? Is that it?'

'What do you want from me? Whatever you're looking for, you're not gonna get it.'

I wanted to jump over the table and punch him in the face but instead I shook as whatever dregs of composure I had left won over.

'Why didn't you come to the funeral? Why didn't you come to say goodbye to them? You owed me – you owed them – at least that much.'

Linc made a snorting sound and picked up his phone, dividing us with the sound of an incoming notification.

'Am I not worthy of an apology?'

'What more is there to say? I stuck it out for our children. I did my moral duty as a man. When you left to go back home, I was relieved, then you had the accident. But it was all for the best. We were never meant to be.'

Have you ever wondered what betrayal tastes like? Well, it's bitter for a start, with hints of copper. It reminded me of blood. It filled my mouth and burned like corrosive on my chest. It affected every part of my body from my fingertips to the needles in the sole of my feet.

It spread like wildfire.

'What the fuck are you doing? Give me back my phone. Now, Charlotte.'

Linc was too late. The phone smashed on the ground before he could finish his sentence. I didn't even realise what I was doing until I had done it. It was like some kind of electric reaction I wasn't in control of. Like my body had switched over to a part of me who didn't care about consequences or repercussions.

The part of me that just wanted to fight. Suddenly I was enraged, for everything that had been taken from me. For everything that could have been but now was impossible. For all the hours, days, weeks leading to this. For what I realised a while back but was only now starting to accept: Lincoln Jackson didn't care that our children had died.

'You promised that no matter what happened we would be together. Why would you do that? Why would you lie to me? Why did you take everything from me? What did I ever do to you, Lincoln?'

'Keep your voice down. You wanted a family. Did it ever occur to you that maybe I didn't? Jesus, there should be a law against women like you getting pregnant.'

I got to my feet, my mouth wet with fresh saliva. After everything this man had done to me, he thought it was OK to just admit that in the middle of Grind of all places.

'You selfish piece of shit – do you have any idea what you've done to me? What I've lost?'

'I couldn't give two shits what you've lost, Charlotte. Why do you think I went to Kilby? I didn't want you anywhere near me. Don't you get it? You need to fuck off.'

A part of me could see the mounting audience reaching for their smartphones, but I couldn't stop myself. I had to say everything I came to say to him. It was now or never. There wouldn't be another chance.

'So, you admit you got Kilby to threaten me? Why would you do that? He wanted to put Zaheen in prison.'

'The girl commits fraud. She's lucky Kilby let her go. She belongs in prison; you all do after what you did to Heidi.'

'What we did to Heidi. Are you out of your mind?'

'She told me you attacked her.'

'Well, surprise, surprise, pathological Barbie is a liar. We never laid a finger on her. She just said that so you and the rest of the world would feel sorry for her. And judging by this conversation, it worked. She manipulated you.'

Then it hit me like a tonne of bricks. It was so obvious I didn't understand how I couldn't see it before. It was Heidi. Suddenly, I was sure of it.

'How much do you really know about Heidi?' I said, sliding back into my seat. I was disarmed.

'What on earth are you on about, Charlotte?'

'Heidi! Your loving girlfriend.' I cleared my throat. What if Linc didn't know what she'd done? 'What if she did it?'

'Did what?'

'Set up the break-in. What if she did it? What if she's the reason I fell? What if she's the reason I lost them?'

'*What?* Are you insane? Why would she do that?'

'So that she could have you all to herself. Can't you see what she's done?'

The expression on Linc's face grew dark, as his eyes darted from me to the other diners then back to me.

'Listen to me, Charlotte.' He grabbed my arm roughly. 'Heidi had nothing to do with your attack. I've warned you once and now I'll warn you again, for the final time. Stay away from me. You come anywhere near us, and I'll have you arrested. Understand?'

I reached out to grab his hand. He was hurting me, and I wanted him to let go.

'Linc – stop.'

He pulled back.

'Stay away from us.'

Linc pushed back from the table and his chair fell over. It smacked the floor as I got to my feet.

'*Linc!* She did this. I know she did. She's been manipulating you from the start. I'm the only one you can trust!' I screamed as he exited Grind and jogged across the road to his car.

I had never witnessed a person so desperate to get away from me. I looked up as people stood around me gaping and glaring.

Then everything went dark.

THE HIVE — **Lincoln Jackson and ex-girlfriend Charlotte Goodwin have a heated argument in Grind Cafe**

foxy_roxy99 — so @charlottegoodwin blacked out in Grind? Someone explain to me why @lincolnjackson dated this nutjob please?? I'll wait!! @thehive

meganlay — @foxy_roxy99 the wait is over, she's a total wreck. If ur gonna ambush ur ex then at least wear a decent outfit

wildbunnycam — @foxy_roxy99 @meganlay It's @lincolnjackson I feel sorry for, look at his face right before he runs out @charlottegoodwin should neva show her face in public again to be honest, she's so desperate #thehive

foxy_roxy99 — @wildbunnycam @meganlay if anyone deserves pity it's @heididolak imagine watching ur bf have lunch with a crazy ex #cringe

thomaskane71 — this is jokes, @lincolnjackson sprinted out the door lol LEGEND

wildbunnycam — @foxy_roxy99 @lincolnjackson could never be my boyfriend @heididolak needs to cancel him immediately

cindyleepk — @jassatimly have u seen this LMAO I swear ur sister went school with her friend Poppy???

jassatimly — @cindyleepk Yup, her, Poppy and the Asian 1 were all in my big sis year, they all hung out with this rich girl Trix that's probably how @charlottegoodwin met @lincolnjackson I gotta get me some rich friends lol

cindyleepk — @jassatimly don't matter how rich you are what I've just seen will live in my mind rent free forever loooooool #toofunny #thehive

CHAPTER TWENTY-NINE

'**W**ELL, IT'S NOT GOOD. AND I totally resent being called the "Asian one" by the way. Racist trolls.'

Zaheen slid the phone back into my palm. My fingers trembled slightly as I accepted it with a wince. A story from The Hive had emerged online a few hours after the video had begun to circulate. It had already been viewed more than five hundred thousand times and the trolls were out for blood, calling me everything under the sun, from desperate to pathetic.

The cloying scent of floral car freshener assaulted my nostrils as a slice of pale moon made visible from the car windows illuminated us. The evening had brought with it freezing rain that momentarily settled into a clear night sky. My head was still fuzzy. I'd collapsed in Grind only a few hours earlier and still felt the overpowering darkness from the moments after Linc left, like without him standing there, there just wasn't enough air to breathe.

We were on every gossip page imaginable arguing in Grind Cafe like a couple of star-crossed lovers that were no longer in love. I vaguely remembered being filmed, and I knew that possibly a few media sites would pick up the story and exploit it as much as they could. But I never imagined I would be portrayed as a deranged woman obsessed with her ex-boyfriend. Linc was a sports icon, practically a household name, and him arguing with me in public was tabloid gold. My superstar ex-boyfriend, the man who had kissed me so generously, the man who fathered the only children I would ever have was screaming at me to leave him alone. It was all caught on camera for the entire world to see. I was humiliated. Had I not been through enough? Everything had been taken from me. I was left with no substance, just dust, blood and flesh. I felt the heat on my face.

The rage hit me so hard I struggled to breathe.

'Char, what were you thinking confronting him like that?'

My eyes couldn't focus on Zaheen's face as she spoke, I just kept staring at the screen until the images blurred.

I repulsed the only man I ever loved.

'I don't really know what to say,' I answered her. But I wish I'd stayed silent. We were a family. At least that's what we were supposed to be, but that was all before Linc betrayed me. Before he betrayed our would-be family. Before everything became about Heidi.

'What the hell were you thinking? You're probably going to be arrested. Kilby doesn't look like a man who goes back on his word.'

'It was a mistake, Zee. I just wanted to talk to him. Make him understand what this has done to me.'

How could I have got it so wrong? Zaheen was right, I would be arrested if the footage got back to DI Kilby and I'd put my friends in jeopardy too, but there was nothing I could do. It was all over the internet, and some bored troll had already taken the liberty of making it a meme.

I was fucked; there were no two ways about it.

'Damn it, Char. You warned all of us to stay away from him then you go and do this. Are you trying to ruin your life with this crusade?'

'*Me?*' I roared at Zaheen and sat up as best I could in the back seat of Poppy's Corsa.

'I get this is hard for you – and trust me, honey, nobody understands better than the three of us what you've been through, it's heart-breaking – but this has to stop before you destroy yourself, or us in the process. Please, I'm begging you.'

The car door swung open, and Poppy and Trix got in.

'What'd we miss now? Has Linc uploaded anything?' Trix said, concern tightening her brow into a thin line.

'No. Not yet. But we should brace ourselves; that man's capable of anything.'

'What'd we do now? We can't hide in my car all night,' Poppy asked, her brow a matching thin line like Trix.

'She can't go home. That's the first place Kilby will look,' Zaheen said definitively.

'Well, dur, we know that. Poppy, she'll have to stay at yours until this whole mess dies down a little. In the meantime' – Trix turned her entire body to face me – 'give me your phone.'

'What the hell are you doing?' Poppy's hands were up, separating Trix from me.

'Something I should have done a long time ago. Phone, Charlotte. Now!'

I handed it to her and she unlocked the screen and proceeded to delete my Instagram and Twitter apps. I could have just reinstalled them later, but it was more of a symbol. Trix had had enough. She wanted Linc and all my problems to go away.

'There – no more socials for you. You're not gonna know where Lincoln is, or what he's doing. That way there'll be no more impromptu visits that end up on the blogs. Don't look at me like that. I'm stopping us from landing ourselves in jail.'

'I'm not a child, Beatrix. I can be trusted with my phone.' I used her full name to let her know I was being serious, but it didn't intimidate her like I'd hoped it would.

'I'm not a babysitter, Charlotte. None of us are. Yet since the night of your accident we've done nothing but babysit you, and I'm tired of it. Where's the Charlotte who held a knife to Michael's throat and threatened to kill him if he ever came anywhere near me again? Huh? Where's that strong, independent, badass woman gone?'

She was right. I did threaten to kill Michael with a kitchen knife after he attacked Trix in a drug-fuelled rage. I protected her and her children with no fear or consequences for my own life. Michael could have killed me, or I could have killed him and ended up in prison for murder. It was me who finally made him leave Trix for good. I'd won that fight, but Linc was kicking my arse in this one and there wasn't a thing I could do about it.

'I don't know what you want me to say. That version of myself is gone,' I confessed.

'All right, Trix, that's enough. She's upset. No need to push it.'

Poppy narrowed her eyes as Trix stepped out of the car. She lit a fag and called us morons over her hunched shoulders, as rain began to drizzle from the slab of dark sky.

'I'm sorry,' I said, my voice strangled and raw with sadness.

'Ay, I got you.' Zaheen wrapped her arm around me as I wept angry tears.

Guilty tears. Tears that just wouldn't stop.

'Hey, today's been tough, Char. We need some gin. How about you come home with me instead? Pops can spend some time with Jeremy, and we can have a girls' night. And don't worry, DI Plum has no idea where I lay my head so he won't find you. I promise,' Zaheen said, before exiting the car and pulling Trix by the arm into the Co-op across the street.

'I just don't feel like myself, and I don't know how to feel like myself anymore. I'm trying. I try every day, but it doesn't get any easier, just worse, as if there's no way out. I just want them back. I just want my babies back. Why me? *Why them?*' I screamed the last part.

I was unable to hold back all the emotions that eroded me from the inside out. I had lost too much to recover and had too many loose ends to move on. I still didn't know who sent the Instagram message, or if Heidi and Linc were in on it together.

I was finished.

'I can't do this anymore, Poppy. I feel like I'm going mad. I just want to wake up from this nightmare.'

'What did Dr Kole say? Maybe we should go see him together. Would that help?'

'That quack. I can't ever see him again.'

What Dr Kole told me kept me up at night. I was scared. Scared of what I was beginning to understand I was capable of.

'Poppy, I had one job – to protect my children, and I couldn't even get that right. And now this video is plastered all over the internet. Everyone thinks I'm fucking crazy. And they're right because I feel like I'm insane.'

'Oh, Char.' Poppy tutted. 'You aren't crazy. You've been through the worst thing any woman could ever go through and you're still standing. You're a fucking hero, and don't you forget that. You hear me, Char? You're my hero.'

I didn't feel like a hero, in fact I felt like the opposite. A failure.

'Maybe you should go with the girls, get something stronger than gin?'

Poppy looked at me bemused but didn't argue.

'OK. You gonna be all right on your own for a few minutes?'

'I'll be fine. I promise.'

I needed to feel safe, but nowhere was safe anymore.

The sun rose, burning away the morning mist, as I knelt before the window surrounded by a massive cloud of cigarette smoke. I could hear Zaheen prattling about outside the door of the tiny bedroom, unsure whether it was safe to enter or better to leave me be. She must have eventually walked away because when I emerged one cigarette later there was no sign of her.

Just a note, lying idle. In almost illegible blue italics she'd scribbled down on the back of a letter that clearly wasn't addressed to her but had somehow made its way to her living room. She'd gone to the shops to get some breakfast but would be back shortly. Ten minutes tops or at least that's what I think it said.

I was finally alone at last. Every square foot of Zaheen's flat felt miles too big around me, like a shirt that wouldn't fit right no matter how it was adjusted. I wasn't on the run from the police; there'd been no enquiries round Trix's which meant there was no one coming for me.

I was safe. Although for some reason, some part of me had never been more terrified in my entire life.

The girls tried and failed to console me. For hours the night before I howled like an injured puppy begging to be put out of its misery. My pain only burrowed deeper inside me because a) I knew I could never show my face again in public, and b) most importantly, Linc had won.

Zaheen's flat was tastefully decorated with white furnishings, oval mother-of-pearl mirrors, and hints of rose and gold throughout, but it couldn't stop me from floating away. Absent-mindedly, I grabbed a black coat that was pegged to the wall behind a door and pushed my feet into a pair of Zaheen's slippers.

A switch had flipped.

The air was a putrid reminder that I didn't deserve to remain alive while my children decomposed in separate wooden coffins that belonged more to the earth than they did to me. It was torture.

I'd realised in the dead of the night, my face mottled in fresh salty tears, that I could be with them. I could leave everything and everyone behind.

An automated voice called out another street name, as I sat back in the busy blue felt chair. The bus was practically empty given it had just gone eight in the morning. The day was icy. Yet I'd left the house in a daze. My mind was fuzzy and distracted. The sudden smell of vomit invaded my nose in waves. It took me a while to realise that I was the one who'd been sick. Stupid hangover.

The elderly woman sitting two seats in front shot me a bizarre look then faced forward quickly once I'd caught her staring. I'd been drunk a long time by then. So, any and all unwelcome attention was met with a look that could only be translated along into, *Mind your own fucking business.*

I stumbled off the bus, regaining my footing as I stormed along the pavement. A sharp gasp escaped me when I saw my reflection in a passing shop window. I was a ghostly woman that looked as haunted on the outside as I was on the inside.

I wasn't myself anymore. I'd transformed into a thin-lipped, yellowed-eyed clone who'd once had everything.

A homeless man offered a paper cup for me to spare change. I almost didn't register the interaction as I breezed past him to enter the train station. I tapped my Oyster card then tossed it away once on the other side of the barrier. I had no intention of tapping out so figured I didn't need it anymore. I moved briskly, trying not to draw attention to myself, which was easy since my eyes were bloodshot and puffy. My face dehydrated.

I didn't care that I looked dishevelled and traumatised; hopefully nobody in their right mind would recognise me. It was like I'd had an outer-body experience where my body just reacted. I was functioning automatically, as if every movement was muscle memory. It had only just occurred to me; I had been doing that since I lost the twins. Functioning. Neither living nor dead.

I threw the diamond bracelet on the ground. It once meant everything to me, a symbol of the love Linc and I shared, but I wouldn't be needing it where I was going. I stepped over it as I walked up the steps to platform one in Walthamstow Central.

I kept moving. The platform was busier than I'd anticipated but after I jumped it wouldn't matter what the onlookers thought.

Or filmed.

If I jumped too soon, or gave the inkling that I was going to, then I would be stopped, if not by a meddling TfL staff member festooned in a hideous high-vis jacket, then by a heroic commuter who would think they were doing the right thing when in actual fact they would be doing the complete opposite.

I didn't want to be saved.

Whatever Linc and Heidi did or didn't do made no difference to me because nothing would bring my children back. Sweat collected at the base of my spine. I could hear my heart hammering away in my chest like it wanted to tear away my flesh. I felt cold and distant, then angry and sad.

I walked up the furthest side of the platform, tackling my thoughts.

'Mummy let you down. I'm so sorry, Mummy loves you so much. Mummy will see you on Rockabye mountain,' I whispered, waiting for the train that would be there in approximately two minutes. Meaning I had two minutes left to live.

Jump!

It first entered my mind as a whisper. It felt easy and nothing had felt easy in so long. I was exhausted. I hated myself. I hated who I was. I hated how I looked and how I felt. So, I stood on the edge of platform one, fingers trembling, eyes unable to see anything other than rusted metal.

This was for the best.

This was how it all had to end. I heard the metal batter against the track as the train approached steadily.

Just one final step and it would all be over.

That's when Sasha pulled me back.

THE HIVE — Lincoln Jackson and Heidi Dolak announce their surprise engagement with an intimate photo. Heidi Dolak captioned the photo YES to indicate her response to the stunning proposal which took place last night on the terrace of Lincoln's multimillion-pound home. No pics of the ring yet, but, as always, we'll be keeping our ears tuned and our eyes peeled

anniekaper2 — Congratulations @lincolnjackson @heididolak so happy for the two of you

milkandhoney — @heididolak will be announcing her pregnancy next, so happy for her

swavey_p — Poor @charlottegoodwin this just isn't her week loool #thehive

kellyhill44 — all in the space of a few months @heididolak you are a savage pmsl

tessrash — @kellyhill44 the best woman won in my opinion lool

lenagyale — @lincolnjackson first lunch with ur crazy ex @charlottegoodwin now a proposal to @heididolak it's like watching *EastEnders* I can't keep up

jessicameadly — so strange but I could have sworn I saw @lincolnjackson with another woman arguing at the Taj this afternoon how bizarre

vancehector1 — When you get caught having lunch with your ex now you gotta propose to save the relationship @lincolnjackson bloody legend man

ruthkeap — congratulations to the happy couple

pamalaberry — even I feel sorry for @charlottegoodwin at this point #bekind

CHAPTER THIRTY

I COULD STILL FEEL THE PRICKLE of sweat at my hair-line as the rain began to fall in sheets. My shame felt like thick oil, suffocating, as Sasha stared back at me, wide-eyed and mouth open. For a moment we both said nothing, unsure of how to decipher what had transpired between us.

Sasha had saved my life at the very moment of the train's approach. Just in time. It was as if she had been standing there, watching me, and then at the final moment, insurmountable, she decided to intervene.

She had kept me alive. But why? I didn't deserve to live.

'Charlotte, say something. *Charlotte*, can you hear me?'

I couldn't. I just shrank a little and let the tears roll down my face, camouflaged by the battering rain.

'What are you doing? Were you about to jump?'

'I … I …'

The edges of my vision blurred. Sasha's dizzying floral pink coat was getting ruined by the onslaught of rain. But I felt paralysed. She gestured for us to take shelter further up the platform and slowly she lagged behind me, as my feet began to follow instruction and pace north before I lost all sense of time.

I didn't know how long I'd been sitting on the bench next to Sasha, but I knew it must have been a while, because the slick film of nervous sweat on the back of my neck had been replaced by the sharp chill of freezing air.

I was supposed to be dead.

I tasted the iron in my blood rise, mingle, then gum together at the roof of my mouth. I had bitten my tongue but couldn't remember doing it, like the memory had been stolen from me.

I was supposed to be dead.

'I take it you heard the news. Is that what brought you here? Lincoln?'

My eyes stayed trained on her.

Sasha was very beautiful, but even her beauty couldn't mask the insouciant expression dabbling her features. She looked cold. Probably even a little annoyed, but she never said it, she just sat there with the knowledge that she knew I didn't want to be alive anymore. Sasha knew I wanted to die.

'What news? What are you talking about?'

'Oh my God, you don't know.'

I could have sworn I detected a fleeting smile trace her lips.

'Here.' She entered the passcode to her phone and handed it to me.

My stomach heaved. Linc had proposed to Heidi.

'When did this happen?' I asked, feeling the sourness itch the back of my throat as I tried not to quiver.

'They both posted late last night. It's been all over the internet. Especially The Hive. It's disgusting if you ask me. How Lincoln's treated you. It's vile!' Sasha said it imploringly, giving me time to let my anger remain vestigial instead of reaching boiling point.

'Look, usually I wouldn't say anything, and I know I don't know what happened between you two, but I know what you were about to do. And if he's the reason you're doing it then don't. Men like him don't deserve women to die for them.'

'I didn't know about the engagement. And you don't know what you saw,' I hissed defensively, slapping the phone back into her hand and turning away.

'I know a suicide attempt when I see one, Charlotte, and if I hadn't stopped you, then we both know you would've jumped.'

She was right. I would have. I would have been dead and Linc would have won yet again. I spent my entire life being emotional armour for other women but for some reason I just couldn't find the strength to fight back. Not truly. Not how I wanted to.

I needed to be strong, calculative, *captivating*, but I couldn't find it in me. Linc had snuffed it out. I wanted to tell Sasha the truth, everything the man I loved had done to me since the day our children died, but Linc had me bound and gagged so tight that there was no way out of my nightmare.

'I can't tell anyone what he did to me, but just know Lincoln Jackson is a bad man. A horrible man.'

'Then why are you letting him win? Why should he be allowed to get away with it? If what he's done is so bad, why give up, Charlotte?'

The ominous feeling Sasha knew more about the situation than she was saying tightened at my throat. I stood then, my stomach too unsettled to stay seated a moment longer. Sasha didn't understand. She didn't know how powerful Linc was. Or what he'd make DI Kilby do to me if I told the world about my accident.

'Can't you see he's already won? If I fight him, I just end up hurting the girls. I can't hurt them. I won't risk them.'

'Then don't. Charlotte, if anyone can bring Lincoln Jackson to his knees it's you. Don't you see you hold all the cards? You're the one person that can hurt him the most. You have to do this. If not for you, then for the reason you were going to jump and let the same people you are trying to protect mourn for you.'

Relief swept through me like a breeze caught by the slash of a steel blade. I'd reached the apex of my grief and now something new was emerging.

A feeling. Like the stillness after a storm has passed.

'Why do you care?' I asked, suddenly turning on the heels of my feet to stare at her unblemished face. Sasha's expression remained undisturbed, but her upper lip twitched, and I knew that whatever she was about to tell me wouldn't be the whole truth.

'You're not the only one going through boy trouble at the moment, you know. And maybe you standing up for yourself might just be good for the rest of us.'

After what Sasha did to Poppy with Brad, I knew it would be a mistake to trust her completely. I watched the way she pressed her fingertips into her wrist and knew that whoever had hurt her had done so very deeply.

'What'd he do to you?' I asked, not removing my eyes from hers.

'What they all do. Promise the world then take it away once they've got what they want. I loved him. I really loved him, and I thought he loved me too. I thought we would go the distance, that we had a future. We were meant to get married one day. I was wrong about him, about us. I was wrong about all of it.' She half smiled but I could see the fissure in the foundation as her lips curled down.

'What are you going to do about it?'

'What'd you think I'm doing here.'

I looked at her perplexed, unsure of her statement.

'He won't get away with it. I won't let him, Charlotte. I'm stronger than that. Stronger than him. And so are you.' Her words were as icy as the rain beating down from the solid hue of grey above.

'I'm going to take you home now. You still living with Trix? Same address?'

'Yeah,' I answered quietly as she paced in front of me, her dark hair thick and lush in a high ponytail that trailed the length of her back like an ebony serpent.

'I heard a rumour Trix's babies' father's in prison?' She eyed me, waiting for me to confirm or deny the tales she'd heard through the grapevine. London was an extremely small place. Everyone knew everyone, and that meant knowing everything.

'Trix hasn't been with Michael in years. So, I don't know anything about it.'

That was a lie. A huge one. Trix and I were the sole reason Michael was in prison.

'Well, hope he gets out. Kids shouldn't have to see their parents behind bars. I should know. My father was in prison most of my childhood.' Sasha rambled on blithely about her adolescence then went on to compare her mother and sister to less attractive versions of herself.

I wasn't listening. Well, not to all of it; in fact, I was about to opt for taking the bus passing some excuse that I needed air or wanted to be alone when we approached her car.

Then I stopped.

'That new?' I asked, noting it was a total upgrade from the Mercedes she usually sported.

'A gift ... from him,' she said, as if I knew precisely who 'him' was, or ought to be. But that's when a thought confused me, like a steadfast brick to the head.

'Why did you come to the station? Were you going somewhere?'

I waited for her reply which came out gently, almost practised.

'No, I was coming back. We've ended things. It's over.'

'Char, what the hell are you doing here? Zee's been frantic. She's called like ten times. Your phone's switched off. We were panicking.' Trix's expression was split: half relieved I was back safe and sound, and half pissed off I was walking through her front door in the middle of the afternoon with Sasha in tow.

'Umm ... I didn't. Sorry. I wanted to come home. Sasha dropped me off.'

'Go easy on her. She's had a rough morning,' Sasha said, veering forward to face Trix dead on. It was odd watching two of the most beautiful women I knew stare at each other in pure disgust.

'Relax, I swear, I wasn't stalking Linc or anything crazy. I just had to get some fresh air. Sasha dropped me home. That's all. Please play nice you two. I have a headache,' I muttered as if I'd been caught in a lie. But it was the truth: Sasha was only there to help, and she'd done that. She'd helped me.

'You seem different today.'

Trix raked her gaze over me from head to toe and back again.

'What'd you mean?'

'I don't know. You just do,' Trix snapped then impatiently turned back to Sasha. 'Look, thanks for bringing her home but I can take it from here.'

'Charlotte, you going to be all right?'

'Yeah, I'll be fine. Thanks for—'

Sasha cut me off. 'Don't worry about it. Anytime. Just remember what I said.'

'I will,' I responded nervously, knowing that whatever happened at the station wouldn't go further than our conversation. Sasha had not only saved my life but lit a vicious fire in my belly that wasn't there before. I was finally ready to fight back.

The door closed behind Sasha before Trix spoke.

'What the hell was all that about?'

I took a beat.

'Nothing. Has DI Kilby been round?'

'No. There's no sign of DI Plum, but—'

'Good.' Blank relief swept over me as I headed for my bedroom, Trix calling determinedly after me.

'I'm not finished. What the hell were you doing with Sasha? Hello, I'm speaking to you. I don't trust her, Char.'

But I didn't answer. There was something else I needed to do.

CHAPTER THIRTY-ONE

THE DECISION TO KILL MY ex-boyfriend was one I came to the day after I tried to kill myself. I was sitting by the window, a cloud partially blotting out the sun, in a shoddy coffee shop somewhere close to Enfield high street. I had reached rock bottom, truly the pit of despair, prepared to end it all because for me there was no reason to live. But then something changed. I'm not sure when it happened; I mean it was hard to pinpoint. Up until then I had only thought about Heidi and how she was standing in my way. Except it wasn't just Heidi in my way, Linc was there too. And then it hit me – why should I die when I can kill!

It was Thursday, and I'd done my best to write it all out in intricate detail on a gritty napkin. It wasn't like I could just walk up to Linc's front door and do my worst. I would have to be smart. Like he'd been. And that meant not getting caught.

But how do you kill one of the most famous men in Britain?

Essentially, my plan had three major flaws.

The first and most obvious was, I needed proof.

If I was going to take down Lincoln Jackson, then I had to be one hundred per cent sure he was guilty of involvement in my accident. The girls had no doubt he was to blame, but while having a detective on his payroll was suspicious, I wasn't wholly convinced I knew what his role in the events of that night had been. I still needed answers and only Linc could provide them.

Then there was Heidi. She had already proved to be a manipulative bitch, but did she have a silent hand in the shadows helping Linc all along? Was *she* really to blame, and Linc just a victim of her cunning?

Linc was pretty dim on the best of days. There was no way in hell he could've planned a fake break-in without help. And I suspected Heidi was that help.

I deliberated hard. I didn't want to hurt Heidi without good reason. It felt tacky, and wouldn't go down well with the public, and I needed the public on my side if my plan was going to work. I didn't just want Linc dead, I wanted a confession too.

That brought me to my second problem. No matter which way I ran through different scenarios, the outcome was always the same. Me getting caught. I could already envision the dumb smile on DI Kilby's face as he carted me off to a filthy cell. There'd be no way out. Linc would have won even in his death. I was the prime suspect in a murder I hadn't yet committed. And that posed risks and consequences that extended beyond me. No matter what happened to me, Poppy, Trix and Zaheen could not be implicated in any of it. I'd made up my mind. This had to happen. It was necessary and logical.

Linc had to confess.

But the truth was I wasn't entirely sure what I was capable of, or how far I was really willing to go. I was the only person who could make it right. And there, stark, staring me in the face. A cold poltergeist. My third problem.

Venue.

If I was going to get a confession, then I needed a place to do it.

'Would you like anything else? A refill perhaps? We're offering a promotion on our spiced pumpkin lattes.'

A stringy girl with painful red acne approached the wooden table. Her hair was far too greasy and clung to the overwhelming scent of coconut, which was probably feeding the pustules festooned on her forehead and cheeks. She stood too close, peering directly over my shoulder.

'No, thanks, I'll be up all night if I have any more coffee.'

Although that didn't sound like a bad idea. There were still gaping holes in my plan and I wanted them at least marginally full before I set anything in motion.

'Well, let me know. We've got a new salted caramel cappuccino too. It's pretty awesome if you're not into lattes and wanna give it a go,' she continued. The assembled smile stuck to her face like adhesive.

'Thanks, but unless you have a manual on how to kill your ex-boyfriend and get away with it, then I think I'm all done here.'

She blinked conciliatorily.

'Been there, sister. I've always thought electrocution was a good method, but now I think about it some more, so is burning alive.'

She straightened herself and let out a nervous smile that exposed a row of off-white teeth.

'What's your name?'

'Jill,' she said in a weedy voice, almost apologising.

'Well, Jill, take it from me, if you're planning on killing your ex then you should pick your poison carefully.'

'Men, they really are God's worst creation. Hey, do you come here often? You look really familiar.'

'Oh, I'm not who I used to be.' I dropped a ten-pound note on the corner of the table and stood. 'Have a wonderful day, Jill.' I padded off through the glass bi-folding doors.

'You too!' she called from behind me, completely oblivious to the idea she had just implanted in my head.

The air hit me like a wall. My thoughts felt weighted and wrong, like I was in a lake with them pulling me down. Everything that had happened up until then had been done to me, I was playing defence in a game where all the players wore masks. Well, it was time to see who I was playing against.

As soon as I got home, I scrolled through Instagram from one of my fake accounts and settled on a few profiles. In order for my plan to work, I would need to make some digital connections. All would be vital, and each would play their part.

First, I would need a police officer, but not just any officer, a seasoned detective. DI Kilby fitted the bill perfectly and I was more than a little excited to start playing with him, since he already had the pleasure of playing with me and my friends at Linc's behest. It was time for a little payback.

DI Kilby had a profile. It was private, but that wouldn't stop me. My fake page was camouflaged as a home food catering service in East Ham, miles from where he lived in Acton, but in less than an hour he'd accepted the request, and just like that, I was in his world. Kilby was smiling with his copper-coated Labrador in a photo posted four months ago. Easter lunch on the Isle of Wight with his relatives. There were other shots too. Nights out with the lads, top golf with his nephews. No girlfriend or kids of his own. A quiet, pathetic observation, but one I made nonetheless. DI Kilby almost looked normal without his damp brown suits and air of superiority. I hovered for a little while, made a few notes then moved on. I had a lot of work to do, and organisation was key.

The other person who would be vital to my plan was a person who worked for – you guessed it – Instagram. This would be a little trickier since I would have to convince Sasha to help me. She had already saved my life and, in doing, flipped a switch inside me that wanted to fight back and win. But would Sasha help me again?

Finally, I would need an employee who worked at the Rosewood Hotel in Holborn. It was a favourite of Linc's, a place he had taken me for lazy weekend romps. He always got the same suite, and just because his girlfriend had changed, his taste certainly hadn't. I would need access to his regular room.

Owen Grain, the senior concierge, would grant me that. Even if he wasn't aware of it yet. I followed him from my real account and waited.

I thought back to the morning on the field after I ran out of the hospital. I thought of the way Poppy, Trix and Zaheen all swore to me that they would do anything just to take my pain away. It was that co-dependent sisterhood that would either bond us forever or shatter us completely. I didn't want their help, but I did need it.

I needed them.

I rose from a restless night. I slept twisted and sticky in dark dreams that felt like syrup. My mind was unable to settle. I wondered if I would ever be able to sleep again or, like emotion, if that would allude me too.

I sat up and rubbed at my sandy eyes. My plan would take approximately a week to execute. I had the people, contingencies sorted. Every possible scenario and outcome had been thought and rethought. I was focused. The risk of leaving anything to chance too grave. Whoever said murder was easy clearly hadn't done the legwork.

Trix entered holding a brown paper bag.

'Do you fancy making some breaky? I'm thinking pancakes. What are you doing?'

'Call it surveillance,' I said, holding up the phone and shaking it.

'All right.' She sat at the bottom of the bed in a copper slip, crossing her long legs.

'Are you sure this is healthy though?'

'Call it a coping mechanism.'

'I suppose I should be happy you used the word "coping". And, if I'm being honest, you've seemed more yourself over the last few days.'

'Trix, you don't have to worry. I think I've finally found a way to get over what happened to me.'

The brown bag rustled as she adjusted herself.

'I mean that's a good thing, right?' She chewed the last bit of her words.

'I feel different. Optimistic even.'

Trix sighed, wanted to challenge my answer, then decided not to.

'What's wrong now?' I didn't recognise the look she was giving me.

'It's just you're smiling at your phone. You're smiling and looking at a photo of Lincoln and Heidi. You've been acting weird ever since you came home with Sasha. Did something happen that day?'

Yes, I tried to kill myself and Sasha stopped me.

'No.'

'Well, I don't trust her. Not after what she did, or have you forgotten she was in Dubai with Brad the day of Poppy's abortion? A woman like that only looks out for herself. So, whatever you have going on, whatever you're planning, I don't want any part of it.'

'Tragedies change people, Trix. They make them someone new, cold. What I want is for Linc to tell the world what he's done. What he's taken from me. I want them, all of them, every person to know what really happened that night.'

I was shaking. But Trix's brow knitted together as I clutched the scars on my stomach.

She wasn't convinced.

'Trust me, Trix, everything's going to be OK. Just wait and see.'

'Wait for what exactly? You know all this cloak-and-dagger bullshit is giving me a migraine. Charlotte, what are you going to do to Lincoln?'

Trix stared me down, hoping I would flinch. I didn't.

If the girls knew what I was really up to then they would stop me from going through with it, and I wasn't prepared for that to happen. Best they stayed in the dark for now. Until I needed them. And believe me, I would need them.

'Everything will be fine, just have a little faith.'

'Promise me you're not up to something stupid, Char?'

I turned, unable to look at her glassy eyes. 'I promise.'

I was lying.

HEIDI DOLAK — I really am the luckiest girl in the world, thank you @lincolnjackson for my beautiful ring, I love you and can't wait to be Mrs Jackson

shmuni — look at the size of that thing @lincolnjackson that can't have been cheap

blxncoo — he could have better spent the money feeding a small village just saying

chikka — this man does not miss wooow its amazing

tys_57 — @lincolnjackson come on mate ur putting the rest of us to shame

janelle.anya6 — @tys_57 damn right, I want a new one for our anniversary and it better look like @heididolak

tys_57 — yes dear loool @janelle.anya6

therealladaa — blimey that was fast what happened to that other bird?

gjones — @charlottegoodwin must feel so stupid looool he's only been with @heididolak 5 mins and he's marrying her

mi_saj71 — congratulations look at that rock

dom_lez — I don't think I've ever seen a more beautiful ring it looks like the one Kanye gave to Kim

CHAPTER THIRTY-TWO

'W HEN DID WOMEN START LOVING sex as much as men? It says here they've done so since the nineteen hundreds. Do you think that's true? Or is it bull like most of the shit in these mags?'

Zaheen was sitting beside me in Poppy's Corsa, dejectedly flicking through *Heat* magazine. She had one leg tucked under the other and innocently sipped an orange Capri-Sun, while speaking softly. I'd spent all night admiring Heidi's ring from every angle available on her Instagram pictures. I scoured the comments and discovered it was an emerald cut with a platinum band flecked with smaller diamonds. Cartier. Not what I would have chosen but irritatingly stunning on the finger of the woman who stole my life. When I got bored of looking at Heidi's boulder, I ran the plan over and over again in my head from start to finish, but still faced two problems.

Needing proof and not getting caught.

Two issues which, when overcome, didn't just make my plan work, but made it brilliant. Everyone would know what Linc had done when I was finished with him.

'I think women have always loved sex. They're just more open about it now. Less repressed. Or whatever.' My answer sounded as boring aloud as it did in my head. Still, it was a fact. Women loved sex.

'Maybe being repressed was for our own good. It's a free-for-all now. A jungle out there. Maybe we had it right before.'

'It's a theory.'

I had no interest in what Zaheen was saying or reading. I was staring out of the window, eyes alert, trained for any sign of Linc or Heidi.

Zaheen put down the magazine and touched my arm. Her fingers were cold and, for a moment, I let them rest there cooling my hot skin.

'Well, shotgun weddings and chaperoned dinner dates weren't the craziest ideas. There'd be fewer single mothers in the world. More families. Sorry, I probably shouldn't read such crap. Although I am here against my will so I guess I can read whatever I like. It's not like you care.'

I was parked across the path at the other end of Linc's house. I was here to solve problem one. Proof.

'Stop being dramatic. I already explained to you and Trix that if I'm going to make Linc confess then I need proof. This is how I get that proof.'

'Yes, but what you failed to mention was that we'd have to come here to get it. You kept that one all to yourself. You're not telling us everything.'

It wasn't a question. Nor would I provide her with an answer. What I could manage was a brittle laugh followed by shallow silence. Zaheen wasn't comfortable with me doing everything I could to prove my accident wasn't an accident. Nervously, I tried to smile, but it must not have been the right social cue for the conversation because her face contorted, and she looked at me weirdly.

'Charlotte, I don't want you to get carried away. We've already witnessed what Lincoln can do. And might I remind you some of us have more to lose than others.'

'I'm not stupid, Zee. I know the risks.'

'No.' Zaheen shook her head. 'I don't think you do.' She straightened up then, teasing a strand of raven hair behind her ear as she looked at me, her brown eyes hard and glassy.

'Char, I'll go to prison. The stuff I do. How I earn my money – I'm a criminal. Lincoln will use that. I'll spend years of my life behind bars. And it's not just my life you'll ruin. Poppy will lose her career. That means everything to her, you know that. And Trix. Trix will lose Kera and Kyle for good. That bitch Jennifer will be their mum and Trix will end up—'

And Trix would end up childless and alone, just like me. She didn't say it, but Zaheen may as well have. I couldn't argue. She was right if things went wrong, I would have to find a way to protect them. No matter the cost.

'You have to trust me. I never wanted this. Any of it. But I promise everything I'm doing now will not hurt you guys. I would never hurt you. You know that.'

'I hope not, and you'd better be right. Lincoln had better be mixed up in this somehow otherwise game over. He wins and all of us lose.'

'In that case, I'll prove it ... stay here.'

'Where are you going?'

'Please, Zee, just stay here.'

I got out. Rounded the car to the boot. I removed an electronic keypad, a pair of leather gloves and a thin knitted mask which I got last week in the Zara sale.

'Char, what the hell are you doing?' Zaheen bellowed, lowering the window frantically.

I ducked under a rather huge tree branch. There was a slim chance that Linc had changed some, if not all, of the security features. But Linc had this uncanny ability to only do something when and if he was told. Since I was no longer in his life to prompt him, I hoped that everything would be how I left it.

I pulled on my mask as I got closer to the entrance, my heart beginning to beat hard against my chest plate. According to Linc's Instagram story, he and Heidi were eating at The Ivy Asia, St Paul's. It felt different as I entered. The house. It was different. A warm scent of sandalwood mixed with bouquets of freshly cut water lilies clung to my nostrils, the smell folding into my senses. It was new and as fervent as Heidi's presence was on the rest of the house.

Everything was different. Except for the security codes that Linc had kept the same. It was easy getting in; I was the one who set the bloody code in the first place. I guess Linc never imagined I would have the balls to come back. I shook off the out-of-place feeling and decided to proceed to the office. I was going to hack his laptop; no doubt he hadn't changed the password for that either – it was always the name of the woman he was currently fucking. I didn't know exactly what I was looking for, but maybe the office was the perfect place to start.

Instead, I took a left towards the kitchen like my body was being magnetically pulled and the rest of me just obediently followed.

It hit me harder than it was supposed to, but I guess there wasn't a deterrent in the world that was going to stop me from seeing where it all happened. It was like a compulsion, but one I wasn't in charge of. I sunk to my knees, skimming them slightly as I landed and the ground fell away beneath me. I remembered what happened that night. The two figures, their voices.

The fall.

I remembered it all.

My fist stung painfully as I repeatedly slammed it against the marble floor until I saw tiny blooms of red. It throbbed, but I could barely feel it. The anger rose like bile, burning my chest. Overcome with sudden panic, I wiped the blood from the floor on my sleeve and headed for Linc's office.

Predictably, Linc's laptop was exactly where I thought it'd be. The password: heididolak – no spaces.

'Too easy, Linc. Too easy.'

Suddenly, I heard the front door creak, then the distinctive sound of footsteps. Linc's voice reverberated through the hall.

'Let's take that dress off then, babe.'

Heidi squealed like a piglet as I looked down at my phone and saw the seven missed calls from Zaheen. She had been trying to warn me. She had been trying to tell me to get out.

'*Fuck!*'

I quickly rounded the desk, hearing Linc's heavy footsteps coming up the stairs. Under the desk I curled myself into a tight ball, as I clasped my hand over my mouth.

This wasn't good. My plan may as well have been over before it had even started. If I was caught, then DI Kilby would be called, and I would be arrested. I wasn't supposed to be here.

The sinking feeling started to settle in my stomach as I got the urge to piss my knickers. The pebble lodged in my throat was a rubbery lump I couldn't shift. My skin felt hot and sticky, my top moulding to my body as it got more and more wet. This was not a good position to be caught in. I could play the scorned ex or the 'I couldn't live without you, so I broke in' card, but I knew none of that would work. Linc may have been dim but Heidi was anything but, and she wouldn't buy what I was selling, if I gave it to her for free.

I settled my breathing and curled my body in rigidly. With any luck they would walk straight past the office and head for the bedroom without sensing anything amiss and because no alarms were set off there would be no reason to check the CCTV. I mean, Linc was about to get lucky, surely the last thing on his mind was emails.

'Ahh, baby, I think I drank too much. My head's spinning,' I heard Heidi delight as Linc planted passionate kisses on her porcelain skin. I swallowed down the vomit that threatened to escape my mouth and bit my tongue until my mouth tasted of pennies.

'That's good, I like you drunk – and wet.'

I rolled my eyes, watching through a slit, as Linc scooped up his soon-to-be bride into a tender embrace.

'Can we film it?' she asked, almost harmlessly at first.

'I've told you before. I'm not really into that, Heidi. What if it gets into the wrong hands? I have a reputation. A career,' Linc continued.

'Oh, come on. I'm going to be your wife. I want to watch it back, see my sexy action man do his thing. It makes me hot just thinking about it.'

Why would she want a sex tape? What the hell was Heidi planning?

Nothing that woman did was done without purpose and motive. Me and the girls had learned that the hard way.

'I think the camera's in the office on the desk. No phones – just to be safe.'

Not the office, I thought, as they arrived at the door, switching on the light and slithering in one after the other.

Shit!

'You know Charlotte used to send me naked videos of herself. It was kind of our thing.'

Linc laughed unexpectedly, sending a flutter through my stomach. Not love but pure unrefined rage.

'Why would you mention her? Didn't we agree never to speak her name in this house again?' Heidi bit out venomously, forgetting for a second to manufacture her usual non-threatening smile. Heidi was her name and docile was her game. But that was only if you couldn't spot the bitch under the surface.

'Yes, we did. But I was just noting the similarities between the two of you. That's all. I guess you have more in common than I thought. You both like to get what you want.'

I almost got up and ripped his head clean off with my bare hands.

Similarities. Was he kidding me?

'You can't compare me to her, not after what she did to you, baby. She almost ruined your life.'

'Well, many women have tried to trap me over the years and she almost succeeded. She almost ruined my life yes. But still what happened – that night, the fall. I'll never forget seeing the blood.'

My fingers trembled as I pressed record on my phone.

'We couldn't help what happened.'

'Yes, but we could've stayed and helped her. We left her to die.'

'We had to. We didn't have a choice. She would have known about the two of us. We couldn't risk it. We did what was best for your career. End of.'

All traces of docile Heidi were gone in an instant. I had my proof. It was them. It had always been them.

'It was for the best, my love. She's a pain in the arse but at least now she can leave us alone. And move on with her life. And we can get married and make our own family.'

Heidi wrapped her arms around Linc's neck creating a noose.

'There isn't anything I wouldn't do for you. I love you, baby. We've been through hell together.' She sounded sickly sweet, like thick treacle. It made my stomach turn, my arms blossomed with goosebumps and my fist dripped with blood. I honestly couldn't understand how they could be so nonchalant about what had happened.

My accident was no accident if they were the cause.

'If anyone ever found out what we did to her, Lincoln, we would go to prison, we'd lose everything. We got rid of the CCTV and the masks, but, no matter what, Charlotte can never know we were involved. She can never know it was us.'

They were too late. I had it, their confession. Recorded. I had it.

'I know. Don't worry, I'll never tell a soul and I know you won't either. Kilby will handle it if there's any more trouble from Charlotte and her friends. Don't worry, we are free. We're safe.'

'As long as I don't lose you, and we get the happy life I've always wanted, then what we did was worth it. No matter what, we never turn on each other, Lincoln. Through thick and thin. Husband and wife.'

'I'll never give you up. You have my word. Even if this all goes wrong, I'll take the blame, I won't let anyone hurt you,' Linc concluded chivalrously.

But they could relax. I had no intention of sending them to prison. That would be too easy, and not nearly as much fun.

The girls were right, Linc was responsible, and Heidi had helped.

I could've killed them both right there. I was certainly angry enough to do so, but I was yet to hatch the rest of my plan, and not even Linc's unknowing confession would make me rush perfection.

I couldn't be sloppy. Not now. It wouldn't serve a purpose, and the act of passion would cost me my freedom. I gripped the laptop, tightening my fingers around the device as I banished thoughts of breaking it over Linc's skull. But then what would I do?

It would be extremely difficult to incapacitate two people, especially when one was a heavyweight boxer. Plus, and probably most importantly, I couldn't figure out who to kill first. Both were as guilty as sin.

While I could easily snap Heidi's neck with my bare hands, I'd envisioned taking my time killing Linc. I wanted to savour the moment, see his surprise. Taste his fear, because in his mind he'd already won. They both had, and that's exactly where I wanted them.

Untouchably smug.

You don't pay a plumber for banging on the pipes, you pay a plumber for knowing where to bang. I would wait. Then, when they were least expecting it, like hellfire I would burn away at all the pain and anguish I'd felt since the moment my children died.

But first I needed to get out.

With blood ringing in my ears, I closed my eyes trying to imagine a way out. Then the knock came. It was Zaheen.

'What the hell are you doing here? Is Charlotte with you?' Linc's voice rebounded like a spring through the halls as I unfurled myself from the laptop beneath the desk.

My brow was slick with a film of anxious sweat.

'No, I've come alone. I wanted to speak to you without Charlotte.' Zaheen paused. 'And Heidi. Is she here? I want to speak to both of you.'

Despite Linc protesting, I could hear Zaheen entering the house. That's when the penny dropped. Zaheen was creating a distraction for me to get away.

'Linc? Baby, who's at the door?'

Heidi adjusted her dress and exited the office, slowly descending the stairs.

'Look, this isn't easy to say but what you're doing to Charlotte has got to stop.'

'I don't know what you're referring to, or what she's told you, but your mate isn't well. She needs to get her head checked. We all saw her passing out in Grind. Do you think that's normal?'

'None of this is normal. Not Charlotte's accident, not you moving on with Heidi so quickly. And not the message Trix and Poppy got that night. The night she was supposed to be meeting you. None of it makes sense. And now you two are continuously parading your relationship.'

'Correction: *engagement*. I'm not Lincoln's girlfriend, I'm his fiancée.'

'I don't care what you are. You're hurting my friend. And it has to stop.'

The crunch of glass against a wall made me jump as I ran through the back door with Linc's laptop and something else in my hand, leaving Zaheen with Linc and Heidi.

I wanted to go back. What if that sound was Linc attacking Zaheen? But she wanted me to get out. She put herself in harm's way to ensure it. And she could handle herself. She would be OK.

The air had been rinsed clean by the rain. I jogged along the path, my skin blazing hot despite the drop in temperature until I made it back to Poppy's car. The key was still in the ignition.

I sat there for I don't know how long trying to eradicate the chill in my bones, until I spotted Zaheen coming out, blood seeping from a fresh head wound.

'What the hell happened?' I asked, as she got into the passenger seat.

'It's fine. You should see the state of Heidi.'

'What'd you do?'

But Zaheen didn't say anything. She just smiled.

CHAPTER THIRTY-THREE

O N THE FOURTH RING SHE answered, sharp and breathless.

'It's me.'

'Charlotte, is everything OK?' Sasha's voice sounded tepid, all traces of the industrious woman who usually greeted me was missing.

'Yeah. Everything's fine. Is this a bad time? Can you talk?' I waited for her to respond, but when she did, I wished she hadn't. She seemed nervous or anxious, but I had no idea why.

'Yeah, I have a few minutes. What's on your mind?'

'Well, it's hard to explain. Especially over the phone.' I justified myself at the liberty of her silence.

'Let me guess, you need my help with something.'

'Yes. I do. And you're the only person who can help me. If you're willing to that is.'

'That depends. What's in it for me, Charlotte? Last time I got you Michael's address he ended up behind bars, and I didn't even get so much as a thank you. Now you want me to risk my job again.'

I paused.

Sasha seemed less compliant than I hoped she would be, but I couldn't afford not to have her on-board. She was a vital part of my plan.

'I managed to get Linc's laptop. Can I bring it to you this afternoon? We can talk properly then.'

To be honest, I had expected more questions from her, like how the hell did I get his laptop for one, but Sasha didn't seem to care. Instead, she let out a low, exaggerated sigh and said: '*No*. No, I'll meet you somewhere at one maybe two depending on traffic. I'll text you the address.'

The sound of a howling wind echoed through the phone. I don't know where she was, but I knew she wasn't at home.

'Thank you, I really appreciate this.'

'Don't thank me yet. I haven't agreed. I'm just willing to hear you out.'

After I got back from meeting Sasha, I was surer than ever that my plan would work. She had the laptop and I'd even managed to pacify her annoyance and get her even more onside. Together we came up with an even better way to not just make Linc confess but hit him where it hurt and have the entire world watch in the process. People underestimated Sasha; she was more than just a pretty face and a few hundred thousand Instagram followers. She was smart. Tech smart. And thankfully a real friend.

I didn't divulge that ultimately my plan would lead to Linc's death. I thought it was better to keep that golden nugget to myself for as long as I could, but the plan had evolved and was spreading among the women in my life like furry green mould.

Poppy, Trix and Zaheen were waiting for me when I arrived back at home. Poppy's lips were tightly pursed together as if she had a wasp in her mouth. Her cheeks were red and flustered but her blue eyes were ablaze. I knew that face. I knew that look. I had seen it before. Poppy was mad and I had a feeling I was the reason why.

Poppy led the crusade. First a rehearsed speech about how hard she'd worked to get to where she was and leave her past behind. She was proud of being a nurse and didn't want my rash actions to change that. What she couldn't understand is I didn't want that either. The last thing I wanted to do was ruin Poppy's career. Her life. Those deep blue eyes, I'd stared into for twenty years, welled up as she begged me to let go and move on from whatever pain was inside me.

But I couldn't.

Zaheen was up next. No tears or theatrics. That wasn't her style. Just a few carefully chosen words about sisterhood and support bubbles. She must have googled the latter before I got back because it sounded wrong coming out of her mouth. I could tell not even she believed what she was saying. Zaheen was an advocate for justice, and how could she not be after what Badoo did to her. Deep down she wanted the same justice I did, to punish the men who'd hurt us. But it was left to Trix, the mother of two, to deliver the final words on the situation. There was just one problem. She couldn't answer my question.

When I asked Trix if it was her, if it was Kera or Kyle, or, God forbid, both, would she be able to let it go? Would she move on? Who would she become?

A furious row erupted. Tears. Crushing words. It took six hours, three packets of cigarettes and an entire bottle of peach gin, which we drank from the neck in Trix's kitchen, before the smoke cleared and our beating hearts settled. We laid our cards flat out on the table, from Brad to Michael and Linc twisted in between like a perverted game of poker and went to bed. There was no resolution that night, but no one left either.

The morning sun teetered at the edges of the blinds. I could smell stale coffee, long ago brewed, reminding me the girls were downstairs, quietly hating me. They were still mad. Mad at me for what I had to do. I didn't blame them. I was somebody they loved dearly and I was broken, and they couldn't fix the quiet desolation. No one could. They couldn't see it yet, but the only way Zaheen, Poppy and Trix could save me was by helping me. And when all was said and done, that would be a decision they would have to make on their own.

'Charlotte Dianne Goodwin, get your behind down the stairs now.'

Trix bellowed my full name. Not a good sign, but by the time I made it downstairs and into the kitchen in joggers and a matching grey crop top showcasing my scar, Poppy, Zaheen, and Trix were perched on the breakfast stools with fresh, steaming mochas and stern expressions staring back at me.

'Morning, all. Bit early for intervention part two, wouldn't you say?'

Gingerly, I lifted an apple from the fruit bowl. I had no intention of eating it but tossed it from palm to palm in an attempt to thwart their glares.

'We made yours a triple shot mocha. You look like shit but then again nobody slept last night,' Poppy said, her pale underwear peeking out beneath one of Trix's old tops as she kept her breathing slow and calm.

'We just want to chat. We're worried about you. With everything that's happened ...' Zaheen trailed off.

'Don't be worried. I'm fine. In fact, I have never felt better.'

'See that's what I'm talking about. It's creepy. Char, you went from the bowels of depression to erratically happy in a matter of days and you expect us to just believe you're fine.'

'That's what I said, *Trix*.' I stressed her name.

Poppy's golden hair caught a luminous ray of light that filtered through the bi-folding doors as she stood.

'But you're not fine. I can see it in your eyes.' Poppy's hand felt like ice against my skin so I withdrew.

'I'm tired, but I'm fine, I promise.'

'Bullshit. Last time you said that I ended up bitch-slapping Heidi at Lincoln's front door because you decided to do a little breaking and entering – poorly might I add. This stupid plan of yours has already got out of hand. You're asking for trouble.'

Zaheen was usually the one up for a half-thought-out idiotic plan of action but she seemed just as pissed off as Poppy and Trix. And, in truth, I took advantage of Zaheen because I knew the others would refuse to help me break into Linc's house. I was sorry for that.

'You put Zee in danger. Lincoln's already proved how dangerous he can be and there you go giving him a loaded gun.'

I tried not to let my face react to Trix's words.

'He's already destroyed you, it's just a matter of time before he comes for the rest of us, and you just won't quit. Dammit, Char, please tell us what to do. Tell us how to save you from yourself before it's too late. What we didn't tell you last night is that this has to end. You've put your life on hold for long enough. Forget this plan and just live. You've missed so much already.'

'That's true, I wanted to introduce you to Jeremy weeks ago, but you've just not been in the headspace for it to be honest,' Poppy added.

'Then there was Kyle's birthday last week. You missed that too,' Zaheen finished, making it a resounding three against one.

'We took him to London Zoo, it was supervised, of course, but Michael's cousin still works there so he gave us a VIP tour down to a close-up with the lions. We didn't mention it to you because we were scared you'd have a meltdown and ruin it for Kyle. That's what you've become, sweetie – a liability. Our liability.' Trix dumped the rest of her coffee down the sink in an attempt to hide the tears skimming her cheeks.

'I think what Trix means is that we love you and you're not present in our lives anymore. Our priority since your accident has just been to try and support you. But we can't support this. We can't support revenge.'

It was hard hearing this from Zaheen, but I understood their reservations. I knew they were scared.

'Kera and Kyle are my priority, not some revenge plan for your ex-boyfriend. I'm sorry but I won't be a part of this. Let it go,' Trix spat.

'You once told me good girls don't make history.'

Poppy avoided my eyes.

'Your point?' Zaheen responded.

'All I want is for Linc to confess what he did. You all saw it before I did, you knew deep down something wasn't right about my accident. The Instagram message, the fact there's been no police investigation – the whole thing's been off. The only way I get answers is if Linc confesses everything. And I can make him do that. There's a way to know what really happened that night. All I want is the truth.'

'Except the truth can ruin our lives. Please, for our sake, let it go.' Trix smoothed out her tawny hair.

'So you're asking me to pick between you guys and justice for what happened to my children?' My skin crawled.

'No, Char, *God, no.* We are just saying for now it's best to let it go.' Poppy took my hand again but this time I didn't pull back.

'I just want them back. I miss them every day. I just want them back.'

'Oh, sweetie, they can't come back. I wish they could, like that boy at work, I wish they would just wake up. But they won't. They're gone.'

I wept into Poppy's chest, as an idea flashed into my mind. There had to be a way I could protect the girls and still make Linc pay for what he did to me and my children. The stakes were high. Poppy, Trix and Zaheen had all agreed almost in tandem that I should back off.

But I wouldn't.

'You all right, babe?' Zaheen said, standing at my shoulder.

'I'm fine.' I strained a smile. 'In fact. Let me make it up to you lot for looking after me. Let me do something nice. Like a dinner? No – a picnic. Like we used to. Just for you, the three best friends that have stuck by me through everything.'

As the words spilled from my lips, I knew from this moment that things would never be the same.

LINCOLN JACKSON — I'm incredibly honoured to be the recipient of this year's Sports Athlete of the Year Award. This is a huge achievement and I'm thrilled my beautiful fiancée @heididolak and I will be attending the award show on Thursday evening. Tune in to see what we're wearing

y_a_z_y — anybody else bored of watching @lincolnjackson and @heididolak play dress up?

penny118 — @y_a_z_y I know it's like seen one Armani tux seen them all mate looool

anna_ pretty — the things celebs think we care about but we don't

thehive — congratulations @lincolnjackson big news!!

frida49 — can't wait to see @heididolak dress I hope one of the good designers dress her

ramone21 — congrats champ!

bossburts — don't know who voted for this numpty

vlogspot — well deserved congratulations

sunshine_xo — well I know what I'll be watching Thursday night

branded_usa — @sunshine_xo and I know what I won't be watching lool

cove_girl — congratulations @lincolnjackson I voted for you

CHAPTER THIRTY-FOUR

A PITCHER OF FRESH POMEGRANATE JUICE, ice cold, sat next to an exotic fruit platter with honeydew melon and dragon fruit. It was Zaheen's favourite. Silky poached eggs and smoked salmon accompanied sourdough pulled from the grill and placed in a basket, which I covered with a linen napkin to keep the bread warm. A mermaid salad with fresh capers and anchovies peeked out of the quartet of bamboo bowls. Enormous dried pampas grass burst from clay vases. I dotted sweet basil and jasmine candles and large throw pillows in the space, deliberately creating an oasis in Trix's living room. It was an indoor picnic with a twist.

I proceeded methodically to lay everything on the table. It was after eleven and Trix was upstairs getting ready while Poppy and Zaheen were on their way. After that morning nothing would be the same. Neither for them nor myself. So, one more picnic. One last chance to prove myself to the women I loved, admired and protected through the years. One last chance to say goodbye.

'Wow, everything looks amazing. You really went all out.'

Trix was in a cream jumpsuit that snatched in at her waist. She had made an effort with her hair, nails and subtle blush makeup. She looked amazing. Happy I was pretending to be who I was before I met Linc.

'I wanted to make a fuss. You lot have been so good to me, it's about time I say thank you properly. You know, for everything.'

I'd spent the last three months trying and failing to put the pieces together from my accident, and although there were still a few loose ends – like who sent the Instagram message to Poppy and Trix the night I fell – it wouldn't stop me from going through with what I had to do.

'Should I pour the mimosas?' Trix asked eagerly, as the door buzzed.

'No, let me, you get the door. I'm doing them with pomegranate juice instead of orange, a little twist I got in *Cosmo*. I think you'll like it.'

'Oh, I'm excited. It's just like old times.'

Trix disappeared into the passageway as I cautiously made the drinks. After I assembled them I put three on the table and kept mine close to hand, making sure they didn't see me.

'This looks out of this world,' Poppy squealed, holding up a bottle of Moët. Her hair was loose and hung at her shoulders.

'If this is how you make it up to us then keep it coming, I can't believe you've done all this. It's amazing.'

Zaheen wore a mint-coloured dress, her dark hair complementing the pastel shade.

'We should have a toast,' I announced, lifting my flute, as they quickly got theirs in hand to do the same.

'To the three women who have stood by me through the worst thing that's ever happened. I owe you three my life. I'll never forget what you did for me, or how you tried to save my children. I'll love you forever.' The last part was hard to say. My voice cracked and I was sure they heard it.

'Oh, stop it, Char, you're going to make my mascara run.' Trix sipped her drink, swiping away tender tears. 'You're right about the pomegranate juice though. Keep it coming. This is so yummy.'

'Take it easy, Trix. Wouldn't want you to pass out,' I said without a smile.

'On cocktails? It's like you don't know her at all,' Zaheen said, laughing then reaching for a chunk of dragon fruit. She pushed it into her mouth, before making a satisfied moan, then took another.

'I know I'm meant to be the one from Ireland, but our Trix puts me to shame,' Poppy whispered into my ear, bumping my shoulder with hers.

My mind drifted as I watched the girls get comfortable around the Japanese floor table I'd got from Amazon. They looked so happy picking at their food; that moment made me feel like I could burst. But it was short-lived. Everything I needed to go through with the plan, including Linc's laptop, which was with Sasha, was in place. Even the gun I'd found in his office. I had everything I needed squirrelled away ready. But I had to wait until they fell asleep. I needed them out of the way.

An hour passed, the food was gone, the juice drunk. I watched as, one by one, Poppy, Trix and Zaheen fell asleep. Trix dropped face first into her dessert, but I didn't move her. Instead, I gazed at their slumber-calm faces; their beauty and their loyalty were something I would never forget. They were my equals, but would they be willing to do whatever was necessary for me to survive? I had been their saviour, their protector once upon a time when they couldn't protect themselves.

I took out a paper and pen. I had two stops to make, first Sasha and then Chinatown, but first I had to write a letter to the girls. I just hoped that they would choose to save me, because when they woke up the show would begin.

CHAPTER THIRTY-FIVE

I WAS HAVING A FANTASTIC DAY.

But time was tight. I only had a small window of opportunity, and if I missed it, even marginally, all of it would have been for nothing. My stomach knotted as I rounded the familiar corridor seeking out suite 308.

That's where Linc and Heidi were, peacefully unaware of what was about to happen. Linc knew how to celebrate and his ego afforded him the best – the best service, the best suites – so when he tweeted about the awards I knew where he'd be staying.

I could have stopped. Turned around and headed back to the home I shared with Trix, Costa coffees and pains au chocolat in hand. They might have suspected they'd been drugged but I could slip under Trix's duvet and lie there, at ease with the rest of the world.

Except I wasn't at ease. My children would still be dead. I would miss the way the girls stared at me as I brushed my hair or fixed brunch while we all recovered from hangovers. I could be performing any number of mundane tasks, but they would always look at me as if it were the first time anyone had ever done it. They loved me, and I loved them. I loved all of them so much, and today I would either break their hearts or have them break mine.

Transfixed, I stared at 308 scrawled on a gold plaque mounted on the wall beside the door. Then I raised my hand and knocked.

'We don't need any cleaning.' The voice rumbled from behind the door. Then firm hands fiddled unsuccessfully at first with the handle, but then he got it right and the door swung open. Linc's body blotted out the light.

'Sorry to disappoint you, but I'm not the bloody maid.'

His face drained to a shade whiter than white, the caustic lines set deep into his forehead didn't soften as I advanced forward, closing the door behind me.

'W-what are you doing here? You're not supposed to be in here.'

Linc took an unsteady step back as his cortex tried to regain some sense of what was happening. He was clad in ivory chinos and an open robe exposed a rippled slab of taut muscles. He looked sharp, I thought, clean. I could smell his signature scent drift as he moved back from the gun I had pointed to his head. His gun.

'You know what I'm doing here. We need to talk. Why don't you and Barbie – *Heidi, get out here* – have a seat.'

'Char—' Linc protested, his eye taking in the expanse of the room. It was beautiful, a rectangle with high ceilings and a dizzying black and white striped carpet. A desert yellow couch, two armchairs matched in the same shade and a large flat-screen TV blaring *Sky Sports News* made it look like any other high-end suite used by the inordinate amount of famous and wealthy clientele. But this suite was singularly special. It would be the last place Lincoln Jackson would ever take breath.

'Sit the fuck down, Linc.'

Heidi paced in from the bathroom, makeup brush still in hand. She noticed the gun first, then was so overcome with fear she trembled and sat in the armchair furthest from me. I could already hear the tremor of sobs cracking her vocal pipes. Within seconds, the dam broke, her tears made their great escape, floods streamed down her half made-up face, as if someone put a battery in her back and switched on a fountain. But Heidi didn't say a word. She just sat idle and waiting.

'Nice to see you again, Heidi. Although you probably don't recognise me without my mask.' The gun was trained at her torso. 'Of course, that *was* the only part of your story that was true. The masks. Everything else not so much.'

I turned back to face Linc as I continued talking. It wasn't wise to take my eyes off him for too long. He was stronger than me and, although he was frightened, his defensive instincts could kick in at any moment.

'That's why you're here? Because Heidi told her followers that you attacked her?' Linc snorted.

'Don't be silly.' I smiled back at him. 'I'm here to murder both of you of course.' I let the words sink in before I continued. 'Because of what you did. What you both did.'

'What are you talking about? We didn't do anything.'

Linc's face was hard like a stone, small beads of sweat slickening his brow. I took out my phone and threw it on the coffee table.

'Maybe this will refresh your memory. Press play.'

'*Ch*—' Linc started.

I took the gun off safety.

'I said press play, arsehole.'

'Just do what she says, Lincoln. Please, I'm scared.' Heidi sounded inconsolable, like she had pebbles lodged in her throat.

'Listen to Snowflake, because she gets the bullet if you don't comply.'

Heidi let out a pathetic yelp which gave me a wave of satisfaction.

'Oh, don't cry. Linc was always partial to horror films. Now he gets to star in his very own.' The confession of him and Heidi played, and once it had, the words felt absorbed, like there was nothing left to say.

'You left me to die. Didn't you? You left your son and daughter to die.'

Linc eyed his phone.

'Don't even think about it. Best we put the phones in here.'

Reluctantly, Linc drowned his and Heidi's phones in the silver ice bucket I handed him. I couldn't risk alerting the police, so I made it impossible for either of them to call for help. We were in a private suite on the third floor of the Rosewood, so even screaming for attention was inconceivable due to the padded walls that gave their guests added privacy. Owen, the concierge manager, helped me to book out the only two other suites on the floor. We were completely alone, but I erred on the side of caution and disconnected the landline. Just to be safe.

No one would be coming up here anytime soon. No one was close enough to hear them scream.

I had Linc and Heidi all to myself.

'I think we should play a game. Linc, do you remember how fond I was of games?'

'Charlotte, what I did was unforgivable. I don't know what I was thinking. I was depressed. Staging that stupid break-in with Heidi was the worst thing that I've ever done. You have to believe me, I'm so sorry.'

'*Shhh*. There'll be plenty of time to beg for your life later. Right, so shall we play?'

My face remained undisturbed as I spoke, not wanting to give anything away.

'Honestly, Heidi, can you pull yourself together? You're starting to bum me out. *Here.*' I threw her the box of complimentary tissues that came with the suite. 'Dry your face.'

'What's the game?' Linc asked, most probably trying to buy himself a little time.

'Attaboy. That's the spirit. We are going to play a game of truth. How it works is, I ask a question and you both tell me the truth. Simple! Except if you lie then I shoot you in a place that will cause you so much pain you'll beg me to kill you.'

'You're insane,' Heidi spat, in what I could only presume was a moment of momentous bravery.

'You would be too, if your ex-boyfriend and the woman he left you for staged a break-in that killed your children and left you for dead.'

'Charlotte, please, it's not what you think.'

Linc's eyes were downcast as he took a seat next to Heidi.

'Let's begin before I get bored and shoot you for the fun of it.'

My voice was tight, as I tapped the barrel of the gun against my temple and took a deep breath.

'First, when did you two decide to be a couple?'

'It was December. The third, I think. Something like that. It was a Thursday. He told me he loved me for the first time.'

'Thank you, Heidi. I'm glad to see you participating. Is this true, Linc? Did you tell Heidi you loved her three days after I told you I was pregnant?'

'I was in shock. I wasn't ready to be a dad. You saw what was happening in the media. The public hated me for that stupid tweet. I hated me. I couldn't love them. I couldn't love you. Not the way you wanted me to.'

'So, you break up with me. You don't leave me for dead and make me barren in the process.'

'I didn't mean to do that. I was scared. I'm sorry, Charlotte.'

'I'm so glad you said that because that's question number two. What were you trying to do? What was your goal? Were you trying to hurt me? Did you want me dead?'

'*No!* No, I could never hurt you. Not that way.'

He was lying.

'I just wanted you gone. I didn't want to hurt them, but they were inside you. So, when you fell, I just panicked and left. I thought you'd be OK.'

I couldn't believe he'd said that aloud, but in some odd way I respected him for it. For his honesty. Maybe this was the first time Linc was being truly honest with himself.

'Charlotte, I'm not a bad person. We both did wrong. I'm so sorry for all your pain.'

But then there it was. The empathiser. The hero, ready to own up to his wrongdoings. You'd almost believe the silver-tongued Judas and get lost in the thicket of his gingerly spoken words. You could physically hear him choke up at that last part. The part where he all but admitted caring if I would be all right. This wasn't an apology. If I didn't know better, then I would have mistaken it for one, but I did know better.

I knew, just like everything else Linc ever said to me, this too was a lie.

'Was any of it real? Did you ever love me?'

'Charlotte. Of course, I loved you. If things were different, if I could go back, I'd have done it all differently. I'd have stayed. I'd have been with you. With them. A proper family.'

I almost laughed at his transparent attempt to manipulate me. Even Heidi had figured it out and stayed mute, as Linc handled me with the limpid tenacity of a Tennessee stage mom.

'I don't know what to say.' I did, or perhaps I didn't, since laughing hysterically wasn't actually saying anything at all. 'Can I ask you something? A final question.'

Linc's eyes looked like black beads as they narrowed in on me, sharp and in full colour.

'Shoot.'

Hopefully his pun wasn't intended.

'Why do you have a gun?'

He stopped, his eyes tracing Heidi's face.

'What gun?'

'Don't play dumb, Linc. The gun I'm holding. It's yours. I found it in your house the night I recorded your confession. The night I broke in.'

There was no response, but their faces turned paler.

'So, if you felt so guilty about what happened, if it hurt so much, then why do you have a gun?'

'It's not mine.' Linc's jaw tightened.

I let the words sit there for a moment before saying.

'So, if it's not yours—' I waved the gun in Heidi's direction. 'Then it has to be yours.'

Heidi shook, her face puce and hot.

'What were you planning? Were you going to kill me? Make it look like an accident? You manipulative bitch.' I tasted sour bile, felt it rise up in me like a typhoon.

'I had to protect us. And, look, I was right. You're going to kill us. I told you she was dangerous. I told you she would hurt us. We should have finished you off when we had the chance.'

'What are you doing? Shut up! Charlotte, I don't know what she's on about. I never knew about the gun.'

'Quiet, Linc. The women are speaking.' I adjusted myself. 'And for what it's worth, you should have finished me off, because I certainly plan on ending you.'

They both looked at each other, but it was Linc who spoke first.

'She said you wouldn't get hurt. When she first suggested it to me. She said you wouldn't get hurt.'

I could almost hear Heidi's heart break in the silence that lingered after Linc's words were spoken. Despite the awful things they had done together. This was the first time Heidi truly saw Linc for what he was.

This was the first time she saw the monster.

'Charlotte, please. It was all him; he convinced me. He said we could be together. He lied to me. He lied to the both of us. He set it up, I just went along with it.'

'Shut up, bitch!' Linc hissed, clenching his teeth as frothy speckles of saliva perched in the corner of his mouth, making him look like a ravaged mutt.

'Charlotte, she's lying. She's trying to save herself. I swear on our son and daughter, it was all her.'

'Linc, why are you doing this? She's going to kill us both. Just tell the truth.' Heidi lunged for him, but I cocked back the gun.

They both stopped dead in their tracks like cats that had been caught stealing food off the kitchen counter.

'I've made my decision.'

Heidi's ocean blue eyes focused solely on me as I lifted the gun and let off a single unexpected shot, right in the centre of her head.

My ears rang as the bang suddenly sounded, like thunder. I looked at her face. She was still pale; her eyes still blue, her lips still rose. Nothing had changed, nothing had moved or splattered unnaturally out of place, she was just still. Frozen. Like that's how she had always been and would always remain. Like my children. The expression on her face was hard to read. Perhaps it was shock, possibly confusion. Or maybe it was fear. The neat pinhole in her forehead leaked angry red. It was a little at first, then a lot, but still, her face didn't change. She just stopped.

'You believe me, Charlotte, thank God.'

Linc sounded strange, his words as tense as his body. I picked my words carefully before speaking.

'Oh no, Linc, I don't believe you.' The gun leaned heavily towards him. 'I just really wanted to kill Heidi.'

CHAPTER THIRTY-SIX

'**D**on't look at me like that, Linc. You heard Barbie, it was her or me. Killing her quickly was me being kind. But don't worry, it's not a courtesy I'm planning on extending to you.'

A violent eruption of vomit left Linc's mouth, soiling his ivory chinos at the crotch. Every part of his body seemed out of place, kneeling to a woman didn't quite suit him. He looked fidgety, like his fight or flight instinct was about to kick in.

'Jesus, Linc. You're a boxer for Christ's sake. You should be used to a little blood.'

He heaved, his stomach visibly wrenching in front of me.

'Guess not. No matter. You'll just have to die in your own filth. Which is awfully poetic since that's exactly what you are. Filth. Scum. Human waste. Feel free to stop me when you hear the word that best describes you.'

The two steps I took back provided some much-needed distance between me and Heidi's body. If Linc felt jumpy, it would be pretty much impossible for him to subdue me without getting at least one shot off in time. I had him right where I wanted him and there was nothing he could do to stop me. No one could.

'Charlotte, please. It was Heidi. I just did what she told me to.'

'*Killers.* That's it. You and headshot Barbie over there, are killers. *Baby killers.* That's the worst kind in my opinion. You could have saved them if you'd helped me that night instead of walking away.' I waited, watching his tiny features expand and deflate with shaky breaths.

Even held at gunpoint, he couldn't face me. He could barely look me in the eye. He just kept staring at Heidi.

'Maybe we can work this out. Please, there's still a way out of this. I know you're grieving. This is pain – we'll say what happened here was an accident. Heidi committed suicide. Please, I miss them too. I loved them. They were my son and daughter. They were ours. The only thing in the world that belonged to the both of us.'

A volt of rage shot through me so fast I failed to register the connection between the gun and Linc's face until I saw the driblets of blood.

'My nose! My fucking nose!'

It occurred to me then that Linc would say just about anything to stop me from killing him. I stopped, stepped back and conspicuously admired what I'd done to his face.

'I've had enough of you, and your lies. You didn't give a shit about our babies or about me. I don't even think you cared about Heidi. Not really. You must think I'm a fool. Do you really think I believe that you would lie for me? That you would lie to the police?'

'Charlotte, please. I'm just trying to explain, myself and my actions. I'm not proud of what I did. I've been broken ever since. I left you to die. The guilt, it's been bad for me too.'

'*You?* You've been broken. Jesus, Linc, you're engaged for fuck's sake.'

We were both silent.

'Well, you were engaged, but I think it's safe to assume the wedding's off.'

Agitated, I paced back and forth. I had to start the live in five minutes according to my watch.

'Only you could make the death of our children all about you.'

'That's not what I'm trying to do. I'm trying to apologise. Right my wrongs. I did a terrible thing. I can't take it back, but I wish every day that I could.'

'You got DI Kilby to threaten me, Linc.'

'I knew him from school. He was a few years above. We kept in touch. He's got me out of a spot of trouble on occasion. He has a gambling problem. I-I offered to pay off his debt if he shook you up a little. Made you scared so you didn't out me to the media or something. I don't know, it was a stupid mistake. You'd already signed the NDA, but I know you, I knew you would do something reckless.'

'Reckless. Me? This is karma not irrationality. DI Kilby threatened to have Trix's children permanently taken away from her. He said he'd put Zaheen behind bars.'

'I didn't tell him to do that. I wouldn't. A mother needs her children. I see that now.'

'You only see it now because I have a gun pointed to your head. You don't give a shit about my friends just like you don't give a shit about me.'

'Your friends.' He scoffed. 'Maybe you have more enemies than you think. Wolves disguised in sheep's clothing.'

He smiled through a mouth of red, his words stinging like venom.

'Maybe one of your friends was jealous of you. Jealous of us. Maybe they hate you. You stupid, stupid girl. Even now you don't know who to trust. Do you think I was only seeing Heidi? I was only with her for the photos. My image is everything, you know that. Heidi was the best looking, that's all. Still is, even at this view.'

Suddenly his words felt like weights as we both stared at her.

What was he talking about? Did Linc use Heidi just to further his career?

'You really are a son of a bitch, aren't you, Linc?'

'Yes, baby, and, guess what, you loved every second of it. You all did. If I wasn't Lincoln Jackson, would you still have wanted me? Would you all have craved to be Mrs Jackson like well-heeled bitches in heat. No, I don't think you would. You were with me because of who I am, and what I had . . . but then you got pregnant.'

'And you couldn't let me have them.'

'You said it, *baby*. You were bad for business.' His mouth twisted, contorting his face like some feral animal.

'You're sick!'

'Yet here you are, like a dog returning to its own vomit.'

I threw him a black zip tie, fatigued with his efforts to prolong his death.

'Put it on. I want you to confess. And we'll let them decide if you live or die. We'll let them choose.'

'Who?' he said, slipping his hands through the zip tie as I stepped forward to tighten it.

'The Hive!'

Ceremoniously, I brewed the tea in silence. When I'd finished, I took out the second phone I'd concealed in my inside jacket pocket, mounted the phone on a stand and began streaming live.

'Reecehamilton33 voting die just for bants – what'd you think, Linc? Do you think your beloved fans will let you die? Just a few minutes left then your fate's decided.'

Silence.

'Did you really think I was gonna let you walk away, or did you underestimate me? Does it terrify you to know that they're here watching us, right now? Mum and Dad together at last.'

'Do you think I was happy when you left?' Linc's face strains up towards me as he lies restrained on the ground.

I reach for the phone on the tripod. My hand shakes as I point the camera back at Linc.

'I don't think you felt much of anything when I left. You just let me walk right out the door.'

'What was I supposed to do? You wanted to leave.'

'That's because you made it impossible to stay. You gave me no choice.'

There are over a million people watching The Hive Live as I say my words. A rush of emotions run through me heating my skin. Linc is guilty.

'Was our entire relationship a joke? Was any of it real?'

Linc swallowed and looked into my eyes, but his face seemed blurry and I had to blink a few times before he became fully formed. The tea was starting to mess with my head.

'Yes. The truth is I was always sleeping with Heidi from the very beginning. She was always there. You just didn't see her because I didn't want you to.'

'So why start a relationship with me? Why pretend to love me?'

'It's complicated, Charlotte. There are things you don't know or understand.'

'*Complicated?*' I stand and pick up the gun from the coffee table. 'If I shoot you in your leg would it still be complicated, or would that uncomplicate things a little?'

'Charlotte, don't. Jesus, what do you want me to say? I liked you, I really did, but I just wasn't in love with you, not the way you wanted me to be. I'm sorry but I can't help how I feel. Or how the public perceived you. My boxing career means everything, and you and those babies were threatening it. When it came down to it, I picked my career. There are people watching now that will agree with that, you'll see. They'll save my life because they love me.'

His rejection feels like I've been set on fire. My organs feel like they're twisting. It was all a lie, every word, every precious moment. It was all a lie. And now the entire world knows it. Lincoln Jackson was never in love with me.

'What are you doing, Charlotte?' Linc's voice is a white noise as I kneel over Heidi's body.

'Finally, a shade of the truth. Who knew you could be honest? You once said to me, mark my words, the next diamond I put on your hand will be a ring.'

I prise Heidi's engagement ring from her cold finger.

'You've already broken so many promises to me.' I stand, gun in one hand, ring in the other, cock my head to one side and slowly jut towards him.

'This is a promise you're going to keep.'

'My hands are tied so I can't put it on. Nor would I want to. I don't love you.'

I put the gun to his head and watch him close his eyes.

'Open.' I shove the ring inside his mouth, splitting his lip in the process, then traced the blood with my fingertips. I pushed the gun deeper into his temple. 'If you bite me, I'll blow your head off.' I thrust my ring finger into his mouth, forcing him to gag. When I pull it out the large diamond is covered in blood and saliva.

'You're insane!' Linc shouts, spittle landing on his chest. But I can't hear him anymore. I feel like I've been dragged under-water like a fish in an aquarium. Everyone watching, everyone staring. But just us together here forever.

'*Yes.* Yes, Linc, I'll marry you.'

THE HIVE   **LIVE 1.9M**

_russell66 — come on we can't let @lincolnjackson die he's one of the greatest fighters in the world #votelive

margaretkhan — a woman losing her children is the saddest thing in the world #votedie #thehive

lesley_earth — I feel sorry for @charlottegoodwin if she could have more children I would vote live but she can't sooo ... #votedie

yungertaco44 — let's save the champ #votelive @charlotte-goodwin we are coming for you

navalkaren — everyone please save @lincolnjackson #votelive

pixiebatta — why are @thehive screening @lincolnjackson murder, this is sickening #votelive #thehive

willmarcus2 — @pixiebatta my thoughts exactly #votelive

jackbeaken55 — what an embarrassing way to go #votedie #thehive

My vision's blurry, my hand's shaking from the weight of the gun. I put on the safety, not sure if I was going to shoot Linc or myself. The nightshade that was in the tea begins restricting my reflexes. If I stand for much longer, I'll fall. So I sit, cross-legged and upright.

'Please don't kill me.'

'Why not? Why should I let you live? Tell them. Beg The Hive to save your life, *baby*.'

'What'd you want me to say? You want a confession, but there isn't one I can give you. It was Heidi. It was all her. I'm so sorry.'

I play the recording again, this time for my audience so they can hear it from Linc's lips. He killed our children.

Heidi's body slumps forward, burying her face in the carpet with a thud.

'I see your dead fiancée's making herself comfortable. What's that, Heidi?' I mockingly stay silent as if I'm waiting for her to respond, no longer caring if the people gawking at their screens have a stellar angle.

'You hear that, Linc? Heidi thinks it's bullshit. Heidi thinks you came up with the plan to scare me on your own. Heidi thinks you're a *killer*. I'm inclined to believe Heidi since you're responsible for her death too.'

'You killed her – you're the murderer, Charlotte.' Linc's voice trembles viciously.

'*Me?*' I say, hoarse, truly horrified by his accusation. 'I may have shot her, but you put the gun in my hand. You brought her into our lives, you conspired with her. @gloriafurls88 agrees. She thinks I should just kill you now, to hell with the vote. Oh, Linc' – I tut as I read through the torrent of words – 'these comments are not good at all.'

The rage feels bile-like, it makes the back of my throat convulse. I'm running out of time.

'You killed Heidi, Linc, not me.'

'I may be responsible for Heidi's misfortune, but before this vote is over, I want you to know this is on you. I can't have children because of you.'

I hold the gun to his head. 'You really are a bastard.'

'And you're insane,' Linc spits.

'No – I'm pissed.' I shoot him a look filled with contempt, fury and anguish. 'You took them from me. The only thing I've ever done right, and you took them from me. Why? What the fuck did I ever do to you? Why did you hurt me?'

'Does it matter?'

'To me? Nothing's ever mattered more.'

'Why should I tell you anything? You've already executed your leverage. Think what you want, I cared about Heidi more than I ever cared about you. I cared about them all more than you.'

'Maybe now you know what it feels like to lose someone you love. To not be able to protect them, or save them, although everything inside you wants to keep them safe. That's what I tried to do the night our children died. The night you and Heidi waited for me in the dark. The night you took everything from me then left me to die.'

'Please, Charlotte. There must be something I can do. There must be some way to make this right. There must be something you want more than anything. Tell me what it is?'

'I need you to stop breathing. That's all the relief I need.'

I'm lying. There will never be relief. Not for me. I died in pain the night my children left my body. But there will be justice for them, and that will have to be enough.

It occurs to me that I wasn't the only person who's been left in the dark.

'You don't know who sent the Instagram message to the girls, do you?'

'Yes, I do. She saved your life. She alerted Trix and Poppy. It's the only reason you're still alive. I'll tell you if you let me go. Funnily enough it was actually all her idea now that I think about it. I can't believe I didn't see it up until now. She set me up!'

'*No!* This ends with you. I don't want to know who sent the message. You can save them a seat in hell! After all that's where you'll be going. Time's up. The vote's in.'

I look at him, my eyes sallow, cut with red capillaries. There's no love here now.

'This could have all been so different. We could've had a real family. We could've been happy.'

'Charlotte, you don't look so good. Put the gun down – let me call a doctor.'

His genuine panic surprises me.

'It's too late.' I cock back the gun, letting a bullet descend into the chamber. There's no going back.

'Charlotte, I'll do anything. Please, I'll do whatever you say. What about the vote? The Hive can't really want you to kill me? People love me.'

'Actually, they don't. It's fifty-fifty.' I breathe out. 'This means, no one cares if you live or die, Linc.'

I squeeze the trigger and watch his face freeze in a strange expression. The bullet paralyses him instantly, but just like Heidi he doesn't move. Instead, he lets out a strange gurgling noise. I don't know how, but somehow, I know his lungs are filling with blood. Linc claws at his chest but his brain struggles to locate the trauma. Sinking to my knees, I watch on impassively as Lincoln Jackson suffocates to death, choking on his blood and lies.

Now, I'm famous.

CHAPTER THIRTY-SEVEN

RELIEF FLOODS THROUGH ME AS I loom over Linc's and Heidi's motionless bodies. Maybe there's a small part of me that believed I wasn't capable of murder. But this is what I set out to do. This moment is the one I've been waiting for. I'd rehearsed it. This is my stage, and everything I do now counts. My phone buzzes as the tiny voice in the back of my head grows more dominant. It tells me, in no uncertain terms, to hold the gun to my temple and let all the pain slip away.

It's Poppy calling. Then I see the texts from Trix, followed by a voice note from a panicking Zaheen. They watched the Instagram Live. *Thank God!*

I know my plan must be difficult for them to process, especially from their perspective. I designed it to show all the ugliness in Linc, but in parallel it showed all the ugliness in me too. I just hope it wasn't too much for them to stomach. Women usually hurt themselves or extensions of themselves when they're in pain. It's how we express anger. It's how we hide our turmoil.

I don't do that. Not anymore. I go right for the throat and confront my pain head on. Exactly how a man would. It's hard to focus my thoughts in one direction, when all I want to do is crack open my skull and let every thought I've ever had unspool onto the black and white carpet. It's one thing to murder someone in secret, but murdering someone live on Instagram – hell, that takes balls. As I light a cigarette, I notice the congealed blood embedded in my fingernails; I can't stop trembling. My stomach heaves as my eyes dart back and forth between their corpses. After a few minutes, I gather up my body, unnerved, and pull a sheet over them, because the more I look at them, the more they stare back at me.

'So, here we are, back at the beginning of this horror story, or in many ways we've come to an end. I warned you that it wasn't what you were expecting,' I purr, just as I'd practised. It's important to get it right. I won't get another chance. 'This was my truth and I thought it was about time you heard it. All of it. I hope I've convinced you all that a truly horrible man died today. He doesn't deserve to be remembered. Or mourned. He's the reason our son and daughter are dead; Heidi too. You may not agree with my actions, but I know at least fifty per cent of you would have done what I did today. And to the other fifty, I ask you, what if it was your child? What would you do? Who would you become?'

I think it's better to focus on Linc and what he did. Some comments call for me to run, but there's no point in running or hiding. That's not part of the plan. I have to stay.

No deviation.

Planning the perfect murder takes discipline, logic and just a tiny bit of luck. Mine is in the form of the three women watching. They are my hope. They heard Linc confess. They know he's guilty. That's all that matters now. They know the truth.

'This was the right thing to do. I understand it may not look like it, especially to you, The Hive. It's hard to see the good person I am when I'm sitting here covered in Linc's blood – but to the people who know me best, who know my tragedy, I ask you to look past what I've done and see what I've been doing my entire life. People do bad things because innocent people don't have the strength to do it themselves. Evil or mercy? That decision belongs to you.' I wink directly at the camera. The blood's drying, falling off in thin red blood-flakes.

I raise the cold cup of tea to my lips, encumbered, breathing in the exotic flavour. This is for the twins that never got to take a breath or say their first words. This is for the kisses they will never get and the sounds they will never make. This is for the smiles that will never be seen and the love that will never be reciprocated. This is for all of them and me. One final act to end this nightmare.

Then there is nothing.

falcon36 — I can't believe wat I've just watched. This has to be a sick joke #riplincolnjackson #thehive

theoriginalblade — @falcon36 I don't think so mate, she shot @heididolak first then killed Linc live @charlottegoodwin is a madwoman #charlotteunhinged

falcon36 — @theoriginalblade do you think she's dead? I don't know what was in that cuppa but hopefully it was poison, I can't believe people actually voted to kill @lincolnjackson you people are sick #thehive

vpeak88 — @falcon36 @theoriginalblade that's an awful thing to say @lincolnjackson deserved everything he got, he killed his own children, and lied to the police about the attack when he and @heididolak were the ones that did it #evillincolnjackson #thehive

theoriginalblade — @vpeak88 @falcon36 have you bloody lost ur mind? @charlottegoodwin was clearly losing it, we all saw the video in Grind, I guess if she can't have him nobody can, but the vote . . . that was cruel

vpeak88 — @falcon36 @theoriginalblade that's the thing with you men, you will never understand a woman's love for her children, it's poor @heididolak who got mixed up in all this mess, but if she did what @charlottegoodwin said she did, then maybe she deserved it and FYI the vote was genius she let us decide for ourselves

pmeap — @vpeak88 @falcon36 @theoriginalblade exactly can you imagine the pain @charlottegoodwin must have been in!! If that was my baby daddy I would kill him not sure about the vote though @thehive how could you live stream this????

jassatimly — @cindyleepk welp she killed the bastard!! Death by social media, if that's not poetic justice then I don't know what is PMSL

cindyleepk — @jassatimly I know what a nightmare, I can't take my eyes off the screen, she actually shot @lincolnjackson in the chest #charlotteunhinged #votedie

martelsanchez — I think I'm in shock this is a tragedy this is why we should #bekind

omarbruce54 — rip @lincolnjackson fly high champ #votelive #thehive

CHAPTER THIRTY-EIGHT

THEIR EYES BLINK INTO FOCUS as the image of Charlotte stock-still and slumped takes on full shape. The last hour has transpired for them in a dream-like state. The room is quiet despite the three women sitting around the Japanese floor table, their phones purposely propped up in the centre on a stand like an abnormal centrepiece. There are pillows and plates of discarded food littered among them. The eggs are congealed, the air crackling around them as they stare at each other disbelievingly.

'Did I just watch what I think I watched?' Poppy's hand is fixed to her mouth, her pale skin glowing white.

'You mean did we just watch our best friend murder her ex-boyfriend live on Instagram, yup, Pops, I think we did.' Zaheen trips over her words, her breathing unsteady as she stares at the image on the phone screen stroking it delicately with her fingertips.

Charlotte isn't moving.

'I think she's dead. I think she killed herself. What the hell was in that tea? What the hell has she done? Please, Charlotte, wake up. Open your eyes, sweetie.' Poppy weeps as her body convulses. 'We should have saved her. Why didn't we save her?'

Poppy continues, dabbing her face with a cream napkin then discarding it.

'She didn't want us to. That's why she stopped us, so we wouldn't get in her way. Didn't you think it was strange she only had one drink. She drugged us so we wouldn't stop her. She made sure of it with this bloody picnic then she made us watch. Charlotte, what have you done?' Trix's voice shakes as the doorbell sounds.

'*Fuck!* That's probably the police. What are we going to do?' Zaheen gets to her feet. Her nose is filled with the smell of nervous sweat hovering at the top of her lip. 'What the hell are we going to do?' Zaheen repeats, the sound of panic ringing in her throat as they listen to the door buzz again.

'Just stay calm. Charlotte would never implicate us in anything. She drugged us to keep us out of the way. All we have to do is tell the truth and we won't be in any trouble, OK?' Trix says, stumbling as she gets to her feet.

'We just have to tell the truth. We had nothing to do with what happened to Lincoln and Heidi. We had no idea about the vote. We're innocent, agreed?' Poppy's blue eyes narrow in on Trix, who looks as if she's ready to say something but decides better and stays silent.

'Agreed. Just get the door before they break it down for fuck's sake. This is a nightmare,' Zaheen spits amidst the simmering tension, the three of them staring at each other groggy and disorientated.

'I'll go. It's my house after all.' Trix smooths down her hair, steadying herself as she approaches the front door. She takes a deep breath, feeling her stomach sink as the reality of what her best friend has done sets in. Charlotte was dead but had left her and the rest of the girls to clean up her mess. Why did she kill Lincoln so publicly? Had she really been in that much pain? Had Trix missed it? The door goes again. There's no more time for her to think. She grabs the handle and pulls it open, the rush of fresh air hitting her along with waves of nausea.

But it's not the police.

Instead, Sasha stands in front of her, clad in a black tracksuit and dark shades.

'We have to talk. It's about Charlotte.'

Sasha pushes her way inside as Trix steps back, too stunned to say anything.

'I take it you watched. Of course you did, the entire world watched Charlotte kill Lincoln.' Sasha bites down on her lip. She's been crying all morning and doesn't know if she's strong enough to deliver the letter. Charlotte's letter.

'I didn't know what she was going to do. When she asked for my help she said she wanted to make Lincoln confess. I never knew she was going to kill him and Heidi – and I never knew about her babies. She never told me what happened.'

'You've got to be kidding me. What the hell are you doing here?' Poppy appears in the passageway, her body tense. She wants to tackle Sasha but she's still too out of it. The sleeping pills and alcohol swirling through her bloodstream.

'Great, so you're all here. Look, I'm not here to cause any trouble. I don't want any problems. Or anyone to find out I was involved in this.'

Sasha advances into the kitchen as Poppy and Trix slowly follow her lead.

'Charlotte came to me for help.'

'So you offer her an ear, you don't help her murder two people and off herself in front of the entire world. She was our friend and now she's dead and it's all your fault.' Zaheen's words are strangled with emotion.

'You should have told us what was happening,' Trix barks.

'I'm . . . I'm sorry. I thought I was helping her heal. I thought she was just going to embarrass Lincoln online, his reputation would be tarnished and that would be that. I never dreamed this would happen. She tricked me.'

'How dare you come in here, playing the victim card. She didn't trick you, Sasha, you were a willing participant in this mess. Our best friend is dead, and you come here for what? To get your kicks in.'

'Calm down, Zee.' Trix blocks Zaheen with her forearm.

'No, I won't calm down. Charlotte is dead, our friend is dead, and she didn't even say goodbye, instead she let us and the rest of the world watch like some sick spectators.'

'You think I wanted this? I never meant for any of this to happen. Charlotte said you'd be left out of it. And just so you know she did say goodbye. She gave me this letter for you. For all of you.'

Sasha puts the letter on the island.

'I didn't read it; Charlotte said it was private. Between the four of you. Just like it's always been. Thicker than thieves.'

'You were never one of us because you couldn't be. What we share is deeper than you'll ever understand.' Poppy paces back and forth, picks up the letter and approaches the stove, switching it on.

'What the hell are you doing?' Zaheen eyes dart from Poppy to Trix.

'Ending this nightmare once and for all. Heidi's dead, Lincoln's dead and Charlotte's ... Charlotte's gone. To hell with her goodbye. She drugged us.'

'*Stop!* Don't burn it.' Zaheen pushes Poppy, shoving her into the island.

'You two stop it. Get a hold of yourselves,' Trix screeches, separating the two of them.

'The police will be here soon so we need to get our stories straight. We need to stick together. For Charlotte. I don't know why she did this, but she has, so stop acting like children because it's not helping. And I doubt people are going to believe we slept while our friend went nuts.'

Trix thinks that is true. She thinks this is a misshapen puzzle of Charlotte's creation. Even then, she can't see the full picture, everything just out of focus. Pixilated and ballooned by all the commotion and media attention. It is chaos.

'I think you should read the letter. Charlotte really wanted you guys to read it. It was the one thing she asked me to do, and I want to honour that. I want to honour her.' Sasha switches her handbag from one shoulder to the other, remembering her last conversation with Lincoln at The Taj the day Charlotte tried to jump at Walthamstow Central. The day she unknowingly set Lincoln Jackson's murder in motion.

'Please just read it. For Charlotte.' Sasha leaves, the weight of her words like a ghostly presence in the room.

CHAPTER THIRTY-NINE

One Year Later

THE HIVE — It's been a year since the tragic passing of Lincoln Jackson and his fiancée, Heidi Dolak. Today we remember the Instagram vote that made the world stop

myworld450 — I remember watching charlotte pull the trigger RIP Lincoln Jackson what a way to go

millashah — rest in peace Charlotte Goodwin you made history girl #thehive

sean_lyim — can you believe this was a year ago today @hanna_lyim

gballbigg — and there's been like 10 copycat livestream murders since, ladies this is not the way to dispose of your exes looooool #thevote #thehive

bossburts — I was happy a year ago and I'm still happy now good riddance @lincolnjackson

joancreek46 — rest in peace @heididolak and @lincolnjackson gone too soon #thevote

titan213 — I hope charlotte goodwin rots in hell for what she did I'm talking eternal torture

mazzydean — do you know what's mad Instagram removed charlotte's account, but let @thehive keep theirs like that was gonna make the videos disappear LMAO gotta love a corporate attempt to distance themselves from a total cock up

yannablake — I've lit a candle for @lincolnjackson for 365 days I'll love you forever till we meet again in paradise #thehive

d_go_gotta — that vote was insane charlotte goodwin has to go down in history as being the craziest bitch of all time it's a shame she didn't get away with it

GOLDEN RED LIGHT SATURATES THE rooftop eatery, bathing us in a sea of luminosity as the sun begins to dip. Red oak tables line floor-to-ceiling windows; they're encased together in intimate sections sprawling across the wooden floor. My fork catches a glimmer of light as I set it down on a matching gold-trimmed plate. There are speckles of asparagus and dribbles of silky Béarnaise sauce left but nothing else. Cocktails with matte lipstick stains accompany the plates as well as four women.

I've been living in Japan for almost six months now. Prudently, I invested the money I stole from Linc, buying land and building plush sibling villas in Santa Teresa and Costa Rica. Individually, they were worth a tidy seven figures each. I quickly sold both, then used the profit to buy land in Puerto Rico, New Mexico and the Caribbean. House development is something I'm good at, something I wish I had known in my previous life.

Within half a year, I've managed to double my money, and in two I'll have tripled it. It's a tiny achievement compared to everything else I've managed to get away with, but still one I'm proud of. My appearance has changed drastically. I'm now a balayage of strawberry blonde and ash hues of white cut sharp into a graduated bob that makes me look a little older than my thirty years. My eyes have been altered. Synthetic blue implants were put into my pools permanently transforming the shade from blazing walnut brown, to piercing ice, a shade or two lighter than Poppy's. Madly enough, I got the idea from an Instagram post I'd seen while in Costa Rica. Body sculpting evened out my curvaceous figure while an abiding no carbs diet took care of the rest. It was the perfect way to conceal my real identity. I'm leaner, more tanned and stripped bare of everything I used to be.

I wasn't Charlotte Goodwin anymore, I was Vicky Knight.

'I swear you've got more beautiful. Japan really agrees with you. You look fabulous.' Trix unexpectedly squeezes my hand, reminding me I kept a tiny piece of my old self alive in the form of my three best friends. The women that brought me back from the dead.

I should probably explain. After I drugged the girls, I made two stops before going to Linc's hotel suite. First, I met Sasha. I had to give her the letter and make sure she was ready to start the Instagram live on The Hive's profile. The next was to the belly of Chinatown to visit the boy Poppy had called Lazarus.

He gave me a rare form of nightshade grown exclusively in the mountains of Laos in exchange for five thousand pounds. All the money I had left in the world. It was agreed with the help of the boy's grandfather that the quickest way for the nightshade to enter my bloodstream was to ingest it. So I brewed it in tea and drank it in front of the entire world. There was just one problem: my body would need a shot of adrenaline within seventy-two hours if I was to wake up.

317

So I left the girls a letter, I let them decide if I should live or die.

'Stop it, you're gonna make me go all red. You know I just saw your feature in *Teen Vogue*. Big move. Children's Fashion Newcomer of the Year – I'm so proud of you.'

'I swear I got more sleep when I was just Kera and Kyle's mother. Running an online fashion house and being a full-time parent – well, let's just say I haven't slept in the past year.'

Trix had used her share of the money to start an online retail store with Jennifer's help. It seems my death had given both parties the opportunity to set aside their deep-rooted differences and let bygones lie, creating something they could both be proud of in the process.

Not only was Trix's relationship with her mother flourishing, but so was her relationship with her children. Her virtual boutique was so popular she dressed every celebrity tot in the Hollywood Hills and then some. But her children were her inspiration. They were her world.

'It's hard being the boss.' Trix beams softly in the sun, no trace of the jet lag she complained of when they arrived yesterday for the one-year anniversary of the vote. The day I killed Lincoln and Heidi and got away with it.

'I'll drink to that,' I agreed, admiring Trix's half up, half down hairdo.

Then my eyes shifted to Poppy's golden crown. She wore a bohemian lilac matching set, her skirt split to reveal one pale leg.

I don't think I'll ever forget the moment I came to and felt Poppy's hands claw at my throat, while Trix and Zaheen tried to restrain her. I'd never seen her like that before. Ravaged and angry. She didn't understand why I did what I did. The letter I gave Sasha wasn't a goodbye. What was written was a set of instructions. One for each of them.

First was Zaheen's: she was to steal the money in Linc's savings accounts. I didn't want to steal from Linc, but I needed means to start my new life and Linc had them – and I knew he wouldn't have use of them anymore. So I had Zaheen take the money from him.

Next was Trix's instruction, and it was a little tricky, but if anyone could steal my body from the police morgue undetected it would be her. Of course, I left her help in the form of a brown envelope hidden under my mattress. The envelope had photos of DI Kilby and the commissioner's underage daughter, Violet, I'd found on Linc's laptop. Seems it was more than just a gambling debt keeping DI Kilby under Linc's thumb. I gave Trix the tools, but the tranquilliser she got from Michael's cousin who worked for London Zoo – well, that was her own doing. After she blackmailed DI Kilby into handing over my body, she drugged him, and as a result he didn't remember what he'd done. Despite the footage of him wheeling my body out of the morgue two and a half days after I committed murder. Trix delivered my body to a warehouse behind Tottenham Stadium with three hours to spare.

Finally, and most importantly, I needed the shot of adrenaline to bring me back to life and I knew Poppy could procure some from the hospital, but she had to decide. They all did.

'God, the sashimi looks so good. I miss raw fish.' Poppy rubs her protruding stomach and smiles.

'But it's all worth it.' Trix reaches for her sake, knocking it back in one, reminding me that some things never change.

We are spending seven nights together in one of the most upscale penthouse suites in Tokyo. It's the only time I've been able to spend with the women who saved my life since that fateful day. I took it very seriously, imagining we'd repeat these once-in-a-lifetime excursions and luxury spa treatments in exotic locations every year as a sort of tribute to the people we were, and who we are now. We are stronger, we have a renewal of life, but I suppose that's what happens when you get away with murder. Social media, the police, everyone thought the Instagram Live was because I wanted to die in a blaze of fame. It wasn't true.

The live stream, the vote, it had nothing to do with glory or attention. I killed Heidi Dolak and Lincoln Jackson publicly on The Hive because I needed Poppy, Zaheen and Trix to be there with me. They, and they alone, were my audience. They were the people I needed to see the truth. They were the people I needed to convince to let me live. And I did. They saw everything, every facet of the truth; they were my judge and jury, and they decided my loss outweighed my sins.

They exonerated me.

In the first days after I had left London on a fake passport Zaheen got from Badoo, I headed to Brazil. I have flashbacks of shots of top-shelf amber tequila and blurry images of flamingo-pink carnival costumes, complete with feathers and rainbow glitter. It was a week to remember, yet I couldn't remember much.

Next it was Colombia. Vast sweeping views of the rainforest and wildlife hikes through national parks. I stayed in a luxury compound in the mountains, spending the week celebrating

Poppy's engagement to Jeremy the surgeon through a secure video chat.

I let a pink and blue balloon float away in the sky that week, and lit candles to remember the children I'd lost.

Aspen was cold but beautiful. It marked six months since the death of Linc and Heidi. I glowed, basking with excitement as I was told via text that Zaheen had financed a tech start-up company that was about to be sold for millions. There was no doubt in my mind Zaheen would do well, everything she touches turns into molten gold. She was the only one in the group whose net worth, I suspected, would surpass my own.

Finally, I visited Negril, Jamaica. I ate salt-fish fritters on the beach and sipped piña coladas from young coconuts while steel pans played a rendition of Bob Marley's 'Every Little Thing's Gonna Be All Right'. I jet-skied by day and enjoyed bonfires on the beach while I indulged in succulent jerk chicken and rich pumpkin soup by night. I talked for hours to local fishermen, our toes embedded in the golden sand until the sun broke the clouds and resort staff materialised shooing us to clean up the mess we'd made. I made weeping phone calls to the girls that night.

I was lonely. It was selfish of me to assume Zaheen, Trix and Poppy would want to spend more time with me. I mean how much time is sufficient enough to spend with your murderous, supposedly dead, best friend?

'Did you hear about DI Plum? I'm sorry, Kilby. He's a number one *New York Times* bestseller as of this week.' Poppy's voice is low, but still audible enough for us to hear her. Her lilac top moves out of place forcing her to adjust it. It wasn't a comfortable choice since she's expecting her first child in four months' time, but she looks happy and peaceful.

'You're lying?' Zaheen covers her mouth with her dazzling ombre nails.

'Yup, the book's called *Missing Body*. Ten thousand yen you can guess who it's about?' Poppy hisses, then mockingly blows her lemongrass tea that's turned lukewarm.

'You know, to this day he still doesn't have a clue why he wheeled your body out of the police morgue? He just has the CCTV footage of him doing it. It'll be good to know his theory after all these months,' Trix quips, a smile starting to emerge on her plump lips.

'I've always wanted to know how much tranquilliser you gave him?' My brow furrows.

'Enough to take down a bull! Besides, you gave me the idea when you drugged us. I wanted to incapacitate him just in case. I was blackmailing a cop, but I had no idea he was going to lose his memory. It was a happy coincidence,' Trix replies in a voice that is in no doubt pleased with herself. It may be the most exciting thing she'd ever done, but only because she got away with it.

'My God – and the internet calls me evil.' My mouth makes a perfect 'O', as I smooth the brittle hair away from my face while contemplating shaving it off completely.

'You killed two people,' Trix whispers unflinchingly. 'I just drugged a bent detective enough so he wouldn't remember that week, let alone that day.'

'That's my girl, you'd think you were the criminal,' Zaheen says chirpily, as my eyes slide over Poppy.

She didn't get it before. She never understood the love I had for my children. But now she's going to become a mother for the first time she understands. She empathises with my pain, because she knows she would do anything to anyone who hurt her own child. That's why Poppy forgave me.

'I think Kilby would have done it even without the drugs. It's one thing to accept a bribe, but the pictures of him and the commissioner's daughter in very compromising positions meant he had no choice but to give me your body. It's a good job Lincoln never got a chance to use it first.'

'You're right, Trix, we are the lesser of two evils. And you may have got her body, but I got the money and Char—I mean Vicky out of the country. *Swish!*' Zaheen grins, using her chopsticks to reach for the last maki roll.

We laugh hysterically getting the side-eye from a young Asian couple three tables over. Nothing to see here. Just four women discussing the murder and robbery they casually got away with.

'Oh, please, I'm the one who stole the adrenaline to bring you back from the dead.' Poppy pushes out her lip.

'I wasn't really dead, just somewhere in between,' I admit.

'Whatever you say Lazarus two-point-oh. But at least Kilby's getting paid for his efforts, although I still think he should be behind bars.' Poppy exhales.

'We made him lose his job and spend six months in prison for improper disposal of a dead body even though they never found a body. I think we can call it even. For now at least.' Zaheen raises the ice water to her lips.

'I suppose that's the penalty for colluding with Lincoln Jackson,' Trix chimes.

I flinch. Even after all these months it's hard to hear his name aloud.

323

'You know, Jeremy thinks I should go to therapy, says the pregnancy's turned me into some sort of demon.' Poppy rubs her swollen belly, and it makes me twist in my seat.

'He was so happy to drop me at the airport yesterday, I could tell by his shifty little face.'

'Thank God my kids are growing up. Kyle is starting Year Two in September and Kera just got into her first-choice secondary school. It's nice having her home and not at boarding school. I'm taking her to Milan to celebrate for half-term. Even Michael's being a decent human being for once. He sees them one weekend a month. Seems jail helped him turn his life around. He's Catholic now,' Trix says with a bead of pride.

Then they all look at me and I can tell what they are thinking.

'Hey, don't do that. I'm happy for you guys. Really, I am. I'll never have a family of my own, but I'll always have you three. My sisters . . .' My words trail off, as Zaheen presses her cheek against mine.

'You know we love you, right?'

'I know, Zee. Speaking of love. I got you all a little something.'

I remove four identical elegantly packaged silver boxes from my purse.

'You shouldn't have.' Poppy rips open hers first. 'Oh my God. It says "the marshes". I can't believe you remember that. I love it. I'll never take it off my wrist.' Poppy squeals as her mind is brought back to the secret spot we used as a hangout to smoke weed and stay out late drinking cheap bottles of vodka. The best parts of our youth.

'I could never forget. You know I used "the marshes" as my password for like forever. Changed it now though, but it always held a special place in my heart. It'll always be home.'

'It was mine too,' Zaheen chimes, clinking her glass with mine.

'I'm ashamed to admit it's still my password. Jeremy can't figure it out although he tries, bless him.' Poppy's laugh is delicate and soft.

'That was our place. So many memories.' Trix smiles, her lashes extending with her words.

'Yeah, until our foursome became a *fivesome* and we had to find another spot, but there'll never be anywhere like it.'

One thing about the night my children died always bugged me. I never knew who sent the Instagram DM to Poppy and Trix asking them to come to Linc's house. It niggled at me for months, especially after Linc told me one of my friends was actually my enemy.

But I never figured out who else knew what Linc had done. Until just now. It was so obvious. We weren't always a foursome. There was one other member of our group, one other friend. One other person responsible for the death of my children.

EPILOGUE

I F YOU CUT OFF THE head of a snake, then another will grow in its place. The rain hits concrete creating silver ribbons that glimmer slightly from the dim orange lamp-posts floating above me. It's the middle of winter. I walk down the cobblestone pathway leading to the house with the red door and terracotta plant pots outside. Slabs of pitchy cloud block out the sky; despite it only being four thirty in the afternoon, it feels much later. It's a miserable day. Cold and damp. Not that I mind since I don't plan on being in the capital for any longer than I have to. Grey and dreary. London's the same as the day I left it, brooding and temperamental. Tokyo feels closer to a lifetime ago, rather than three months, and the girls could not know I'm here. Or why I've come.

The wind undresses me, leaving the lapels of my coat flapping relentlessly behind me. My stomach's stronger than it was an hour ago due to the triple shot of vodka I greedily knocked back in one swig.

I miss my home. My possessions mainly. I spend a lot of time ensuring I have the perfect abode. Unblemished things and creature comforts from my travels to anywhere, and everywhere that isn't here. They make me forget about the murders.

Some nights I forget about Linc and Heidi altogether. But recently I can't sleep, dark, sticky dreams haunt me. Dreams of Heidi's face – cold and hollow, black holes replace her eyes and mouth. But I can still hear her taunting me in the shallows of my mind. Her voice a perfect blend of spite and indignation. She laughs at me. A blood-curdling laugh that makes my entire body contort. Then Linc appears, his flesh removed, pink and raw. The smell so unbearable it makes my eyes sting as I watch the wriggling maggots fall away from him in grape-sized clumps. I want to be sick. I can taste the acrid sourness scratch the roof of my mouth. Heidi kisses Linc anyway. I see the inside of Linc's jaw. White and shiny teeth through slashes of broken flesh. I watch the tissue that used to be his tongue move against hers, and even without her lips, I can see Heidi smiling back at me.

There should be three of us.

Ghosts in my dreams; there should be three. Linc, Heidi and the other person.

My friend.

I tried to fight it at first. The urges, but it unsettles me. Like my skin isn't my own. I hate unfinished business. Injustice makes me recoil. I guess it's much easier not knowing the truth, but once you get it, what do you do with it?

'Hey, I'm so glad you could make it at such short notice. It was the craziest thing. Everywhere was fully booked up. Can you believe it?'

It's odd hearing her talk about hiring me on a whim when I surreptitiously called all the nail salons in her area and booked up all the appointments. The art to successfully getting away with any crime is preparation, and mine was diligent.

'We can't have you not looking your best, it's your engagement party. Let's give them something to remember. You here alone?'

'My thoughts exactly, and, yup, all alone. To be honest, I'm happy for a little peace and quiet. You can set up in the living room.' She waves me off, as I trail behind her, a grey suitcase rolling along with me.

'Are you married?'

'No, I'm afraid I'm not that lucky. No children either.'

'Out of the two of us, I think you're the lucky one. I've been planning this thing for five weeks. I even had the tomatoes flown in from Italy, not that my husband-to-be cares about the tiny details. Honestly, he even suggested marrying me in a community centre just to get out of wedding planning.'

'That would be a tragedy,' I say, taking my time to unpack my utensils. Polish, file, restraints. Kitchen knife.

'Oh, trust me, the only tragedy is my future mother-in-law's hideous wine-coloured dress that she insists on wearing tonight. It completely clashes with the colour scheme.' She smiles and it's amazing she doesn't recognise me. I remember being so close with her but that was a long time ago. She's changed. *I've* changed.

'That sounds awful, but it's best to let her get it out of her system now, before the real big day.'

'Wow, that's so funny. That's exactly what I said to my fiancé.'

She looks good. Slender, well tanned and maintained. The house is an old Victorian that has been renovated with modern fixtures and a huge imitation marble island. Floor-to-ceiling windows create light but kept the look minimalistic, while from the corner of my eye I spot a glass wall made of bottles of wine at the back of the house. Maybe after I kill her, I'll pour myself a nice glass of Merlot.

'Well, we should get started, I don't want you to be late to your own party. I'm sure your soon-to-be mother-in-law wouldn't like that very much,' I say, smile, then tilt up my lashes.

'You know you look familiar. Have we met before? I can't shake the feeling that we know each other.'

I dip my head, shying away so as not to make eye contact with her. The element of surprise is still on my side.

'I just have one of those faces. Take a seat for me.'

She sits eagerly in front of me, her mind thankfully preoccupied with better things than placing my face. Sasha was a lamb coming to the slaughter.

'What colour did you have in mind? Nude, traditional white? Or something bolder, like red?'

'My dress is baby pink so I was hoping like a rose or blush.'

'Pink it is.'

I'm a little disappointed she doesn't go for the red, but I don't let it show. It's hard enough to stop myself from giving up the rouse and strangling her with my bare hands.

After all it's what she deserves.

'You know, it's bugging me. Are you sure we don't know each other?'

I can't hold it in any longer.

'Perhaps socially, *Sash*.'

She freezes, her brain struggles to recollect itself, because it can't be real. It can't be me. Charlotte Goodwin is dead.

'*C-C-Charlotte!*' she says, fear etching her words.

'You're not going mad. It's really me.'

'Why are you—'

The knife sinks into her skin like playdough. I twist, feeling the vertebrae in her hand protest against the steel. She screams and my eyes roil in her pain.

'I wouldn't move if I were you.'

'Somebody help me!' She's whimpering.

'Why did you send the Instagram message to Trix and Poppy? Why did you save my life when Linc and Heidi left me to die?'

Her face is a picture. Both surprise and anger ebbing away at her features as she realises why I'm here. She meets my eyes.

'Because if I had never gone away with Brad, you never would have met Lincoln. I needed you out of our lives, but I didn't want you to die. If I knew you'd go on to kill him, I would never have sent that message. I loved him.'

'So you were the other woman?'

Sasha pauses at my question. There's so much blood. I must have nipped an artery when I stabbed her in the hand.

'You don't get it. We were soulmates before you, before Heidi. The only reason he followed you back on Instagram was to get back at me for leaving him for Brad, and I only did that because he was cheating on me, and I found out the week before. I was trying to make him jealous. It was never about hurting you or Poppy. He promised me he was going to end things with you after your first date, but then you were photographed together. And The Hive got wind of it.'

'So Linc had to keep me around just so he didn't look like a playboy,' I said, coming full circle and realising that from the very beginning my entire relationship with Linc was a lie.

'But then you got pregnant. Lincoln was out of his mind. He thought you'd ruin him so he came up with the stupid idea to scare you with Heidi, but you fell and lost the babies.'

'Let's not forget he made me barren,' I spit, clenching my teeth.

Sasha doesn't look so good.

'He called me that night, told me what had happened. He couldn't call the police as he would have been implicated. So I told him to leave, then I messaged Poppy and Trix on Instagram and made it look like you did. I knew Poppy was a nurse. I knew she would save you.'

'Except you killed my son and daughter trying to save Linc in the process.'

There's blood at my feet. Sasha's bleeding out quickly.

'Don't you think I regret it? Lincoln proposed to Heidi. I loved him and he used me. That's why I helped you. That's why I saved your life, Charlotte.'

'Pity there's no one here to save yours.'

'Please, somebody help me! I don't want to die.' Her mouth bloats with blood as I slash her neck, muffling her cry. She sounds like she's drowning.

'*Shh.* Save your strength. Before you bleed to death, I want you to answer one last question ...' Sasha falls from the chair grappling the severed tendons in her neck.

My trainers make a squelching noise as I kneel watching Sasha's warm blood pool around me.

'When the worst things have happened, who do you become?'

THE HIVE — Influencer Sasha McLean was tragically murdered in her home last night. Her fiancé is said to be devastated as police currently have no leads or suspects in custody

trinitymacky — influencers getting murdered seems to be a thing these days first @lincolnjackson and @heididolak now @sashamclean #RIP

skyreen — never liked her anyway to be honest

_hylton44 — RIP @sashamclean my condolences to her family

whiskylee — do you ever report any good news @thehive

trey11 — @whiskylee last year they got hacked and livestreamed a double murder and a suicide, so perhaps not lmao #thehive

whiskylee — fair point mate looool @trey11

nisha_green — what no live footage?? @thehive we expect better of you kmt

phizzytank — damn she was cute as well rest in peace

kandiee — nah these influencers are dropping like flies @gingerpink

gingerpink — I saw her poor family laying flowers outside her home #stopkillinginfluencers #bekind

bethhenry — @thehive I think I need a social media detox smh

ACKNOWLEDGEMENTS

FIRSTLY, I'D LIKE TO THANK God, I'm forever grateful for my many blessings. One of the happiest days of my life will always be the day I got represented by Kate Burke and the entire team at Blake Friedmann Literary Agency. Thank you for championing *The Hive* – without you none of this would have been possible. I can never express my gratitude enough to Kelly Smith and Zaffre for making *The Hive* shine as brightly as it possibly could. It's an honour and a privilege to be published by Bonnier Books UK.

I want to thank the girls and my muses: thank you, Maz, Shani, Mina, Jaydine and Emily, for not only believing in me but pushing me at every step and hurdle. Thank you, Team Good Guys, for always being there (drink in hand) when I needed you. Thank you to THMG girls, Benisha, Amy, Emily, Kristin and Fayza, for turning a blind eye when I was writing at my desk.

Thank you to my family: Anna, Lee, Philip, Lisa, Jasmine, Kirsty, Kara, Sarah-Ann and Preston, for all the round table conversations and love you've shown me throughout my entire life. Thank you, Sav, for encouraging me to reach for the stars while simultaneously being the rock to keep me grounded.

Thank you, Dad, for always being there for me when I needed you most. Mum, thank you for your unwavering support and constant love. I'm the woman I am today because of you.

Thank you to Nadine Matheson, who mentored me, you are an inspiration, and helped me believe that one day I would become an author. My dream came true.

Finally thank you to every reader. I hope you love *The Hive* as much as I do.